HELL HAS NO FURY

Also by Keith Lee Johnson

HELL HAS NO FURY

Keith Lee Johnson

www.urbanbooks.net

Urban Books
10 Brennan Place
Deer Park, NY 11729

ISBN-13: 978-1-60162-019-4
ISBN-10: 1-60162-019-5

First Printing October 2007
Printed in the United States of America

10 9 8 7 6 5 4 3 2 1

Submit Wholesale Orders to:
Kensington Publishing Corp.
C/O Penguin Group (USA) Inc.
Attention: Order Processing
405 Murray Hill Parkway
East Rutherford, NJ 07073-2316
Phone: 1-800-526-0275
Fax: 1-800-227-9604

Dedication

To *New York Times* Best Selling author, Eric Jerome Dickey, thanks for publicly acknowledging me in my home town, Toledo, Ohio, when you were here, in interviews you've done on radio, at the library in Memphis (April 2007), and the Barnes & Noble interview.

Acknowledgments

To Him, who is able to do considerably more than I can ask or think, I give you thanks.

To my mom, who I speak with nearly every morning for over an hour, thanks for your invaluable wisdom and guidance over the years.

To Martha Weber, thanks for all the hard work you put in on this novel. I think we have a winner in this one. Hopefully the sales numbers support this so that you'll get the credit you deserve.

To Carl Weber, thanks for taking the project on and getting it out there.

To Kung Fu Master, Jeff Weasel, who taught me what little I know of the art, thanks so much.

To my man, Phillip Thomas Duck, author of Apple Brown Betty in stores now, thanks for being there in season and out of season.

To Alisha Yvonne, author of *Naughty Girls* in stores now, thanks for all the books you sell for me at your Memphis Urban Knowledge Bookstore.

Special thanks to Tabitha, manager of Borders Bookstore in Toledo, Ohio. Thanks for always looking out for me from the beginning. I won't forget you.

To all my coworkers who *bought* and read every single book. I can't thank you enough and I appreciate each of you.

To all my fans, thanks for all the emails, and thanks so much for buying and reading all my novels. You are appreciated.

To all the beauty salons in Toledo, Thanks for allowing me to put stand up posters in your shops.

And last but not least, special thanks to my man Fletcher Word of the Sojourner Truth Newspaper in Toledo, Ohio. BIG, BIG, THANKS for all the articles and publicity.

Prologue

For some insane reason, people always think they can wrong others and somehow get away with it. They think that if they carefully construct their heinous crimes, they can outsmart their victims and the legal system pursuing them. Having gotten away with their crimes for so long, they begin to relax. They no longer look over their shoulders for ghosts they don't believe exist. For that reason, it never occurs to them that there will be a day of reckoning for sins committed in the flesh. Perhaps they convince themselves that what they've done wasn't evil. Or perhaps they believe that what they've done was a victimless crime, comparing their actions to greater evils like rape and murder, and in so doing, justify what they've done so that they can sleep at night. But while they sleep, those who have been seeking them have now found them, and there is no escaping their hot wrath. Such is the case of a husband and wife team who were living a rather extravagant life at the expense of others in the California desert.

Terrified, the wife, who was completely nude, ran downhill on a winding driveway away from her spacious home in the Mojave Desert, not far from the China Lake Naval Air Weapons

Station. Miles from the nearest neighbor, no one heard her horror-filled screams for help. She looked back at the pursuing convertible that had just turned the corner, its wheels screaming, its engine revving.

"Oh, God! No! They're coming! They're coming! Help! Somebody please help me!" the woman screamed.

She'd had a five-minute head start, but now the maniacs who had beaten her husband to a pulp were chasing her. Surrounded by the consuming quiet of the desert, she heard her heart racing as it thumped hard and fast.

A couple of hours earlier, the woman and her husband, both employed at the Naval Air Weapons Station, were prisoners in their own home, being brutally tortured for information by three masked assailants who woke them up while they were sound asleep in the comfort of their bed. At first the couple pretended they didn't know this day was coming, pretended that the people who had invaded their home had gotten them mixed up with someone else. But shortly after their clothing was ripped off and the beating began, suddenly they knew a lot more than they claimed, and their secret life away from the Naval Air Weapons Station was no more.

After the couple told everything they knew, the masked assailants pulled weapons from a satchel and beat the husband. As they pulverized her husband with a pipe wrench, a bat, and brass knuckles, the woman realized the assailants were not paying attention to her, and she escaped out the front door. Running out of the house in the nude was secondary to staying alive. And she ran as fast as her bare legs and feet could carry her. Faster than she'd ever run in her life, she ran, heart pounding, arms flailing, her feet kissing the Mojave asphalt over and over. She heard a car start in the distance, and if it were possible, she ran even faster.

Now the convertible was right on her heels, speeding up and slowing down, playing a deadly game of chicken with her; threatening to make the woman a permanent part of the pavement.

She looked over her shoulder again. "Please, God! No! I don't wanna die!"

Although she wanted to live, her body was about to betray her. Fatigued, she was slowing down and the convertible was getting closer. So close, in fact, that she could hear the occupants laughing hysterically as they gave chase. Up ahead, she saw the lights of the La Fiesta Sandwiches & Things restaurant on North China Lake Boulevard. The popular eatery normally closed at eight. The woman wondered if the owner was still there. With renewed energy, she quickened her pace. With no bra on, her considerable breasts were in the way, flopping around, nearly pimp-slapping her. Desperately wanting to survive the terrible and frightening night, she was determined to make it to the La Fiesta and live.

The driver of the convertible saw the restaurant lights too and knew the woman was going to try to get there for help. Playtime was over. It was time to end her miserable existence. The driver pressed the gas pedal to the floor, the engine revved, and the car rocketed forward. *Varoom!* Suddenly, metal collided with flesh and bone. *Bam!* The driver and the occupants laughed from their bellies as the bumper hit the naked woman, sending her flying over the top of the car, landing on the trunk, and crashing hard on the hot Mojave asphalt. The convertible slid as it screeched to a halt. The occupants looked back at the naked woman, who, by some miracle, was still alive.

The woman was still trying to get away from her masked assailants. As she tried to get away, she wondered if her husband was still alive, and if she herself would survive the night. The woman crawled as quickly as she could, dragging her broken right leg, which was barely attached to the rest of her body. She heard the engine rev prior to hearing the convertible's tires screech. On instinct, she turned her head toward the sound of the coming vehicle. The rear bumper hit her right in the face as it backed over her. *Varoom!*

The woman wasn't moving this time. She was dead. But the driver screeched to a halt again, put the convertible in drive, and floored it again. *Varoom!* The naked woman was run over a third time. Her body kind of bounced a little when the speeding vehicle ran over it.

The convertible continued on down North China Lake Boulevard.

The masked occupants were on their way to Las Vegas.

There were other people to visit.

Part One

Who is Bruce Michaels?

Chapter 1

The Phoenix Perry Dojo
Arlington, Virginia
June 2005

I was wearing a blindfold as I practiced Kung Fu with Kelly McPherson, my FBI crime-fighting partner. Besides beating up on the wooden dummy, the blindfold was the only real challenge available to keep my martial art skills sharp. Although Kelly had earned the rank of black sash, she was still no match for me. I had trained for twelve years in a Shaolin Temple under the tutelage of legendary Kung Fu Master Ying Ming Lo. Master Lo was more than a martial artist; he was a philosopher. He taught me many lessons. I was his best student. Now I was about to teach my best student two of those lessons. I enjoy teaching students who are serious about the art, but I admit that I have to wear a lot of hats; I'm a wife, a mother of two, a martial arts instructor, and as I said earlier, an FBI agent. Were it not for my in-laws, who always seem to have time for my children, I wouldn't have time to train, let alone instruct others. My husband, a former FBI agent, helped out quite a bit too, which made the two days that I spent at my school possible.

I often listened to music when I trained advanced students like Kelly. It served as a distraction and forced us to concentrate. I wanted my student to be single-minded when we sparred. I preferred to listen to Motown oldies, but today, after lots of begging, I let Savannah, my twelve-year-old, pick the music. Destiny's Child's *Survivor* soundtrack filled the room, adding the extra challenge I needed besides the blindfold I was wearing. The music made it difficult to hear Kelly's movements. I had to be extremely focused to deal with her attacks. I loved the song, and it was apropos to the lessons I was about to teach Kelly. Fluidity of movement and situation adaptation are the keys to being an effective martial artist. Nevertheless, surviving an unexpected attack required more than martial arts training; it required a strong will to live.

Even with my eyes covered, I could see as clearly as any human being with 20/20 vision, dealing with Kelly's attacks as if I could see them. I was forced to depend on my other senses. In my mind's eye, I could see Savannah and her schoolmate, Luther Pleasant, standing in the opening of the dojo, watching with eager anticipation, wondering what was going to happen. I could smell the banana Luther was eating. I could hear my own heart beating at a slow, steady pace.

Although I would never seriously hurt Kelly, I had given her permission to use all the weapons in her arsenal. This was going to be all out fighting—the only way to learn the art. We were both wearing black Kung Fu uniforms and black Pine Tree shoes. I was considerably shorter than Kelly, but my height wasn't a disadvantage. I was relaxed, but ready for her to attack—my hands at my sides. Kelly jabbed at my head. With very little effort, I moved my head slightly, allowing the blow to come as close to my face as possible without being touched.

Suddenly, Kelly was punching and kicking in combination. Each blow had serious intentions. I effortlessly avoided the attack. As she was about to go on the offensive again, I stepped forward and launched my own attack, purposely moving at a slower pace, knowing she would be able to hit me. She did. Suddenly, I felt the power of a well-placed palm strike to my sternum. It hurt and I went down. I heard Kelly laughing under her breath, which I understood. I laughed too when I finally knocked down my master some twenty or so years ago. It felt good to finally get a blow in on the person instructing you, who was usually able to hit you at will. I lifted the blindfold and looked at her as laughter spilled out of her wide mouth and rang in my ears.

"I'm sorry, Phoenix," Kelly said, still laughing.

I didn't say a word. I just pulled the blindfold back down and stood up. I walked over to where she was standing and threw a series of punches, which Kelly blocked with ease. Then she kicked me in the jaw—hard. The blow dazed me, and I went down a second time. I tasted the salty, warm blood in my mouth.

There was no laughter this time.

Kelly raced over to me. "You okay, Phoenix? I didn't mean to do that. It just happened all by itself. I'm so sorry."

"Don't be sorry," I told her. "That was lesson one. You now know more about your capabilities. Now for the second lesson. You ready?"

"Yes," she said in an excited tone.

Chapter 2

Before Kelly finished saying "Yes," quickly, almost too fast for the eye to see, I hit her in the forehead with the second tier of my knuckles, as if I had knocked on someone's door. I lifted the blindfold and watched my friend grab her forehead. She looked astonished by how fast I could move without telegraphing the blow. I had given her a teasing demonstration of my mastery of the ancient Chinese art. I smiled, pulled the blindfold back down, and attacked again, moving forward steadily, backing her up as she futility attempted to defend herself against my powerful onslaught. Then when she least expected it, I knocked twice more on her unguarded forehead.

"Shit!" Kelly shouted.

Before the profane word finished rolling off her tongue, I knocked three more times. The blows sounded like I was connecting with wood. With the blindfold still covering my eyes, I said, "What did I tell you about swearing around the children?"

Kelly became furious, as I knew she would, all of which

was a part of the lesson. "Goddammit!" Kelly shouted. Suddenly, none of this was funny.

I pretended to be angry and faked a menacing scowl. Then I walked toward her at a quick pace, saying, "What did I just tell you, Kelly?" She swung at me, but I felt it coming and ducked. I moved closer—still blindfolded—still pretending to be angry. After she blocked a couple of blows, I backhanded her hard across the cheekbone. "What did I tell you, Kelly? Huh? What did I *just* tell you?"

Growing more and more frustrated, she came after me, attempting to kick and punch me, but I was elusive. Then I backhanded her on the other side of her face. She'd lost control after being on the receiving end of a humiliating slap to the cheekbone. Foolishly, she ran at me at full speed, just as I knew she would. I waited until the last possible second and stooped low. As her body collided with mine, I lifted her off her feet and sent her flying across the room. I removed the blindfold, threw it to the floor in mock anger. With my face twisted in an angry scowl, I hurriedly walked over to her, still pretending this was a real fight.

Kelly was back on her feet, but she had lost control. Her martial arts skill had abandoned her. I could hear her taking rapid, deep breaths, evidence of simmering anger. This was now a street fight, and she resorted to surviving, rather than relying upon the skills she acquired over the years. She swung, but she was so angry, so out of control that the blow was coming at me as if it were in slow motion. I grabbed her arm, stepped in and slapped her several more times, which dazed my crazed student. Then I tossed her on the floor. She was disoriented and lying on the floor, moaning. I turned her over onto her stomach and sat down on the small of her back, making it extremely difficult to get on all fours. I grabbed a hunk of her thick, golden hair and pulled. Her neck reddened as the strain of my pulling mounted.

"I could kill you, Kelly," I said in a calm voice. "This is the second lesson, and you'd better learn it because it will save your life on the street. In real combat, there are no second chances. There is no laughing. This is serious business. When we're on the street chasing the bad guys, they won't hesitate to kill you. Or me for that matter." I was still pulling her hair. "Do you understand?"

"Yes," she said. A tear rolled down her cheek.

I let her go. We stood, faced each other, and bowed.

"I know this was humiliating for you, but it had to be done," I said. "Now . . . en garde."

"Phoenix, let's take a break. I'm too frustrated to continue," Kelly pleaded, almost whining.

I looked her in the eyes and said, "No break. Get it together. Now! Your life is on the line, Kelly. A criminal isn't going to give you a break because you're frustrated. He's going to kill you. Now . . . . quiet your rebellious and ambitious mind and focus on the moment. You're a well-trained martial artist. You're a tiger on the prowl. *Act* like it." I paused for a moment to let my words sink in. Softly, I said, "En garde."

Tears of frustration slid down Kelly's rose-colored cheeks.

"En guarde, Kelly."

"I can't. I can't. I just can't."

"Close your eyes," I said softly, almost whispering.

She did.

"Feel the energy in the room," I went on. "Do you feel my energy?"

Kelly remained quiet for a few seconds and took a couple of deep breaths. I could feel her spirit settling down. Reticently, I moved around the room, giving her no indication that I was no longer where she had seen me. With her eyes still closed, she moved with me, knowing exactly where I was, as if she could see me through closed lids.

"En garde, Kelly," I said.

I quickly moved toward her, swinging wildly, like an untrained attacker would. Kelly easily blocked everything I threw at her. I took a step backward.

"Now open your eyes."

Kelly smiled.

We hugged each other. No words were necessary. She understood now—at least I hoped she did. The only way to know for sure would be on the street, in real combat, when her life was truly on the line. In *real* combat, it would be sink or swim in a single moment. Kelly grabbed her gym bag and left. I sensed some residual anger, but I knew she'd be okay after a hot bath.

Chapter 3

During the summer of 2001, I'd worked on two of the most frightening cases I'd ever had in my career as an FBI agent. Coco Nimburu and the Connelly twins terrorized the DC area. So, when I learned that I was pregnant, I welcomed the chance to get off the street and take it easy for a much-needed change. Coco Nimburu was a deadly Japanese assassin. Not only was she beautiful, she was blessed with a great body and she was an incredibly gifted martial artist. She was a Ninja, and ironically, a nymphomaniac. Prior to killing her male victims, she used a little-known but very effective art that required strategic placement of seven golden needles which resulted in a permanent erection. She thoroughly drained her male victims, leaving them completely fulfilled before snapping their necks. She was also a master of disguise, and had fooled me and Kelly several times.

The Connelly twins and their cohorts were even more twisted. Home invasion was their claim to fame. They maliciously stripped the clothes off their victims, hung them upside down, and lashed them with a bullwhip made of kangaroo hide, which is ten times stronger than cowhide. After seeing what was left of one of my neighbors, I was motivated to solve the case and put the twins behind bars where they belonged. I needed a break from the carnage of those two cases, and an unexpected surprise made the break possible.

Three weeks after September 11, 2001, my doctor confirmed that I was pregnant. Sydney Drew Perry was born in the spring of 2002. My husband decided to give him my deceased father's name. By January 2002, I was doing a nine to five desk job at headquarters, coordinating for the newly formed Office of Homeland Security. Even though I'm not a desk jockey, I kind of liked the gig. The time I was able to spend with Keyth and Savannah was so precious. And truth be told, as I said earlier, I really needed a break.

Sydney kept me busy the last couple of years, but I managed to read and polish my book, *The Nimburu Chronicles*. Because of the notoriety of the Nimburu case, I received several substantial offers from publishing houses. My agent thought we had enough offers to hold an auction. To my delight, the best offer was six figures with a movie option and the opportunity to be the fight sequences coordinator. I think Coco would have been proud, given her secret desire to be a Hollywood actress. The problem, however, was that film options were tenuous at best, my agent told me. She went on to say that she had a client who had a film optioned ten times, and the movie still hadn't been made. So I didn't expect much, in spite of the movie option on the table.

In the meantime, I'd been spending my evenings with Savannah and Luther Pleasant, training them for an upcoming martial arts tournament I scheduled at my school in Arlington, Virginia. Hopefully, I'd be able to attract enough attention, as the tournament was really a ploy to find three or four students willing to commit themselves to the study of the art. I was planning to reopen the dojo. It had been closed for four years, thanks to Coco Nimburu, who had killed four of the five students I had during that chaotic 2001 summer, in an effort to motivate me to come after her.

I expected Savannah and Luther to easily win in their brackets. Luther had been beaten up by a couple of girls on the way home from school, and Savannah had to step in and save him from them while I was chasing the bad guys. After I solved the Connelly twins case, I decided to train Luther. As I expected, he was an excellent student. I'd been training him for four years. Because of his commitment to the art, he had surpassed Savannah, but she was a better fencer.

From my office, I kept hearing the constant thud of someone being thrown to the mat in the dojo, so I went to the doorway to see what was happening with those two. They were going at it like cats and dogs, much like me and Ze Quan Lo, my master's son, when we were their age. I looked at them, each one determined to defeat the other. Somehow, Savannah had gotten Luther in a headlock.

"I got you now!" Savannah screamed with glee.

"Let me go, girl!" Luther yelled. "Don't make me do you like your mom did Ms. McPherson up in here."

I watched them to see what was going to happen. Those two were going to fight no matter what. In a few years, they would probably fall in love. But first Savannah had to learn to respect Luther. She'd had a hard time dealing with him earning his red sash before she earned hers.

"You can't get out of this," Savannah said, laughing.

As she finished her sentence, Luther swept both her legs with his arms and picked Savannah up. Then he allowed himself to fall backward onto the mat. Savannah screamed like she was on a rollercoaster, zooming down a steep hill at ninety miles per hour. She let out a loud "Weeeeeee," as they tumbled to the mat. It reminded me of our trip to Universal Studios, when Keyth and I took her there after the Nimburu case.

When they hit the mat, Savannah let him go and they were back at it again. Luther had performed a very effective move for the situation he found himself in, which is why he advanced so much quicker. Early on in his training, he learned to improvise, and not to be bound to any one way of fighting.

"If you're so good, let's get the foils out," Savannah challenged.

"That's the only way you can beat me now and you know it," Luther shot back.

"Chicken!"

"Okay, come on then!"

The phone in my office rang. I had forwarded the calls from my home phone to the dojo. I yelled out to the children, "Put on your uniforms and masks."

"Oh, Mom," Savannah whined.

"Don't 'Oh, Mom' me. Put them on," I said as only a mother could. As I reached for the phone, I heard Luther say, "I guess she told you, huh?"

I picked up the receiver, and in my best professional voice said, "You've reached the dojo. Grandmaster Perry speaking. Is this call in reference to our upcoming martial arts tournament?"

"Phoenix, this is your Aunt Ruth from Toledo." Her voice shook as she wept. "I've got some terrible news. They found your cousin Michelle. Somebody shot her in Las Vegas last night."

"What?"

"I don't know all the particulars, but apparently she was shot during a robbery. I can't believe this has happened. Can you meet us out there? We're flying out as soon as we can get packed."

"Sure, Aunt Ruth. I'll get there as soon as I can."

Chapter 4

Michelle was in a coma. It was hard to believe I hadn't seen her since her husband killed himself a little more than three years ago. She called me a couple of weeks before his death to tell me she thought she was pregnant. I had just given birth to Sydney, and was hoping she was pregnant so I could return the favor of throwing her a shower. Unfortunately, she lost her baby and her husband the same day. Now it looked like she might die too.

I hung up the phone and called FBI Director Kortney Malone to let her know what was going on and that I needed some personal time. Even though she was a by-the-book director, we had known each other for years, and she made allowances for me that she didn't make for other agents. I think the slack I got had much to do with the President having hand-picked me to find out who killed Jennifer Taylor, the first African-American woman nominated to the Supreme Court. Even though President Davidson was no longer in office, he still had lots of influential friends in key political circles. Solving that critical case made my career, and gave me favor with everyone who knew Davidson.

Surprisingly, Kortney didn't give me a speech about not investigating while I was in Vegas. Perhaps that was because I basically told her why I was taking some personal time. Telling me no wasn't an option. She knew it and I knew it. Unlike most agents, I didn't need the job, not for financial reasons anyway. I could very easily accept my husband's offer to help him run Drew Perry Investigative Firm, which my father had established before I married Keyth. I was supposed to eventually run the firm, but Keyth was doing a fine job with it, which afforded me the opportunity to do the thing I love— playing cops and robbers.

Next I called Kelly McPherson, who, even though she was my partner, was assigned to DC Metro as a liaison agent. She was pretty much on her own and made her own schedule. That was one of the perks of the position, which is one of the reasons she took the job. I explained the situation to her, and she decided to take some personal time to work the case with me. Her loyalty to me was absolute. I could always count on her.

Then I called Keyth and told him what happened to Michelle. He agreed to run the tournament for me. I would have canceled, but Savannah and Luther were looking forward to it. I hated the idea of missing their first tournament, but I would watch the video when I returned.

Kelly was going to meet me at my home. Thank God Dorothy and Clyde, Keyth's parents, were already at the house taking care of Sydney. Sometimes I didn't know what I would do without Dorothy. She loved the kids and loved spending time with them. What I loved most about Dorothy was that she didn't make me feel like I was less than a mother for working when it was clear that our finances didn't require it. Kelly and a lot of other women caught hell for having a career, even when they had to work.

I booked two tickets on the 5:20 PM flight to McCarran International. The only seating available was in the first class section, but I wasn't going to complain. First class was better anyway. Plus, I was charging the cost to Drew Perry, and planned to write off the whole investigation. The seats were more comfortable, and there usually wasn't a crying baby in that section. As a mother, I don't mind my own babies crying, but I don't want to hear other people's children when I'm on a long flight somewhere. And I definitely don't want to inhale baby smells either, okay? Don't hate me for that. I'm just being honest.

After I made reservations, I packed a couple of bags as quickly as I could, taking only the essentials—three changes of clothing, and the usual toiletries a woman needs. Then I tossed in the Egyptian Musk oil. Thirty minutes later, Kelly rang the doorbell. I kissed my children and told them I loved them. It was tough for all of us, but especially for me, as I saw the tears form in my son's eyes and then slide down his sad face. Savannah, on the other hand, was thoroughly disappointed that I had to leave yet again. It didn't matter that it was family this time. The only thing that mattered to her was that I would more than likely miss her first tournament. I had missed her first violin solo at Matthew Henson Academy because I was too busy chasing the bad guys. Then I missed her first feature performance with the school's orchestra because her little brother was ready for the world. Now I was about to miss her first martial arts tournament. I looked at her and she looked at me. My heart broke a little each time I left her, as she was fast becoming a teenager. I didn't want to miss so much of her growing up, but I was a born FBI agent. I walked over to my daughter, who didn't want to hug me, and I hugged her until she hugged me back. Then Kelly drove us over to Reagan National Airport.

Chapter 5

The 757 landed at precisely 7:14 PM Pacific Time. As soon as I heard the steward say it was okay to turn on our cell phones, I flipped mine open and called Keyth to let him know we'd made it in. His cell went straight to voicemail. I left a message to call me. For some reason, the flight crew was taking a while to open the door, so I called my home. No one answered. I left another message and wondered where everybody was. It was after 10 PM, so I would hope the kids were in bed by then, but knowing my husband, he probably took them and his parents to eat in Crystal City or something.

The blazing desert heat slapped us the moment we walked through the aircraft door. When speaking of the Vegas heat, I often hear people say, "It's a dry heat." Dry or not, it is smokin'! I had never been to Vegas before, and a part of me wanted to enjoy myself and see all the glitter and glamour, particularly at night, when the city's beauty is at its best, I hear. Now that I was there, I'd learn why people from all over the world were so quick to board a plane to Sin City and why it was so cheap to do so.

As we disembarked, Kelly practically ran up the gangplank into the airport, dropped fifty cents into the first slot machine she saw, and pulled the arm. She was just about to drop another fifty cents into the machine when I caught up to her. I heard the coins register. Kelly pulled the arm. She'd lost again. I looked at her as if to say, "Are you through?" She rolled her eyes and was about to put in another fifty. I grabbed her arm and said, "This isn't a pleasure trip."

Kelly frowned. "You can fuck up a wet dream, Phoenix."

I laughed. "That's my sole purpose for being on earth."

"Just once more. Three times is the charm," she said confidently.

On her third attempt to strike gold, she put in eight quarters. I looked at her, puzzled as to why she thought she had a better chance of winning a two-dollar bet when she had already lost a dollar on two tries. I was thinking that if she had to play that foolish game of chance, she should give herself more tries. Putting in eight quarters for only one pull was silly if you asked me. But hey, it was her money.

She pulled the lever. The tumblers rotated, and suddenly bells started ringing, the red light on top of the machine swirled, and a ticket came out of the machine. A young woman came over to Kelly and gave her the money she'd won.

"Whoa hoo!" Kelly erupted. People were coming from everywhere to see how much she had won.

I looked at the machine to see the amount she would collect. The amount was fifty dollars; a nice take for three dollars. Now Kelly was probably going to think she was destined to break the bank at craps or something. I looked at her. She had one of those "Now shut up!" looks on her face. I shook my head and said, "You know you're buying dinner, right?"

I rented a burgundy Chrysler 300 and drove straight to the Desert Springs Hospital on Flamingo Road, which was about seven minutes from McCarran. The attending doctor was at the reception desk, speaking to a nurse. When he heard me mention Michelle's name, he turned around and said, "Are you a relative?"

"Yes," I said. "I'm her first cousin." I offered him my hand. "I'm Phoenix Perry, and this is Kelly McPherson. We're federal agents."

As usual, men ignore me with their eyes when they see Kelly, who is tall and slender, with the neck of a swan. The doctor was looking at her, but talking to me when he said, "Your cousin's lucky to be alive."

I wasn't bad on the eyes either, but men went for the blondes, I guess. I cleared my throat to get his attention. When he looked my way, I said, "What else can you tell us about the shooting, doctor?"

The doctor must have realized how foolish he was acting, and now looked at me when he addressed me. "Michelle was shot at point-blank range. The EMS team had gotten to the house just in time, but there's no guarantee she'll ever come out of the coma. I'm sorry."

I thanked the doctor and went to Michelle's room. He and Kelly were still talking when I left.

Chapter 6

A uniformed police officer was stationed outside Michelle's room. I asked Kelly, who had caught up with me, to find out what the police were doing while I looked in on my cousin. When I walked into the room, I saw Aunt Ruth and several other family members sitting next to Michelle's bed, talking in hushed tones. As I approached my sleeping cousin, I noticed that Michelle was cuffed to her bed. I wondered what that was about. Was she a suspect in the robbery? If so, why? Michelle had plenty of money. Why would she have to rob anybody?

"Hello, everybody," I whispered.

I wasn't exactly sure why I was whispering, other than the fact that they were. Michelle was in a coma. We wanted her to wake up, didn't we? Yet we were all whispering like we were at a Wimbledon championship tennis match.

Aunt Ruth stood up. She looked so much like my deceased father it was uncanny. We hugged, and she began to sob on my shoulder.

"It's so good to see you, Phoenix. Seems like we only see

each other when someone dies. I saw you at Sydney's funeral. Again at Bruce's. And here you are now."

"We're gonna change that, okay, Aunt Ruth?" I said. I felt guilty, but the truth was, they lived in Toledo, Ohio and I lived in Arlington, Virginia. On top of that, Keyth and I worked a lot of hours. We barely had time for each other, let alone extended family. Nevertheless, she was right. I only saw them when there was a family crisis. "Now . . . why is she cuffed to the bed?"

"The police think she was in on the robbery." That was Michelle's brother, Jake, who had walked in with a can of grape soda in his hand. He took several deep gulps before speaking again. "I heard the cop outside tell some white chick that."

"Um, the white chick is my partner," I said facetiously. "She's an FBI agent, Jake."

"Oh, Kelly's here?" Aunt Ruth asked, though it was more of a statement. "Thank you, Jesus! Between the two of you, you all can get to the bottom of this mess. I don't believe Michelle would be involved in a robbery, let alone a double murder."

"A double murder?" I repeated.

"A white couple was killed, Phoenix," Aunt Ruth went on. "A well-to-do white couple at that. They say they've matched Michelle's fingerprints to a tire iron used to torture the husband. They didn't find her prints on the shotgun that blew the man's face off, but they found powder burns on her hands, so they know she fired a gun recently. They say she was wearing a scarecrow's mask when they found her."

I wanted to say, "Michelle is through then," but I held my tongue for once and said, "If all that's true, she's going to need a good lawyer."

Sterling Montgomery Wise came to mind. I met him when Coco Nimburu was in town back in June 2001. Kelly and I saved his life, so he owed us a favor. He was famous for having won a nationally covered murder case in San Francisco in the late nineties. If Michelle needed an attorney, I believed he would take the case. I walked over to the door and closed it. I didn't want the cop that was guarding Michelle to hear my next set of questions.

I said, "Is there any chance she could have done this?"

Jake was the first one to speak up. "Before Bruce killed himself, I would have said no. But since he died, Michelle has been getting crazier and crazier. Hardly came around anymore. I tried talking to her about it, but she always told me she was doing fine. If I tried to see her, sometimes she wouldn't even answer her door. And I knew she was home. She started taking a bunch of trips. Told me it was because of her job with Excalibur Foods."

"You make that sound suspicious, Jake," I said. "She's a food broker. I'm sure she travels all the time."

"All I'm saying is, she hasn't spent very much time with the family, and she's never at home. When she is home, she rarely answers the door, or the phone. Used to be a time when she told us where she was going, when she was leaving, and when she would be returning."

"Jake, she's twenty-seven years old," I countered. "Isn't it possible she could be seeing someone? It's been three years since Bruce died. She knows everybody loved Bruce. Anybody she brings around would be heavily scrutinized by you and everyone else in the family."

"Maybe that's what happened, cuz. Maybe she got hooked up with some fool who got her into drugs or something. For all we know, he could have been a criminal or something. All I know is that when Bruce died, she changed. I think a part of her went to the grave with him. I've heard that when a spouse dies, part of the living spouse dies too."

"I'll look into it and find the truth of all of this. I promise."

"Where will you be staying when we need to get a hold of you?" Aunt Ruth asked.

"We're staying at the Mandalay Bay Hotel."

While I didn't say anything to Kelly or my family, I couldn't shake the idea that my cousin seemed to be mixed up in a double murder.

Chapter 7

We took our bags up to the two-bedroom suite and looked over a list of thirteen restaurants the hotel offered. It was 9:00, and I hadn't eaten since breakfast. We decided to go to the Bayside Buffet for dinner. It closed at 10, so we hustled down to the restaurant. Fortunately, there wasn't much of a line and we were able to get a table quickly. I loaded my plate with sweet and sour chicken, a few pieces of perch, corn on the cob, and string beans. I didn't bother waiting on Kelly to come to the table. I was starving, so I sat down and started shoveling food into my mouth like I had been in a Baghdad prison for the last fourteen years.

Kelly came back with a modest amount of food. For a split second, I felt like a pig for eating so much, but kept right on eating. Every now and then I'd moan as I wolfed down my delicious grub.

"So, how did it go with the cop?" I asked Kelly. "Or were you out there flirting as usual?"

"No, I wasn't flirting, Phoenix," Kelly said, smiling.

"Not even with the doctor who couldn't take his eyes off you, even while addressing me?"

"Not even the doctor, if you must know. He did try to get a piece, though."

I laughed and said, "And you're not going to screw him?"

"No, Phoenix. I called Sterling before we left town. He's flying down from San Francisco."

"Why don't you two settle down together? You obviously have a thing for each other. It's been going on since the Connelly case, hasn't it?"

"It's a flame, Phoenix. Nothing more. A girl has to learn to keep that kinda shit in perspective. I see Sterling because he turns me on, not because I love him. When he stops turning me on, I'll stop bangin' 'im. It's that simple. Until then, I'm going to keep ridin' him like he was Seattle Slew."

I shook my head. I guess I shouldn't have been surprised at her cavalier attitude about sex. She'd been that way since she recruited me from Howard University fifteen years ago. She was flirting with the students and the faculty when I met her. However, she was tired of dealing with upper management and took the step down from Special Agent in Charge to liaison agent with DC Metro. Though we'd never discussed it, I got the feeling she would have quit the Bureau if it weren't for our relationship.

I said, "Speaking of Sterling, when you talk to him, ask him if he could take on my cousin as a client. She's going to need a very good attorney."

"Why don't you ask him yourself?"

"Because I'm not going down on him," I whispered. "You are. As long as you are, you have his attention."

We laughed.

"Anyway," Kelly began, "the cops think Michelle killed the husband, even though they didn't find her prints on the weapon."

"And they think that because . . ."

"Because there were no other bodies. And there weren't

any shotgun pellets in any of the walls. Whoever shot Michelle, shot her at point-blank range."

"So we're talking about at least one other person at the house that night. What about the wife? How was she killed?"

"A knife in the eye."

I cringed when the visual flooded my mind.

"But the cops think a hit man killed the wife. They think Michelle and the hit man had a beef over the wife or something. They can't prove it, but they think the hit man had sex with the wife, and that's what set Michelle off."

I didn't like the thoughts running through my head. I remembered that Michelle's husband, Bruce, had blown off half of his head with a shotgun. I began to think the unthinkable, wondering if the weapon belonged to Bruce.

"Kelly, did the cops run the serial number on the weapon yet?"

"The serial number was filed off. Why, Phoenix? What are you thinking?"

I changed the subject. "Why do the cops think the hit man, if indeed there is one, had sex with the wife?"

Kelly stared at me for a long few seconds to let me know that she knew I had changed the subject. Then she said, "They found her upstairs, naked, with a knife wound in her eye. Whoever threw that knife knew what the hell they were doing. The wife evidently got the drop on the hit man. She still had a Beretta in her hand when they found her. The thing that sticks out in my mind about all of this is that the husband was downstairs in his pajamas. Did the wife sleep in the nude, or what? And what about that knife wound in the wife's eye? Can Michelle do that?"

Even though the question was rhetorical, I felt the need to answer it. "Hell no!"

"Two out of two FBI agents agree."

"We better get to the crime scene and investigate for ourselves, Kelly. Something doesn't seem right."

Chapter 8

The detectives working the case were gracious enough to give us copies of their preliminary report of the crime scene. We didn't dare tell them Michelle was my cousin. They would have given us a lot of crap about *me* being too close to the case. Blah, blah, blah. What the hell ever! I didn't want to hear it, so Kelly did her flirt thing and they willingly cooperated. After reading the report, which didn't tell us much more than what the cop at the hospital told Kelly, we drove over to 5900 Glenistar Gate, where the murders took place. I still needed to see the house—needed to get a feel for Rick and Suzette Nance, the murder victims. According to the police report, Suzette and Rick Nance owned a 7-Eleven store that also offered gas. I felt bad for the couple, but this was my cousin, and I was going to try to find something on them to clear her if I could. I needed to know who the Nances were. I wondered what they really did for a living.

As far as I was concerned, the Nances had to be doing something wrong—at least that's what I wanted to believe. I wanted to believe that because the alternative was too frightening to contemplate. If the Nances were simply living the American

Dream, and Michelle had killed Rick for nothing . . . It was just too unthinkable, which is why I shouldn't have been investigating this case.

I turned onto Glenistar Gate and parked the Chrysler 300 in front of the house. The Nances lived in a very upscale neighborhood. I wondered what the houses sold for. If I had to guess, I'd say they were going for well over $850,000. I planned to check their tax records and see if they could afford to live in this house based on their reported income. I had to give Michelle every chance. Based on the preliminary report, I think my cousin killed a man. But I would never say it aloud. I had to find a way to understand why.

We ducked under the yellow police tape and entered the luxurious home. I said, "Which one do you want, Kelly? Upstairs or down?"

"Down. I'll start in the dining room."

I climbed the staircase and saw more yellow tape, cordoning off another crime scene. Again I ducked under and went into the master bedroom where Suzette Nance was found. With the exception of the small bloodstain in the carpet, it looked like any other bedroom. According to the police report, there was a safe in the floor of the walk-in closet. After pulling on a pair of surgical gloves, I went into the closet. I just wanted to have a look around, not expecting to find anything. However, I was wondering why a storeowner needed a safe in the floor of their closet. Wouldn't their money and jewels be more secure in a safety deposit box? On the other hand, maybe they kept their important papers in the safe in case the house burned down.

The safe was still open and empty. The police confiscated the jewelry, which had an estimated worth of $75,000. I squatted to take a look inside, wondering how much money the robbers stole. They didn't take the jewelry. Why? They were robbers, weren't they? Or were they? Was this a hit of

some sort made to look like a robbery? Did Michelle pum-
mel Rick Nance? If so, why?

I went back into the bedroom and examined the area
where Suzette Nance was found, wondering how the killer
got the drop on her. I pulled my nine from its holster and
pretended to point it at the robber.

*Now, how did you get the drop on her? You couldn't have been
standing right in front of her. Were you sitting? Where was the
knife? She couldn't have seen it. Otherwise, she would have pulled
the trigger. Or did she freeze? Is that what happened? Did you freeze,
Suzette? Did you get the drop on him, Suzette? That's it, isn't it?
You got the drop on him, didn't you, Suzette? He relaxed, didn't he?
Yes! He relaxed and you got your gun, didn't you? But where was he
while you were getting the gun? Still in bed? Getting dressed?
Hmmm, so you were supposed to be getting the money, and you got
the gun instead. When you came back with the gun, he was getting
dressed and you didn't see the knife, did you? But still, how did he
get the drop on you?*

I holstered my weapon, went to the other side of the bed,
and looked back at where Suzette would have been when she
was killed. I sat on the bed, and that's when it hit me. The
killer wasn't facing Suzette. He was getting dressed, probably
had the knife on the floor or something. That's how he
caught her off guard. With his back facing her, Suzette probably thought she had him covered. That's when he threw the
knife.

Chapter 9

38865 South Carefree Drive
Tucson, Arizona

The intruders had been waiting in an Escalade for more than an hour, basking in the cool air it provided. They were parked a few houses down the block. It was a little past 2 AM when the only light in an upstairs bedroom went out. The house was dark when Frank, Nancy, and Lena, wearing expensive Halloween masks, crept past the swimming pool and prepared to enter the Pinal County home through the patio doors. The trio brought a glasscutter, but their victim had left the patio door unlocked. Frank looked at Nancy and Lena and said, "See, girls, this is how I know we're doing the right thing. When women leave their doors unlocked, it's always an invitation for people like us to go in and rob them blind. Don't you agree?"

Nancy said, "Uh-huh. Sure do."

Lena said, "Yepper! Let's do what we gotta do."

Carefully and very slowly, Frank slid open the patio door

and entered the quiet residence. They tiptoed through the
kitchen, down the short hallway that led to the staircase, and
climbed the stairs to the bedrooms. They could hear Cody
Mills moaning softly, as if she were afraid her neighbors
would hear what she and the man she was with were doing.

Frank laughed to himself just before bursting in, immediately flipping on the light switch. He pointed a gun at Cody.
"You scream, you die. Got it?"

Cody gasped and pulled the cover up to her neck and
nodded.

Lena and Nancy walked in and closed the door.

"Come on outta there, mister!" Frank said. "Ain't no need
in hidin'! Besides, we just want the money."

Embarrassed, Cody finally said, "There's nobody here but
me."

Nancy walked over to the bed and snatched off the covers.

Cody was wearing a gown, which was pulled up over her
waist. Her panties were down to her ankles—her vagina exposed. She was about to pull down the gown to cover herself
when Frank cocked the gun and said, "Don't . . . move."

Nancy sat down beside Cody and looked into her eyes.
"No man, huh? Gotta do it yourself? Well, here, let me help
you. Now just relax, okay, honey?" Nancy put both middle
fingers of her right hand into her mouth and moistened
them while Frank and Lena watched. Then she put them between Cody's legs.

"No . . . please . . . don't," Cody pleaded, tears forming.

"Relax. You're gonna love this. I promise," Lena added.
"She's real good at this. I swear. She's gonna do you right."

Cody was about to move Nancy's hand when Frank pointed
the gun at her again. "Didn't she tell you to relax? Now . . .
you be still until she's finished. If I have to tell you again, I'm
gonna let this gun tell you."

Cody forced herself to relax, thinking that if she cooperated, they'd take what little money she had and leave. Before long, she was moaning again, softly at first, then much louder. Her face twisted against her will.

"That's it," Frank said. "Just relax, honey. It won't be long now."

Almost as soon as Frank finished speaking, Cody's body started to writhe and jerk all by itself.

"Ahh. All finished? Now, wasn't that nice?" Nancy asked. She pulled her hand from Cody's vagina and wiped it on her mouth. "Lick it off."

Tears formed again and rolled down Cody's plump cheeks. Feeling totally humiliated, she said, "Please . . . take the money and go. I won't tell anybody about this. I swear to God I won't. Just don't hurt me."

"Oh, we know that, Cody," Nancy said. "We know you're never going to tell anybody we were ever here. Soon as you finish cleaning my fingers, we can get down to business." She backhanded her. "Now lick, you fucking cow! You oughta be glad I took the time to get your fat ass off. Nobody else was gonna do it." She backhanded her again. "Now open that sewer you call a mouth." Cody opened her mouth and Nancy stuck both fingers in. "Taste good . . . don't it?"

Cody nodded—tears continued to flow.

"Where's the money, bitch?" Frank demanded.

Nancy pulled her fingers out of Cody's mouth so she could answer Frank. "In my purse. Over there on the dresser."

"Check it out, Lena," Frank said.

Lena grabbed the purse and rifled through it. She pulled out the money she found and gave it to Frank. He counted the money and looked at Cody.

"Thirty goddamn dollars! Are you fuckin' kidding me? Nancy, beat that bitch's ass."

"I can get you more," Cody quickly offered. "I can get it from the bank tomorrow. Please don't hurt me."

"How much are we talkin' about? And don't you fuckin'

lie to me. If I find out you lied about the amount, I'll kill you slow . . . over three days. And we're still gonna get the money. Now, how much do you have?"

"About twenty thousand dollars."

"Twenty thousand? We got a hundred thousand from Ricky and Suzette."

"Rick and Suzette Nance?" Cody questioned.

"Yes, they cooperated. And we know you can't call the police. What bank is the money in?"

"National Bank."

"Here's what we're gonna do. First thing in the morning, we go to at least ten banks. That's two thousand dollars each bank. And there better be at least twenty thousand."

Lena said, "Here's her bank book. Let's see how much there is." She opened it and flipped to the last page. "Twenty thousand, one hundred forty-two dollars. But I think there's more. She's probably got a safety deposit box or something."

"Probably. But we can't risk going in there. Too many cameras and way too many people. Too much can go wrong. I say we take the twenty and get the hell outta here. That means we gotta stay here for the night and check out of the hotel tomorrow."

Chapter 10

I was energized by the conclusions I had drawn. Though they were far from proving anything, they made me feel as if we could eventually find something that would help Michelle if she came out of the coma. I went downstairs to tell my partner the theory I'd come up with. I walked into the office at the end of the hall, where Kelly was sitting at the Nances' computer.

"You find anything?" I asked

"No, nothing on the computer. But we should pull the hard drive and send it to headquarters."

"The cops didn't pull it?"

"No. They think Michelle and some guy did it. They don't suspect the Nances of anything. They're hoping to get some DNA evidence from Suzette's body that would prove their theory. If she wasn't raped, if she didn't have sex with someone other than the husband that night, they'll probably put it all on Michelle, if they don't find someone else to go down with her. Frankly, from the way they're talking, I don't believe they're even interested in trying to find the supposed hit man If the real killer doesn't get religion and come forward, she's done. Case closed. They'll get her for murder one and accessory to murder. They'll probably give her the maximum sentence too."

"Good thing she's got two bona-fide G-women looking out for her best interests, huh, Kelly?"

"You got that right. How's the family doing? I mean, what are they saying about all of this?"

That was Kelly's way of asking me if they think Michelle did the deed as suspected. That's one reason why she's my best friend. We mesh, almost like we were kindred souls. She knew how to ask me without asking me, giving me a chance to tell her what they said, and then she would draw her own conclusions. But no matter what we found, incriminating or otherwise, I knew I could depend on her all the way.

"You've never met Jake, Michelle's brother, have you?"

"I don't think so . . . no."

"Well, he thinks Michelle might have done this."

She stopped opening computer files and swiveled her chair to face me. "Why?"

"He says she's been acting strange since her husband killed himself a few years ago."

"Strange how?"

"That's just it, Kelly. I don't agree that she's been acting strange. He says she goes on a lot of trips. I say so what? She's a food broker. Traveling is part of her job. He says she doesn't answer the door when she's home. I say they're crowding her. Listen, Michelle married Bruce when she was nineteen years old, okay? For all we know, she could have found herself a man that she knew the family wouldn't approve of.

"When the family found out Bruce was dating her at eighteen and he was thirty, they all had a fit. But when they found out how much he loved her and that he had some money in his pockets and promised to pay for her college education, they changed their tune. The truth may be that the girl hasn't really had a free moment to herself and she was enjoying her bit of personal sovereignty."

"So, what are you saying? She's been doin' a Zane and gettin' buck wild?"

I laughed. Kelly had a way of cutting through all the bullshit and getting to the core of things. "Probably so."

Kelly's cell rang. "Hello." She mouthed, "It's Sterling!"

"So, you're at the hotel? I'm on my way, okay. Oh, and Phoenix's cousin is going to need a good attorney. She's being accused of murder. I'll give you the details later, okay, babe?" She closed the phone and returned it to its holster.

I said, "Um, so, we're finished here, huh?"

"Yeah. I'm going back to the hotel to get seriously laid."

"Fine. I'll have the locals pull the drive and I'll mail it to headquarters in the A.M. Maybe we'll find some dirt on the All-American couple and help Sterling find reasonable doubt."

Chapter 11

Sterling Montgomery Wise was sitting all by himself at a $200 minimum bet blackjack table near the gaming room entrance. He was very well dressed, sporting a white collarless shirt, black slacks, a black tuxedo-collared dinner jacket, and black alligators—his alluring cologne subtle. He was well muscled and wore his hair short with rippling waves. Sterling was definitely a specimen, and he had some serious cash to top it off. I almost envied Kelly. She walked up behind him and put her 38-Cs on his back. I kind of laughed.

"Sit down for a few. I'm on a roll," he told Kelly. His words were easy and relaxed.

Kelly sat on one side of him. I sat on the other. It was almost two in the morning, and the casino was still busy. As soon as one group left a gaming table, another came in to take their place. The dealer slid Sterling an ace of spades and an ace of diamonds. He split them. The dealer slid him the jack of spades and the ten of clubs. He won four hundred dollars just that quick.

"So, how you two ladies doin'?" His smooth baritone sang to us.

Kelly said, "I don't know about Phoenix, but I'm marinating just looking at you, lover."

I laughed, but Sterling remained cool and unmoved as the dealer slid him the two of hearts and a seven of diamonds. The dealer, whose nametag read Sharon, was showing the king of clubs. He motioned for a hit. The dealer slid him the nine of hearts. Sharon turned over a six and then hit it with a queen. Sterling won again.

"Agent Perry," Sterling began without looking at me as Sharon slid him a three of hearts and a four of diamonds. "I hear tell your cousin is in much need of a good attorney." He motioned for a hit. Sharon slid him the ace of clubs. "I was thinking we should discuss her case over breakfast." The dealer busted again.

"That's fine," I said.

"Kelly, baby," the words just rolled off his tongue, "I'm staying in the high rollers suite. The desk clerk has the key for you. I'll be up in about an hour. That'll give you time to freshen up. The champagne and strawberries are in the fridge."

Kelly put her hand between Sterling's legs, squeezed, and said, "Don't keep me waitin' too long, lover." Then she looked at me. "And you . . . you can use my vibrator if you want."

I laughed. "You mean you're not going to share?"

"No, my sister. You gotta get yo' own."

Chapter 12

A message from Keyth was waiting for me when Kelly and I got to the front desk. I looked at my cell and saw that I had a voicemail message there too. I figured he must have gotten my message and simply responded to it instead of calling. He probably didn't want to disturb me, knowing I was going to get involved in the case right away. The message said that he wanted me to call him when I returned to the hotel.

We took the elevator up to the parlor suite and walked into our spacious dwelling for the night. Kelly went to her room to pack a few things for her early morning booty call while I set up my laptop. I wanted to check my email. My kids usually sent me love notes. I signed onto AOL then called my husband on my cell. While the phone rang, I grabbed an apple from the silver fruit bowl that sat in the middle of the dining room table, and looked out at the picturesque view of Sin City. The bright lights were hypnotic and alluring. I bit into the apple.

"Hello," Keyth said in a groggy tone.

"Sorry to wake you, babe, but I just got in."

Keyth cleared his throat a couple of times and said, "Don't worry about it. It's nearly six here anyway. How's it going?"

I went over to my laptop and sat down, preparing to open my mail. "We don't have much to go on other than the shotgun and tire iron the police found at the scene." I was still looking out of the window while I was talking to Keyth. That's when I had an epiphany. Seeing all the bright hotel lights triggered it. "Honey, I might have something."

"What's that?"

"Michelle travels a lot and she gets hotel and airline points with Hilton. I'm betting she stayed at either a Hilton or Embassy while she was here." I was about to check my mail, but instead, I typed in www.embassysuites.com to see how many of their hotels were in the city. There were four Hiltons and two Embassy Suites hotels not far from the Mandalay Bay.

"How's Michelle doing?"

"She's still in a coma, Keyth. I don't know if she's going to make it back."

"Pssssst."

That was Kelly getting my attention. I faced her and put up my index finger.

"Let me call you tomorrow, babe, okay?"

"Okay. You know the tournament is tomorrow, right?"

"Yeah. Be sure to videotape it for me. Tell Savannah and Luther I said to relax and be flexible, like water. I love you. Goodnight." I hit the END button.

"Kelly, I'm going to check out a lead with the Hilton people."

"You want me to go with you?"

"Yes," I said in a serious tone to see what she was going to say. I didn't need her on this one. I probably wouldn't find anything anyway. I just wanted to see how she was going to respond, knowing she couldn't wait to get her panties off.

"Are you serious?"

"Yeah. What's the problem? I'm paying for this trip, and

it's costing me and Keyth a fortune. First-class tickets to Vegas and a first-class suite to bed down in. Not to mention the food. So, yeah. I'm serious."

I wanted to laugh when her smile vanished.

Kelly exhaled hard and frowned. "How long is this going to take?"

That's when I lost it. I laughed hard and from my belly. "I just wanted to see how hard up you were. And looking at your face, I think you better hurry up and get yourself a piece."

Kelly laughed with me before saying, "You sure you don't need me? I'll go if you do."

"Naw, girl. I got this."

Chapter 13

Twenty minutes later, I was back in the Chrysler 300, heading north on Las Vegas Boulevard. I turned left on Flamingo and then right on Paradise and pulled into the Embassy Suites parking lot. The whole trip took about four minutes. As I approached the front desk, I was hoping my credentials would be enough for the clerk to let me into Michelle's room. I didn't have a search warrant, so she didn't have to let me in.

"May I help you, ma'am?"

"Yes. I'm Special Agent in Charge, Phoenix Perry," I said, attempting to sound official without being threatening. "I called a few minutes ago. You have a Michelle Michaels registered here."

"I remember speaking to you. I need to see your ID first, ma'am." I gave her my credentials. After looking closely at my ID and badge, she thanked me and hit a few buttons on the computer terminal. "Room 711."

"I'm going to need a key. The woman is a suspect in a murder case. And right now, Ms. Michaels is in a coma at the

Desert Springs Hospital. I need to know when she checked in and when she's scheduled to check out."

The clerk programmed a key and handed it to me. "She checked in two days ago, and she's scheduled to check out Sunday afternoon."

"Was she alone?"

"I don't know, but we have the room listed for one person."

I thanked her and took the elevator to the seventh floor.

If Michelle wasn't in Vegas to meet a guy, what was she doing here? If she was here with a guy, why weren't they in the same room? Where is he now? Was he a guest at this hotel? Maybe Excalibur Foods was having a convention here and she was seeing a colleague. That would explain separate rooms.

I removed the do not disturb sign, opened room 711, and walked in. I picked up the phone and called the front desk. "This is Agent Perry. Is there a way to print out early check-outs? I'm specifically looking for people who checked in the same day as Ms. Michaels, but for some reason, checked out early."

"Sure, I can print you a list. I'll have it ready for you when you come back down, okay?"

"Great. Can you tell me if you have an Excalibur Foods convention at this hotel?"

"Hold on, I'll check. We've got several conventions going on, but none of them are for Excalibur Foods."

"Thanks," I said and hung up the phone. Then I entered the bedroom area of the suite. Her bed was still made. If Michelle was meeting a guy for sex, they didn't do it here, I assumed. The bed was professionally made and the do not disturb sign was still on the door. Maids don't usually violate the sign if you're going to be staying in the hotel another night. If the maid did violate the do not disturb sign, why leave it on the door? Maybe they met in his room.

I opened the drawers. Her clothes were still there. She was planning to return to her room. I didn't find her purse, so she probably had it with her. But there was nothing in the police report about her purse.

That means it was probably in the car she drove, if she was alone. I didn't believe she was alone. The cops had checked with all the rent-a-car agencies and cab companies, but she didn't rent a car or take a cab. How had she gotten to the Nance residence without a car? There had to be someone else because the cops didn't find any abandoned cars near the murder scene. Someone could have stolen it, but it was highly unlikely that someone had stolen the car she had driven the same night she was found at a double murder scene with shotgun pellets in her chest. Besides, I don't believe that someone who had discharged a shotgun would have the presence of mind and the gumption to call a cab and then wait for it to arrive, knowing someone may have heard the shots.

I checked the bathroom. Nothing unusual. Nothing unusual in the living room either. I took the elevator back to the lobby and went to the front desk. The same clerk was there, doing something at her computer terminal.

"Hi. Do you have that printout for me?"

"Yes. Here you go." She handed it to me.

"Can I get you to do me two more favors?"

"Sure."

"I need her bill and the credit card number she used."

After hitting a few buttons, she handed me the bill. I looked at it, and it confirmed everything I suspected. Michelle had driven her Escalade all the way from Toledo, Ohio. I left the lobby and immediately checked the parking lot and didn't see it. That meant that the man she was with at the Nance house probably had her car. I hoped he had her purse and used the credit card. That way we could track him.

Chapter 14

Kelly McPherson was a screamer and totally uninhibited in bed. The chemistry between her and Sterling was magnetic—so magnetic that not only did he fly to Las Vegas at a moment's notice, he also made monthly trips to DC to hear those deep, guttural sighs. He loved the way she talked in bed—the way she called his name, and just about anything she said while they gave into their carnality. Though he would never tell her, Kelly reminded him of two former lovers, Cynthia Charles and Chase Davenport. Both women were the kind of lovers that made a man's toes curl. They made his body quiver when he climaxed. What he liked most about all three women was that they kept their relationships with him in perspective. They didn't try to turn it into something it wasn't—like a romance. It was lust, pure and simple. They all knew it. They all loved it. That's why Sterling was surprised when Kelly said, "Let's talk this time, okay?"

They were both on their backs, cuddling, relaxing after a vigorous round of unbridled, lust-driven sex, when the question came out of nowhere. Sterling raised his head from the comfortable pillow and looked at Kelly, puzzled as to why she wanted to talk. After four years of meeting each other for hot sex, she finally wanted to talk about something.

"Talk?" He frowned. "You're not going to try and turn this into a relationship, are you?"

"No. It's just that Phoenix asked me about us. And the truth is we've been seeing each other on a physical basis, and that's fine. I'm not trying to get serious on you or anything, okay? But would it hurt you to tell me something meaningful about yourself? Or maybe something about your family?"

"Something meaningful, huh?"

Sensing that he was about to open up a little, Kelly took a deep, satisfying breath and exhaled. "Yes. Something meaningful."

"How 'bout this. A few years back, my baby brother, William, and his bride, Terry, spent their honeymoon in this very suite—in this bed."

"Really?"

"Yep."

"Why haven't you ever married, Sterling?"

"The truth?"

"No. Lie to me. I live for it."

Sterling flashed his million-dollar smile and said, "Don't be such a smartass."

Grinning, Kelly said, "You know you love that about me."

"I do, huh?"

"That and the way I move when we're doin' the nasty." They laughed. "So, tell me. How come you never married?"

Sterling exhaled deeply and rolled out of bed. The air conditioning was a bit frosty, so he put on one of the white terrycloth bathrobes the Mandalay Bay provided, and went to the window.

Realizing she had asked a question that evoked a painful memory, Kelly put on her robe and stood behind him. Then she wrapped her arms around his waist and laid her head on his back. "Hey . . . you don't have to answer, okay? I didn't mean to inflame old wounds."

"No. It's time I moved on. Everybody says it. Both my brothers, Will and Jericho, bring it up whenever we get together. They want me to be happy. Maybe talking about it will help." He paused for a moment and stared at the city lights. "I've only told one person about what really happened between me and Vanessa. That was my baby brother, Will."

Kelly felt closer to him now that he was starting to open up to her. She pressed herself against him, squeezing tightly, like she wanted to be a part of him. She exhaled lovingly, smiled, and said, "You sure you wanna tell me about it?"

"No, I'm not sure. But since you asked, I'll tell you. About ten years ago, I was dating a woman named Vanessa Wright. She was stunningly beautiful, and she had this dark skin that felt like expensive velvet. She was the cream of the crop—the cream. You understand what I'm saying?"

Kelly didn't have a jealous bone in her body. She believed she could compete with any woman, no matter how beautiful the woman was, because not only was she attractive, she was sexy too. Besides, Sterling had never hid the fact that he still had protected sex with a variety of women.

"Yes." Kelly exhaled, feeling closer with each word he offered.

In spite of what she'd told Phoenix and Sterling about not getting serious, she was ready to settle down. She was in her early forties and getting older every day, it seemed. She didn't have much of a life, and didn't have much to look forward to. All she had was her house, which she paid off with the alimony payments she received from her first husband, two children she hardly knew because she thought she deserved a life too, and one friend. Phoenix was the only woman Kelly ever trusted.

Sterling continued, "Listen, Kelly, what I'm about to say is going to sound arrogant, but I don't give a fuck. The truth is the truth. Women say the same shit about men, and they're right about us. What I'm about say is right about them. You can get mad if you want, but after you hear what I have to say, you'll know I'm telling the truth. When it comes to a man of means . . . a lot of women think that because they have a vagina, a man like me is supposed to accept anything that comes along. I'm supposed to be so enamored by their sexual weapons that I'm supposed to pay their bills and buy them the moon if they want it. I mean some of these women have no education; some don't even have a job and no prospects. But I'm supposed to want them because they're nice-looking. Yet, they want me because of what I can do for them.

"See, a man like me with deep-ass pockets is a certain kind of woman's dream come true. Not all women, Kelly, but too many, okay? I don't trust no bitch that's all about my dough, or my status as an attorney and sports agent. I don't play that shit. A few years back, a good friend of mine, Nelson Kennard, got all twisted over one of them gold diggin' bitches the night before September 11. She almost fucked his life up because he loved her and she didn't love him. If I hadn't hired Phoenix's husband to check her out . . . well . . . all I can say is Nelson probably wouldn't have found his lovely wife, Grace."

Confidently, Kelly said, "And Vanessa wasn't like the other bitches, huh?"

Sterling laughed. "No. She wasn't. She was the dream— the real deal. Had her shit together. Had her own dough. Didn't need a man with money. But she loved me. I mean she really loved me, Kelly. She accepted me as I was. Didn't try to change a brotha and shit. And get this; she knew I liked to have a little something on the side."

"So, you had your cake and ate it too?"

"Yep."

"Sounds like you had a good deal, Sterling. So, how did you fuck it up?"

He laughed again. "I guess I picked the right person to tell this shit to."

"I'm glad you think so. I do like you, okay?"

"I like you, Kelly. I do. Okay?"

"I know. And don't get all serious on me. Just tell me how you fucked over *Ms.* Wright."

"Vanessa had three rules, and I broke them all at the same time."

"What were the rules?"

"Absolutely no friends. Always use a condom. And never in the home we shared. First, I banged Brandy, her best friend. She was fine as hell. I mean Brandy was bad to the bone. Face, body, sweet ass—she had it all. They had been friends since they were teenagers. I fucked all that up. Used to be a time when I blamed that shit on Vanessa for letting that bitch hang around. Now . . . don't get me wrong, Kelly. It was my fault. I know that now. But Brandy was all over me all the fuckin' time. She wasn't Vanessa's friend. And to be totally honest, I wasn't Vanessa's friend either. Had I been a *real* friend, I would've told her what her so-called *friend* was doing behind her back. But I had to get a piece instead of doing the right thing. I was going to leave it alone afterward. At least that was my plan."

"So, how did she find out about it?"

"I was coming to that. Second, she walked in on it just as I was about to get off. I had one of Brandy's legs over the couch and one on the floor, pumping her hard and steady, moaning from the sensation she gave me—which was exquisite, by the way, probably because it was forbidden. And to show you how callous I was, when I heard Vanessa's key enter the front door, when I heard her and her friends talking about the Mary Kay makeup kits they had returned to get, I knew I was caught, so I went on and busted a nut just before she walked into the room. To top all that shit off, I didn't wear a condom, which was her third rule. When she walked in, my meat was glistening, and sperm was still drippin'."

Kelly doubled over and laughed hard from her belly. She caught her breath and said, "So, you figured that since you were caught, you might as well finish, huh?" Then she laughed again and sat on the bed.

"Well, yeah." Sterling laughed along with her. "Might as well. I was already cold busted. I guess I was thinkin' why get caught and still be frustrated? It wasn't like me and Vanessa was going to screw at that point."

Chapter 15

Kelly looked at Sterling, who was still staring out of the window. In the four years she had known him, she had never seen the serious, reflective side of him. She sensed his vulnerability and was drawn by it. She wondered if he was ready to stop bed hopping and settle down. She also wondered if she was ready to stop playing Russian roulette, going from man to man, taking crazy chances with the AIDS virus still lurking, seeking to snuff out another precious life.

"Hey," Kelly said softly. "You okay?"

He didn't respond. Kelly stood again and went over to where he was standing. She wrapped her arms around him and laid her head on his back again. "You okay, baby?"

Sterling looked at his watch and then out the window again. Feeling vulnerable and exposed, having shown her his heart, he decided to change the subject. "You ever see that new cable show, *No Holds Barred: Celebrities Uncensored?*"

"Never heard of it."

"The show is wild," he said after looking at her reflection through the glass. He picked up the remote control and pushed the power button. "Look-alike actors play celebrities who've been caught in compromising situations or accused of a crime. The look-alikes give candid interviews. It's fake, of course. I'm surprised you've never heard of this show."

Kelly stared at Sterling for a few seconds and said, "Hey . . . if you ever wanna talk about this again, let me know, okay?"

Sterling didn't answer her question. Even though it had been ten years since the break-up, he still loved Vanessa, and he was still hoping that by some miracle, she would one day forgive him and they would get back together and live in Camelot again. Only this time, he'd be true to her. This time, he'd treat her the way he should have when they were together.

He walked to the front of the bed and sat down. "Let's watch this, okay?"

Kelly stared at Sterling for a few seconds and sat on the bed next to him. She knew he was still deeply troubled by losing Vanessa, and began wondering if she could ever get him to take her seriously—serious enough to consider her for a more permanent arrangement. But deep within, she knew she wanted a commitment from him she wasn't ever going to get because he was still in love with another woman.

The show Sterling wanted to see was already in progress when he changed the channel to the premium station. An actor portraying Middleweight Boxing Champion Drew "Body Shot" McGraw, wearing a sleeveless black muscle shirt, a pair of Levi's, and open-toed sandals, was sitting in a chair. He and host Julia Jordan were sitting in director's chairs, facing each other like it was a real interview. Julia was Caucasian. She was wearing a lavender skirt suit and matching flat shoes. Her hair was coiffed, and she wore purple-framed glasses that made her look intelligent.

The camera was focused on Julia, who was asking the champ another question. "As you know, this is no holds barred, so let's cut to the chase. What really happened in that hotel room with that teenaged girl?"

"See, Julia. See, that's the kinda shit I'm talkin' about."

"What do you mean, Drew?"

"You know goddamned well I'm only nineteen myself, so to constantly call her a teenager makes the public think I'm older than I really am. The teenager, as you call her, is nineteen too. She checked me in when I arrived at the hotel. So let's be a little more balanced with this shit, okay, Julia?"

Julia shifted her weight, leaned forward and frowned. Then she smiled flirtatiously and said, "Okay, Drew, fair enough. Let's hear your version. What happened? Why did you let her in your room?"

"Look, goddammit, she called my room and asked for a fuckin' autograph. I said, 'Sure, I'll meet you in the lobby in ten minutes.' She says, 'I'm on my cell right outside your door. Open up.' I knew then that she was there to give it up, so I opened the door and let her in. But I wasn't plannin' to bang her."

Julia rolled her eyes and swiveled her chair from left to right, attempting to maintain her composure, and said, "Oh—come—on, Drew. You just said you knew why she was there. Yet you let her in?"

"Yeah. I let her in. Lots of women come to my hotel rooms. I let some in and nothing happens. Some—well, shit happens."

Julia said, "What do you say to the people who think it's stupid to let women in your room since you're a well-known public figure?"

He looked around for the camera so he could look directly into it. "What do I say to people who think that? I say start using your head for something more than a fuckin' hat rack! Think for yourself for a change! Stop believing every word you hear in the damned media. And whatever you do, don't blame the victim!"

"So, you're the victim?"

"Exactly. Call me stupid if you want, but we were two consenting adults, as they say. She wanted it and so did I." He paused for a second. "When two people meet in a bar and end up in a hotel room, that's consensual sex, right? But if one of the people has twenty million dollars, it's rape. And if I'm stupid for letting her in, she's stupid for coming in, knowing about all the so-called celebrity rape cases, right? Elvis and the Beatles didn't have to go through this shit fifty years ago. What the fuck happened between now and then?"

Sterling looked at Kelly. Even though it was only a mock interview, it pertained to an actual, ongoing real-life court case. Sterling said, "See, this is why I don't want to get married. This bullshit is pervasive. He wanted some pussy and she wanted to give it to him. Now he's up on rape charges because he has money."

"Well . . . he shouldn't think with his dick," Kelly said, laughing.

But Sterling didn't laugh at all. He stared at her for a long minute without blinking and decided that this would be the last time they met for sex. But even so, he kissed her again, hard on the lips, opened her robe, exposing her naked breasts. Before long, Kelly's sighs filled the room again.

Chapter 16

Frank Howard was the only man who had checked out early. When I got back to my hotel suite, I turned on my laptop, tied into the Homeland Security mainframe, and ran a check on him. Howard turned out to be a highly decorated Navy SEAL from Saint Paul, Minnesota. If I had the same Frank Howard that stayed in the same hotel as my cousin, and I believed I did, he certainly had the skill to throw a knife under pressure with deadly accuracy. According to his credit card company, he last used his card at the Embassy Suites Hotel in Tucson, Arizona. I called the Las Vegas Police Department and brought them up to speed, and asked them to put out an all points bulletin on Michelle's Escalade.

I called the Tucson Police Department and told them to get over to the Embassy on East Broadway Boulevard and pick up Frank Howard, and that I'd be there as soon as possible. I let them know he was a suspect for a Las Vegas homicide. I told them it would be a good idea to check the Embassy at the airport on Tucson Boulevard, just in case the credit card people made a mistake. I wanted to cover all my bases, so I ran the names of the three women that checked out early, too. One was from Barstow, California. Another one was from St. George, Utah—both were within driving distance to Las Vegas. The third woman was from New Hampshire, Vermont. I called the desk clerk at the Embassy again. When the clerk I'd spoken to earlier answered, I identified myself, and said, "Is it unusual for four guests to check out early?"

"Not in Vegas, especially if they drove in. It happens all the time when people lose their money faster than they thought they would. When they fly in, they usually stay because it would cost more to take an earlier flight back home."

I gave her the names of the three women and asked if they were alone. She told me their rooms listed two people. I thanked her again and hung up. So far, Frank Howard was my only lead. Since he was a Navy SEAL, the Navy would have a sample of his DNA. If the autopsy report proved that Suzette Nance had sex with someone other than Rick Nance, we could easily prove if Howard had been at the scene of the murders. The only glitch was that it took two weeks to get DNA results. I thought Frank Howard was an excellent candidate to pin the murders on, which is why I shouldn't have been on this case. Truth be told, I was feeling pretty good about the idea of him committing the murders and not my cousin. For all I knew, whoever killed Suzette could have very easily put a gun in my cousin's hands and forced her to blow Rick's face off. I was holding on to hope for dear life, I knew. Nevertheless, that still wouldn't explain how Michelle knew Rick and Suzette Nance in the first place. It certainly didn't explain what she was doing in their home with a Scarecrow's mask covering her face. Suddenly, I didn't feel that much better after all.

As dawn slowly crept through the windows, I had almost forgotten that I hadn't had any sleep. I was up all night chasing the bad guys, while Kelly and Sterling got their swerve on in the high rollers suite. Might as well stay up now, I thought, so I went to the United Airlines website and made reservations for Tucson. Our flight was leaving at 10:30. I looked at my watch. Five-thirty. I packed our bags as quickly as I could and called Sterling's suite.

"Good Morning, Sterling. Is Kelly awake?"

"Yes. We haven't slept."

"You tiger, you!"

"Kelly told me about your cousin's situation. I'm gonna put Le'sett Santiago on it. She's an excellent attorney."

"Thanks. I really appreciate this, Sterling."

"Hey, I owe you guys for keeping me alive when that crazy Nimburu woman was trying to take me out. I haven't forgotten that. It's my turn now."

"Great! Thank you so much!"

"No problem. Here's your friend."

"Hello, Phoenix," Kelly said.

I could tell she was smiling. She sounded like spending the night with Sterling was exactly what she needed. As far as I knew, she wasn't seeing anyone in DC, but she didn't tell me about all her relationships anymore because she knew I would tell her to find one person and settle down.

"Musta been good."

"Always," she cooed.

"Listen, while you were doing a Lionel Ritchie, I did some real police work. Found out quite a bit. I'll fill you in later. I have to mail that hard drive to headquarters this morning and stop by the hospital to check on Aunt Ruth and the rest of the family. Our flight to Tucson takes off at 10:30 this morning, so get your last piece before I get back, Miss All Night Long."

"What are we going to Tucson for?"

"I've got a suspect."

"Already?"

"I got it like that."

"I see. Well, are you coming up for breakfast?"

"I'll be back by 7:30 or so. We can eat then. Be dressed and ready to go."

Chapter 17

United Airlines flight 1619 landed at Tucson International airport at 11:55. We took advantage of the flight time and slept for the hour and twenty-five minutes it took to get there. We grabbed our bags, rented a car, and checked into the first hotel we saw, which, ironically, was the Embassy on Tucson Boulevard. The desk clerk graciously gave us directions to the Embassy on East Broadway. I had filled Kelly and Sterling in on my findings over breakfast. According to the autopsy, Suzette Nance didn't have another man's sperm in her vagina. They found it in her stomach. I gave LVPD the address of the crime lab in DC and asked them to send them a sample so they could run the suspect's DNA against that of Frank Howard. I had already put his military picture on the wire. We now knew who we were looking for. I just hoped it wasn't a wild goose chase. For all I knew, Frank Howard could have had legitimate reasons for being in Vegas, checking out early, and going to Tucson. I didn't know if he had Michelle's Escalade or not. But if I'm being truthful, I hoped he did.

When we reached the Embassy on Broadway, I flashed my credentials and asked the clerk if Tucson PD had been there yet. She told me the two detectives by the lobby entrance were waiting for us—a black male and a Latina female. After flashing our credentials, I said, "I'm Special Agent Perry, and this is Agent McPherson."

The female detective spoke first. "I'm Maria Santana, and this is my partner, Travis Best." She shook hands with us and continued speaking with a distinct Spanish accent. "The room is clean. We do have questions about the clothes, though."

"The clothes?" Kelly questioned.

"Our lieutenant told us you were looking for one male suspect. A Frank Howard, right?"

"Yes," I said.

"Well, we found men's and women's clothes in the room. This could be a man vacationing with his wife. We wanted to stick around and question them when they returned. They didn't stay the night in the room, though, and never returned as far as we can tell."

I looked at Kelly. We were thinking the same unimaginable thoughts. There were two of them—a man and a woman.

I said, "Maybe the woman shot Rick Nance. All we know is that Michelle Michaels, an LVPD suspect, fired a gun. We don't know what kind." I knew I was grabbing at straws, but she was my cousin. I'd grab a lion's balls if it helped prove Michelle didn't kill anyone.

That's when I decided to check something out. I went to the front desk and asked the clerk if I could use a computer terminal. I wanted to make sure this was a good lead. Using my password, I tied into the Homeland Security mainframe and checked flight manifests from Las Vegas to Tucson to see if Frank Howard had flown in. If so, that meant the Escalade could still be in Vegas. If not, that meant he could have driven it to Tucson. I didn't see his name on any of the flights that left Vegas for Tucson since the night of the murders.

So I checked to see if he had flown to Vegas from Saint

Paul. He had. I then checked all the rent-a-car agencies to see if he rented a vehicle and drove to Tucson. He hadn't. If he had, there was no record of it. On the other hand, maybe the woman rented the car they drove to Tucson. Even though LVPD didn't find his prints at the crime scene, Howard was still a good suspect in the Nance murder case as far as I was concerned. Too bad it would take two weeks for the DNA results. If they were instantaneous, we still wouldn't know if he committed the crimes, but we would know if he had in fact been the man who'd had sex with Suzette Nance that night. That fact would give me something more to hang on to until we solved the case.

Another set of questions bombarded my mind. If Frank Howard had sex with Suzette Nance, where was the woman who shared his suite and in all probability his bed, while he was making it with Suzette? Was she watching them? Or was she the one who had beaten Rick Nance with the tire iron? And what was Michelle doing while all of this was going on? What role did she play? Maybe Kelly was right. Maybe my cousin was doing a Zane and had gotten seriously buck wild. I went back over to where Kelly and the detectives were standing and told them what I'd found. Best and Santana decided to get a bite to eat at Jason's Deli, a local restaurant not far from the hotel we were staking out. They asked us to take over while they ate.

When the detectives left, I said, "Kelly, I'm going up to the room. I need to take a look around for myself. Who knows? Best and Santana could have missed something. Call me on my cell if Howard and the woman come back. And whatever you do, don't wait until they're in the elevator like you did when we were chasing down Coco Nimburu, okay?"

Kelly laughed hard and said, "You got out of the room in time, didn't you?"

I rolled my eyes at her. I didn't think she'd have any trouble recognizing Howard. We had a copy of the picture he took when he was in the Navy. "You did look at the picture, right?"

"Right," Kelly said. Then she winked her eye and pulled it out of her breast pocket and looked at it. When she saw me staring at her, she rolled her eyes and said, "Don't worry, Phoenix. I'll wait until the elevator reaches the floor you're on and then give you a call, okay?" She laughed again.

Chapter 18

Cody Mills was dressed to kill and sitting behind the wheel of Michelle's Escalade. Frank Howard thought it would be best to have her in the driver's seat when they got to the drive-through window so that one, the camera could see her and two, the teller could see her driving an expensive car and looking the part of someone who had money. He hoped his idea would expedite the transaction.

The plan wasn't working as perfectly as they thought it would. The teller at the first drive-through they went to questioned the very first withdrawal and only gave Cody $2000 because she knew her as a regular customer. She reminded her of the bank's policy, which was to only give customers $500 at the drive through. If a customer wanted more than that, they had to come inside, which made it easier to protect their customers from criminals. Cody knew the bank's policy, which was why she was so willing to comply with their demands to go to the bank. They had only collected ten percent of what they thought they were going to get, and they were totally pissed.

Nancy sat in the front with Cody. She had a pistol in case

their hostage tried to signal the teller. After Cody pulled away from the drive-through teller, Nancy gave the pistol to Frank, who was sitting in the backseat as back-up, while Lena followed them in Cody's black Jetta. Michelle's Escalade offered black-tinted windows for the backseat passengers, and the tellers couldn't see Frank, which was why the teller didn't suspect that Cody was under any kind of duress. The teller saw two women in an expensive automobile, which was normal.

"Do you mind if we stop and get something to eat?" Cody asked. "If it's okay, I'll go through the drive-through, okay?"

Frank looked out the window and spotted several fast food restaurants. "Sure. You've been a good girl, Cody. Pull over at the Wendy's up ahead."

They ordered burgers and fries and ate in the cool air of the Escalade, which also shielded them from the torturous rays of the sun. Lena pulled up next to them. She ordered a salad with a Diet Coke.

"How was the food, Cody?" Frank asked.

"Very good. Thanks for asking. Are you guys gonna let me go now? You have the money. I'm thinking why not part company now? I can drive my car home from here. What do you think? You know I'm not gonna go to the police over this."

"Sure. No problem. I just have one question before you go."

"A question, Frank?"

"Yeah, Cody. It's a question we feel compelled to ask. You don't mind, do you?"

Cody Mills was glad she had cooperated; she was glad she hadn't done anything foolish like trying to signal the bank tellers. She looked at him through the rearview mirror and smiled broadly. "What's the question, Frank?"

"Who is Bruce Michaels?"

"Bruce Michaels?" She looked sincere when she repeated the name. "I have no idea."

"I believe you, Cody. But you really oughta remember the names of the people you rob."

Then the small caliber gun he was holding went off. It made a popping sound, like a firecracker. *Pop!*

Frank had shot Cody Mills in the back of the head through the leather headrest. "Who do you think you're foolin'?" *Pop!* "You knew we couldn't get the twenty K, didn't you?" *Pop!*

When Frank pumped the bullets into her, a gleeful grin crept across Nancy's face, followed by an eruption of crazed laughter that rivaled Vincent Price's evil rendition of the same. He looked at Nancy, wondering how she could laugh about murder. Even though he'd pulled the trigger, he was only giving Cody Mills what he thought she had earned.

Lena pulled the Jetta up next to the Escalade and pushed the power button that controlled the passenger side window and blew the horn. Frank's window slid down. "Is it done?" she asked.

"Yeah, baby, it's done."

"Well, what are we waiting for? Let's get outta here before the cops show up!"

Frank and Nancy got out of the Escalade and into the Jetta. Lena got into the passenger's seat, and Frank drove back to their hotel.

"Did you get her purse, Nancy?" Frank asked.

"Got it."

Chapter 19

"I know this is going to sound stupid," Detective Santana began. "I mean I'm sure you two have already thought of this, but did Ms. Michaels have Onstar in her Escalade? I hear all Cadillacs have the system. It's just a matter of whether or not she paid for the service."

"I don't know," I said.

"Well, if she does, they can locate the car in a matter of seconds. It looks like they're not coming back to the hotel."

I felt a little inept for not thinking of that myself. I needed to justify myself, so I said, "I drive a Mustang Cobra. It never crossed my mind to check for Onstar services. But if I'm ever looking for a missing car again, that'll be my first thought from now on. Thanks, Detective Santana."

"Actually, I wouldn't have known myself, but my cousin just bought a brand new Escalade last week and she told me about the feature. It's free for the first year. After that, you have to pay, she said. Otherwise, I wouldn't have thought of it either."

That made me feel better, but I didn't let on. I called the Onstar people and explained to them that I was a Homeland

Security agent looking for the vehicle. Thank God they didn't give me a hard time. The customer service representative probably thought I was looking for terrorists or something. I gave the representative Michelle's name, address, and telephone number. She told me the car was on North Oracle, twenty minutes away from the hotel. I told Santana what I had learned, and she knew exactly where it was. We hustled out of the lobby and into our vehicles. Our tires burned as we sped down the street. Santana's siren blared. We made it there in minutes. We could see someone sitting in the driver's seat.

"Step outta the vehicle with your hands up," Santana said from her car's public address system. Thirty seconds later, she repeated the command.

Cautiously, we approached the vehicle, weapons drawn. Through the dark tinted windows, I could see that the person in the front seat was a woman. She looked like she was asleep. I opened the door and saw the blood. In the backseat was a purse. I got the feeling it was Michelle's, and took it into custody. After searching it, I found Michelle's driver's license and her credit cards.

Chapter 20

The sirens screamed as Frank Howard stopped the Jetta at the lobby door of the Embassy Suites Hotel. He saw three women and one man get into two cars and hurry onto East Broadway. He was going to check out of the hotel, but thought better of it. Without any fanfare, he drove off and got back into traffic. He didn't know why the police were at the hotel. They could have been there for any number of reasons, but Frank thought it best to keep going. As far as he was concerned, the police had finally found them.

"We need our clothes," Lena said.

"We've got a hundred thousand cash and some change. We don't need the clothes. We need to get the hell outta Dodge. They probably found Cody."

Lena said, "We gotta get rid of this car."

"The car's fine. It'll take them a while to find out who she is. We've got her purse and her credit cards, remember? Which one of you wants to be Cody Mills for a while?"

"Let's find a mall and go shopping," Nancy said. "Might as well run the card up before they cut it off."

"Yeah," Lena said. "I deserve some nice things for a change. I want some diamonds."

Frank said, "Let's call her credit card companies and find out her limit. Hell, we can even find out her passwords and get cash."

"They won't give that out over the phone, will they?" Lena asked.

"Of course they will. They'll go through a number of security checks first, like what's the three-digit code on the back of the card, which we have in our possession. We have her license, so we know her social security number. We have her address and everything. All you've gotta do is say you forgot it. Only a real asshole wouldn't give you the password. Just sound confident and answer every question and be friendly. Then they'll tell you the password and give you the limit."

"Are you sure?"

"Of course I'm sure. Listen, the credit card people don't know the bitch is dead, do they? And the police won't even know her name for a while. She lived alone, remember? Didn't even have a man to fuck her. They can fingerprint her, but if she doesn't have a record, that won't help them. They probably won't even know what kind of car she drives or where she even lives to ask her neighbors. She's just another Jane Doe to the cops at this point, believe me. So the car will be safe for a while too. Just relax. I've got this thing under control, believe me. But just to be safe, I say we gas up the car and get to Albuquerque. I wanna ask Audrey Jefferies if she remembers Bruce Michaels."

It didn't matter if Audrey knew Bruce or not. They were going to kill her no matter what.

Chapter 21

We were at a dead end. The Tucson Police Department would have to wait until someone claimed the body or filed a missing persons report. That would give the killers a minimum of twenty-four hours to get to their next victim—if there was another victim. People know the police will not take a missing persons report until the person has been missing for at least twenty-four hours, so the next of kin probably wouldn't even come forward until the next day at the earliest. Depending on how close she was to friends and family, it might be weeks before anyone she knew came forward. This may be a bit morbid, but I was kind of glad we had another body because it helped Michelle. Who knows? The couple we were looking for could have brainwashed her. She could have joined a cult. If Jake was right, if she was acting strange, they could have had some kind of power over her. For all we knew, this could be some kind of crazy Charles Manson shit—Helter Skelter! Michelle may have wanted to get out and when she exercised her free will, they tried to kill her. Which reminded me, I needed to check on Aunt Ruth and the rest of the family. Maybe Michelle had come out of it by now.

Kelly parked the car, and as we walked into the hotel, she said, "Do you think Santana would make a good agent?"

I smiled, knowing where she was going with the question. "I was wondering about that myself. Let me ask you something, Kelly. Did you feel stupid when she mentioned satellite tracking?"

"Hell yeah. I guess what bothered me was that people think we're the fuckin' CIA when it comes to law enforcement. We don't track cars, we track people. But I didn't let on. I stood there stone-faced, just like you."

"Let's see if she wants the gig. If so, let's recommend her."

"I'm hungry. How 'bout we order some grub?"

"Sounds good to me."

We went up to our room and ordered steak subs. Kelly had an Orange Slice with her meal. I had herbal tea.

I checked my phone for messages, and my husband had sent me a voicemail, saying that he had sent me an email with an attachment of the video he shot of Savannah and Luther. With all the running around we'd been doing, I forgot all about the tournament. I went to the bedroom and grabbed my laptop and took it into the living room, where there was a high-speed modem hook-up, and started downloading the video. Apparently he sent me the entire tournament. Even with a high-speed modem, it would take a while to complete. I needed a hot bath, some food in my belly, and some much-needed shut eye. So I took a hot bath to relax and fell asleep.

My body jerked when I heard Kelly yell, "The food's here."

By the time I entered the living room, Kelly had paid the waiter and placed the food on the table. I sat down and took a bite of my sub.

"Ever been to Minnesota, Kelly?"

"Nope."

"Wanna go?"

"Nope."

"Well, that's where we're going in the morning."

"You think Howard went home?"

"No, but we have no idea where he went. Might as well check out his place. Who knows? We might find a print or two. And if we're really lucky, we might find Frank Howard."

Chapter 22

Frank Howard's House
1501 Albemarle Street
Saint Paul, Minnesota

I knocked on the door and then yelled, "Frank Howard! FBI! You're wanted on suspicion of murder!"

We knew he wasn't there, but hey, it was procedure. Besides, someone could have been filming us with a camcorder. The last thing we needed was to end up on the evening news. I kicked in the door and we entered the premises, weapons drawn. The place was a pig sty. Clothes everywhere, pizza boxes with left over pizza in it, roaches crawled around like they owned the place. And that smell. What the hell was that smell?

We put our free hands over our mouths. Tears formed in my eyes and rolled down my cheeks. I needed a top-of-the-line gas mask so I could see.

We continued on through the thick haze in the shack.

Kelly coughed and said, "You know what I'm thinkin', Phoenix?"

"Oh, I don't know. Somebody's dead, perhaps?"

"And they've been dead a long fucking time! Let's find the bastard and get Saint Paul PD here with some masks. Shit!"

I coughed a laugh. But she was right. There was no oxygen in the house—none. The situation was critical! We needed to find whoever died before we fainted. We walked into the kitchen and saw a decomposing body—a male. He was sitting at the table with his mouth open, as if he was trying to get some air in his lungs. No shirt, Trident tattoos on his arms and over his heart. His face was twisted from both fright and pain. His neck was lacerated with what looked like rope burns. I thought the man was Frank Howard because of the Trident tattoos. Navy SEALs get those, and we knew Frank was a SEAL. Someone had tried to strangle the dead man. Or maybe they used the rope to hold him down while someone plunged butcher's knives into each of his hands. Either way, he had definitely departed this world. I looked under the table. A small pool of dried blood had formed on the floor. It looked like he was shot in the balls post mortem. His body was full of bullet wounds. Whoever killed him was mad as hell.

Kelly and I looked at each other, our hands still over our mouths.

Through my hands, I mumbled, "If this is Frank Howard, who have we been chasing?"

Kelly laughed. "I guess the DNA test won't do us much good now."

Chapter 23

Fox News was all over the story. Someone had leaked confidential information, and an unbelievable media blitz ensued. Almost anybody could have leaked the information, but we thought it was someone from LVPD because that's where Fox broke the story. They reported our names and identified us as FBI agents. They even had our pictures. How they got those, I don't know. That meant I could expect a call from FBI Director Kortney Malone, followed shortly by a serious ass chewing. The good thing that came from the leak was that someone came forward to identify the body we found in Michelle's Escalade.

The victim's name was Cody Mills, and she had been a university professor at Arizona State University. She was subsequently fired when it was discovered that she never earned a master's degree in English, as her resume purported. I wondered what she was doing for a living now. The house she was living in reportedly cost $360,000. How was she paying her house note? Fox News had made a point of reporting that Rick and Suzette Nance were living way beyond their reported income, and suggested that they might have been selling drugs.

The drug trade was the first thing that entered my mind too; however, there was no evidence to lead us to that conclusion. But we believed that money was a motive in the two murders we had so far. We didn't know how much the killers stole from the Nances, but Cody Mills had made a two thousand dollar withdrawal from her savings account, according to the Fox reporter standing in front of a bank. Kelly and I were on the scene when we found her at the Wendy's restaurant, and we didn't find any money in Michelle's Escalade. Nevertheless, I wondered where Mills was getting her money. Was Frank Howard murdered over money too? I didn't think so, judging by the shack he lived in, but you never know. My cell rang.

"Agent Perry."

"I thought you had a family emergency," Kortney Malone barked.

"Director Malone," I said, looking at my partner.

Kelly mouthed, "I was wondering when the call was going to come."

"This is part of the emergency, Kortney."

"So your family emergency is in Las Vegas, and now Tucson?"

"Actually, we're in Saint Paul, Minnesota, and we've made considerable progress."

Kortney breathed hard into the phone. "Phoenix, you wanna look into your cousin's case, fine. I've given you lots of latitude, being the friend of former President Davidson. But you know procedures. You're too close to this thing. I want McPherson on point. You're backing her up on this one. Now report!"

I gave her the details of the murders and convinced her that she was doing the right thing by keeping Kelly and me on the case. She only agreed because she knew I wasn't going to walk away from this. There was too much at stake. Plus, I could tell she wanted me back on the streets, hunting down these maniacs. Truth be told, I was glad to be back. The last three years were great, spending precious time at home, nursing little Sydney, actually contributing to PTA meetings, having dinner with my family, training Savannah and Luther Pleasant, and writing *The Nimburu Chronicles*. But what I loved most was having my husband come home for lunch and having wild, crazy sex in every room of the house.

Chapter 24

Frank Howard had been a Navy SEAL, and now someone was impersonating him. Perhaps the impersonator had been a SEAL too. That would explain how he was able to handle himself even though Suzette Nance had a gun on him. We searched Howard's home and found all kinds of weapons and equipment, including night vision and infrared binoculars, an M16A2 rifle, a submachine gun, and an excessive amount of ammunition. What I found particularly interesting was the assortment of lightweight knifes.

We questioned the neighbors and learned that Howard was divorced and had moved into the house on Albemarle street a year or so ago. He had kept the blinds closed and his neighbors rarely saw him. The neighbors who did see him disagreed on what he looked like. I wondered if he was wearing disguises. We didn't find any in the house. Could he have been a part of the murder spree and wanted out? Or perhaps he somehow found out who was behind it?

"Kelly. The impersonator. Is he hunting the people that killed the real Frank Howard? Or did he torture and kill the real Frank Howard?"

"Maybe after being tortured Howard told the impersonator that he was meeting Michelle in Las Vegas."

"Okay, but how would Frank Howard even *know* Michelle? Where would Michelle meet a Navy SEAL? And why would she meet someone she doesn't know and has never seen?"

"People on the Internet do it all the time," Kelly said flippantly.

I raised an eyebrow, seeking authentication.

Kelly laughed. "I'm not that desperate, Phoenix."

"You think Michelle met him on the computer?" I asked.

"Maybe."

"None of it makes any sense. We gotta find out why Michelle would meet Frank Howard without knowing what he looked like."

"Maybe she did know what he looked like, Phoenix. Keyth emailed you a video last night. Maybe the impersonator emailed Michelle a picture of himself, but said he was Frank Howard. How would she know the difference? The impersonator could have built a relationship with her—made her feel comfortable with him. Who knows?"

"But if it happened that way, the real Frank Howard may have nurtured the relationship, and at some point, the impersonator took over and continued building a relationship, and then emailed the picture."

"Maybe, Phoenix. But even if we're right, it still doesn't explain why Michelle was at the Nance house and why she fired a weapon into Rick Nance's face."

"Allegedly, Kelly."

"Fine. Michelle allegedly blew Rick Nance's face off. Whatever you wanna believe, Phoenix. But I'll tell you what . . . you better wake up and smell the coffee on this one. The only thing we can do to help Michelle is to find the impersonator and the woman he's with. Then your cousin might have a chance to beat murder one charges."

I didn't like what I was hearing from my best friend, but

she was definitely right. Michelle was in trouble—a lot of it. Even if the evidence against her was circumstantial.

"Listen, Phoenix," Kelly softened her tone a bit. "I don't mean to hurt you, but I don't think you're being realistic here. It may be hard for you to accept, but in all likelihood, Michelle killed Rick Nance."

"I know, Kelly," I said soberly. "We need to check Michelle's computer. Ever been to Toledo, Ohio?"

"Is that where Michelle lives?"

"Yeah. But before we go, we gotta check out Howard's ex-wife. What if she had something to do with what happened here?"

"Well, if she did this, she needed some help, which tells us what we already know. We're looking for a man and a woman."

"True," I said. "Judging by his build, Frank Howard must have been strong as a bull. Someone had to hold him while the other person plunged the knives into his hands."

"Yeah, and what about shooting his balls off? Do you think a man would do that to another man? I sure as hell don't. That's the kinda thing a woman would do."

"Kelly, what if he was doing somebody's wife? A jealous husband would do this."

"Yeah, but it would still take two men. Otherwise, how do you explain the rope burns around his neck?"

"Maybe we can find her name and address in this dump when Saint Paul PD gets here."

"Hopefully she lives in Saint Paul."

Chapter 25

Hasty Hills
12915 Secretariat Road
Toledo, Ohio

Frank Howard was orphaned when a fully loaded semi-truck plowed into his parents' automobile. According to his Navy jacket, the driver fell asleep at the wheel. It was a miracle that Frank, a two-year-old toddler at the time, survived in the backseat. No relatives ever came to get baby Frank, and he became a ward of the state. Sixteen years later, he joined the Navy and eventually became a SEAL. I had called the Hall of Records and discovered that the Howards' original marriage certificate was missing. We had no idea who his wife was, but she seemed to have disappeared without a trace. We left Saint Paul and headed for Ohio.

The 727 landed at Toledo Express Airport at 5 PM. We rented a car and made our way to Hasty Hills, where Michelle lived. When we arrived at the front door of Michelle's home, I lifted a potted plant, picked up the spare key, and we entered the residence. I keyed in the code so the alarm wouldn't sound.

The house was immaculately decorated, full of paintings, and expensive rugs that sat atop hardwood floors. Each room looked as if it could have been on the cover of a magazine. The spacious kitchen was equipped with state-of-the-art electronic appliances, an island stove, and a double-wide refrigerator that dispensed ice, cold water, and an assortment of beverages. I wanted to move in.

As we made our way through the house, stopping at every room, I couldn't understand the desperation Michelle must have felt. Did she love Bruce that much? Did his suicide have that big an impact on her? Or did she internalize her grief and become old and bitter in her sphere of consciousness?

We entered Bruce's office, which was just as I remembered it when we were here three years ago. After we buried him in Woodlawn Cemetery, the family reception was in this house. I remembered coming in here to get Savannah, who had sat at the desk and turned on the computer. She had found an Internet game. As I sat down at the computer, I noticed that the computer system was connected to a cable modem. "Kelly, didn't the Nances have a cable modem?"

"Yeah. And so did Cody Mills. So what?"

"Nothing, I guess." I turned on the computer. "Let's see what we find."

I double clicked on the America Online icon. Fortunately, the password was set already. Bruce probably didn't want to put his password in every time he signed on. I had my online service set up like that too. I didn't have anything to hide and I paid for unlimited service, so why not?

I didn't say anything to Kelly, but Bruce's screen name was Scarecrow—not a good sign. I exhaled hard. All my hopes for Michelle's innocence were blown to hell with this new revelation. Michelle definitely had something to do with the Nance murders. I was deeply saddened by this realization.

"Phoenix, Michelle was found at the crime scene wearing a Scarecrow's mask, wasn't she?"

I knew where my friend was going with this and played my part. She didn't want to voice the obvious. I answered her question with one word. "Yep."

"So, um, do you think she was *allegedly* going after the Nances for something they did to Bruce?"

"You don't have to say *allegedly* anymore, Kelly. As far as I'm concerned, this seals her doom. The only thing we can do now is try to keep her outta the chair. That means we've gotta find out why she did it. If we don't figure out this beguiling puzzle before Michelle comes outta that coma, she's through."

I clicked on the mailbox. It was full of spam mail. Nothing important from what I could tell. I opened the old mail first to see who had been writing her. We hit the jackpot. There were several emails from someone named Frank, and a couple from a woman named Lena. Maybe the clothes we found in the Embassy a couple of days ago belonged to her. Both emails mentioned Rick and Suzette Nance and making them pay for stealing from Bruce. Now there could be no doubt. Michelle was involved with the robbery.

I said, "This is going to kill Aunt Ruth."

"I'm sorry, Phoenix," Kelly said.

"Me too, Kelly. We'll pull the hard drive and see what we can find."

"What did they steal from, Bruce?"

"I don't know, but it musta been a helluva lot for Michelle to go off the deep end like that. You know what they say . . . Hell has no fury, especially if the woman's black."

"You think Aunt Ruth knows about someone ripping Bruce off?" Kelly asked.

"I don't know, but I'm going to find out. I guess what confuses me is, whatever was stolen couldn't have been much. They still have this beautiful house and money in the bank. At least that's how it appears. Maybe they were seriously swindled. We'll pull their bank account statements and see how they were really doing financially."

My cell rang. "Agent Perry."

"She's gone, Phoenix," Aunt Ruth sighed. "Michelle's gone. She just slipped away five minutes ago."

After getting the details from her, I closed my cell and wept. Kelly wrapped her arms around me, and she wept too.

Snapshot Sequence 1

Michelle Michaels: A Stickup in Las Vegas

Chapter 26

The Nance Residence
5900 Glenistar Gate
Las Vegas, NV 89143
June 2005 Midnight

Four intruders wearing pull-over-the-head masks slipped inside the house through the sliding patio doors after disarming the alarm system. They were there to rob the owners of a substantial amount of money—money they wouldn't dare tell the police about. The owners of the dwelling couldn't afford the heat. This was going to be an in-and-out quick stick-up. The foursome had agreed not to kill them, even though killing is what they had earned.

Without making a sound, the masked intruders dutifully climbed the winding staircase of the unsuspecting couple's spacious air-conditioned stucco home. The bedroom door was open, and they could hear Rick and Suzette Nance snoring. They were apparently in a deep, satisfying sleep. The intruders crept into the master bedroom and watched them sleep in their canopied bed.

At gunpoint, the intruders suddenly snatched the slumbering couple out of the comfort of their bed and onto their feet. Before their brains had a chance to assess the situation, Rick and Suzette Nance were being hurriedly ushered down the winding staircase and into the dining room.

"Wha . . . wha . . . wha . . . what's this all about?" Rick Nance asked. His upper lip quivered and his voice cracked from the stress.

"Sit down and shut up," the woman wearing the scarecrow mask demanded then pressed a double-barreled shotgun into Rick's forehead.

The moment his rear-end hit the chair, a man wearing a latex Darth Maul mask, complete with red-and-black tattoos and small horns, duct taped him to a dining room chair. Another woman wearing a clown's mask held a small caliber pistol to Suzette Nance's head and forced her to sit. She was very composed, almost serene, as a third woman wearing a black cat mask duct taped all four of her limbs to a chair.

The scarecrow's eyes, which were already full of murderous fury, narrowed a bit more. She wanted to kill Rick, but she could never ever kill anyone, which is why they were all wearing masks. In fact, the shotgun wasn't even loaded. Instead, she would scare him, take the money he had stolen, and give him something to think about the next time he decided to rip off someone else. She put the double barrel on the dining room table, and pulled a silver tire iron from a satchel.

Enraged, the scarecrow shouted, "What's this all about? It's about Bruce Michaels. Remember him?"

"Who?"

The idea that Rick Nance forgot who Bruce Michaels was pushed her right over the edge. She swung the tire iron and hit him in the face as hard as she could. *Wham!* Rick saw the tire iron coming at his head and moved away from its force, but his head still snapped to the right from the blow. Blood ran from his fractured skull.

"When you steal from people, you oughta remember their names!" the scarecrow shouted. She drew back to clobber him again, but Darth Maul grabbed her before she could swing.

Suzette finally lost her composure and screamed in horror when she saw the gaping wound in her husband's head and the dark purplish-red blood dripping onto his silk pajamas. "This isn't happening! This isn't happening!"

"Oh, but it is." The clown laughed a hysterical, crazed laugh. "It is happening, Suzette."

"Please . . . please . . . please . . . don't kill us. I've got money," Rick offered, hoping to negotiate their safety.

"Funny you should mention money, Ricky!" Darth Maul said. "That's exactly why we're here."

"Where's the money, Ricky?" the scarecrow yelled.

"If I tell you, you're gonna let us go, right? You're not gonna kill us, are you?"

The scarecrow swung the tire iron again, hitting Rick in the kneecap. She swung again and hit him in the other knee.

"Aah . . . shit!" Rick screamed.

"No deals and no assurances," Darth Maul barked. "Now . . . where's the fuckin' money, Ricky? Or do I turn her loose on Suzette?"

"The money's in the safe in our bedroom closet in the floor," Suzette screamed. "Leave him alone!"

"My, my, my—these two thieves may actually love each other," Darth Maul said, smiling. "Cut her loose. I'll take her upstairs to get the money. You guys watch him until I come back."

Chapter 27

The man wearing the Darth Maul mask shoved Suzette through the dining room doorway, which led to the staircase. As they climbed the stairs, Suzette disrobed, pulling her silk gown over her shoulder-length raven hair. Underneath, she was completely nude. Prior to going to bed, Suzette rubbed scented lotion into her skin, and the fragrance lingered in the air. The man in the mask smelled her scent, which nearly cast a spell on him. He stared unrelentingly at her bubble-shaped bottom as she took each succeeding step up the staircase, wondering if she'd had cosmetic surgery to make it that round. His erection was full-grown, and wanted an immediate introduction to her kitty-cat in the worst possible way. Even though his mind was screaming, *Danger, Will Robinson!* the masked man allowed his desire for sex to impede his sensibilities.

With the gown off, Suzette dragged it a few feet, and then let it drop as she entered the bedroom. She stopped and looked over her shoulder, tossed her hair, and smiled a bright, inviting smile. She flipped on the light and took a few more steps inside the bedroom. She could almost feel his wanton desire for her. She turned around and faced him, giving him a full frontal view of her sex tools.

Suzette watched his dark eyes lower ever so slowly to her pink nipples, which were erect, probably from the cool air. After a few seconds of visual pleasure, his eyes continued down past her chiseled abdomen, down to her bushy upside down triangle. She watched his lust bubble to the surface as he took a couple of hurried steps toward her.

She extended her arm and said, "Not so fast. I have something you want. You have something I want."

The man stopped his forward momentum and said, "And what's that?"

Suzette smiled. She had the man exactly where she wanted him to be—in the palm of her hand. She believed she could negotiate her way out of the trouble she and her husband were in. Although she hoped it never would, she knew this day might come sooner or later. She knew one day a man would come looking for them, and she mentally prepared for him, knowing most men were controlled by the flesh beneath their waist. Giving sex to stay alive was a very small thing, she had previously deduced. However, she never expected women to show up for their money, which meant she had to be real good, so that the man behind the mask could get his friends to go along with the plan.

"To live," she said.

"Is that all?"

Still smiling, Suzette said, "That and a teeny tiny portion of the money. Is that asking too much?"

The masked man stroked his chin several times, as if he was seriously considering her proposal. "A small portion, huh? How much are we talking about?"

"Half."

"I see. So, you masterminded all of it, didn't you?" the masked man asked, as if his senses had returned to him all of a sudden. "You're the one we've been looking for. Not him, right?"

Suzette nodded. "And you're the one running this show, not the scarecrow, right?"

The man nodded.

"But you're letting her think she's in charge, right?"

He nodded again. "You're one cool customer under pressure, lady. Downstairs, you acted like a woman in fear for her life. Here, you're relaxed and calculating."

"Well, what's it going to be?" Suzette asked, ignoring his assessment of her. "I can give you half of the money and unforgettable sex without a struggle. Or I can give you all of the money, and the fight of your life for the sex. You're going to have to kill me to get that."

With a gleeful tone, the man said, "There's something to be said for lust, Suzette. Forcing myself on you could be a very erotic experience for both of us." He took another step forward.

"Think about this then. If we struggle, I will no doubt get some skin under my nails and provide a physical profile for the police when they come. And while you're thinking about that, think about this. I haven't seen your face or any of the others. I can give you fifty of the one hundred thousand, and unforced sex, take a shower to get rid of the evidence, and you and your friends can leave here without involving the police. You know we can't call them and explain why you robbed us."

"Unforced sex, huh?" the man repeated. Then he reached out and grabbed a hunk of her hair and forced her to her knees. "You've got a deal. And none of the Monica Lewinsky shit either."

Suzette unzipped his denims and pulled out his organ, which was incredibly stiff, like it was an artificial erection aided by Cialis. Without a second of hesitation, she gave him the best fellatio of his life. He howled uncontrollably for thirty seconds, if that.

Chapter 28

The three remaining intruders and Rick Nance heard the bedsprings howl as Suzette and the masked man went at it upstairs. The moment Rick realized what was going on in his home—in his bed—with his wife, he bowed his head and cried out. "Nooooo!" Then he struggled to free himself. The scarecrow picked up the tire iron and started swinging indiscriminately. She hit him in the head, the face, the arms, and the legs. Soon Rick Nance was bleeding profusely, at the cutting edge of unconsciousness.

"Please," Rick managed to mumble. "No more. No more . . . please."

"Don't beg now, you son-of-a-bitch!" the scarecrow shouted. "I'm gonna kill you. Do you hear me? I'm gonna kill you."

"Why? What have I done?"

"Why? What have I done?" the scarecrow mocked. "You see that shotgun over there?" She pointed at the table. "I'm gonna blow you straight to hell!"

"Then do it," Rick said, almost pleading. As far as he was concerned, they were going to kill him anyway. It was better to die now rather than hear his wife having sex with the man who was probably going to kill him.

"No. I want you to listen to it. Listen to him bang her brains out," the scarecrow said coldly. She quieted herself and listened to the loud groaning. "Sounds like she's having a real . . . good . . . time."

The woman wearing the clown mask said, "Michelle, why don't we find the computer and see how far this thing goes? He's not going anywhere. Come on. You can finish him later."

"You are one lucky bastard," Michelle said. "But I'll be back to finish you off."

With that, the scarecrow and the clown left the dining room.

As soon as they were out of earshot, Michelle whispered, "Lena, do you think he believes I'm going to kill him?"

"Uh-huh. You really scared him."

"Good. I can't wait to see his face when he realizes the gun isn't even loaded. I just wanted to teach him a lesson. It's my only revenge. Maybe he and his wife will learn something from all of this shit. And me, I can go on back to Toledo knowing I did all I could do to avenge Bruce."

Chapter 29

The man wearing the Darth Maul mask convulsed. Every muscle in his body seemed to tighten when he released a second time. Sex with Suzette was good—very good, he thought. Even with a condom. Good sex notwithstanding, the masked man wanted the hundred thousand. He eased off Suzette and panted a few times, catching his breath, wiping the sweat off his throat; wearing the mask while having vigorous sex caused him to perspire heavily. He turned his head and looked at the woman who had pleasured him. She was just lying there, staring at the ceiling, waiting for his next move. That's when he realized that all of her moaning and groaning was just an act, probably to make the sex better for him. It didn't matter if she enjoyed it or not. He had gotten his, and that's all that mattered—except for the money.

"Where's the bathroom?" the man asked. "I need to get rid of this rubber."

Sweetly, Suzette said, "I can get rid of it for you and bring a towel, if you like."

"How 'bout we go into the bathroom together, Suzette? That way I know you've gotten rid of it."

A little frustrated that he didn't believe her, she said, "But I told you we won't be calling the police. We can't."

"So, I'm supposed to trust you? A thief?"

"Fine. Come on. It's this way," Suzette said, and led the way.

Once they were in the bathroom, the masked man stood over the toilet and let Suzette pull off the condom. She was very careful not to let any spill, like she had done this a thousand times. She grabbed a lavender terrycloth face towel, wet and lathered it until it was soapy. Then she carefully washed him while giving him an erotic massage at the same time. As she removed the soap, Suzette felt him stiffening again. She continued the massage until he was fully erect, and took him into her mouth again. Suzette was so aggressive that he couldn't maintain his balance. He staggered backward until he fell up against the bathroom door. Suzette crawled across the floor on her hands and knees like she was a ravenous tiger on the prowl for the day's meal. When she reached the masked man, she fellated him as if she was enjoying the tastiest Popsicle she had ever tasted.

"You . . . really . . . wanna . . . live . . . don't you, Suzette?"

She didn't answer. She just kept slurping until she drained him. As he felt his seed leaving his organ, the masked man found himself slowly sliding down the mirrored door until he was sitting on the floor, basking in the unforgettable moment. He felt incredibly weak—so weak, in fact, that if she attacked him, it would be a real struggle to defend himself.

"Well?" Suzette said, looking at him through the mirror over the basin. She was putting some Crest on her toothbrush.

The man looked at her reflection through the medicine cabinet mirror. "Well, what?"

Suzette stopped brushing and looked at him as if she couldn't believe he was playing this game with her life. She had put out and put out good. She had kept her end of the bargain. Now it was his turn.

"One question first," he said. "Do you fuck him the way you just fucked me?"

"Better. That was nothing compared to what I do to Rick."

The masked man shook his head. "Weak man like that? How does he keep a sex kitten like you satisfied?"

Suzette spit in the basin, and then looked up at him through the mirror. "By being trustworthy. That's how. Now . . . you're going to let us go, right?"

"Sure, baby. I'll let you go."

Chapter 30

Michelle and Lena found the Nances' office, which was packed with wall-to-wall file cabinets. Lena turned on the Gateway computer. She was going to search for people the Nances were in business with while Michelle rifled through the file cabinets. As soon as the computer's desktop was visible, Lena saw the Nances' Yahoo! buddy list, which meant that their system was connected to the Internet by a high-speed cable modem. Three folders labeled contracts, expenses, and pictures were on the computer's desktop. Lena was just about to open the contract folder when two instant messages chimed in from people on the Nances' buddy list. Michelle heard the familiar sound and went over to the computer to see what was happening. Both women were reading the messages at the same time. The last one came from a buddy on the list named Al Mundy.

The message read: *Are you guys going to make it to DC for the conference? Everybody's going to be there. This is where we're staying.* A blue link for the Crystal Gateway Marriott Hotel in Arlington, Virginia, appeared in the instant message box. Lena and Michelle looked at each other and smiled. The next message came from someone named Filcher. It read: *I got another sucker to cough up $5,000. The fool actually thanked me for taking off a $1000. LOL!!*

Michelle said, "This is all the proof I need. We definitely have the right people."

"We oughta kill every last one of them, Michelle. Don't you think they deserve to die for what they've done and what they're doing?"

"Yeah. But not by my hand. Let's open their America On-line file cabinet and see if we can find out more about their friends."

"Maybe they're in the pictures folders," Lena offered.

"Open it."

Just before they opened the pictures folder, an invitation from Al Mundy appeared, asking to meet in a private chat with Filcher. They ignored the invitation and the subsequent instant messages asking if the Nances were there. After clicking on the pictures folder, the file opened and they saw more than fifty picture icons. They quickly scanned the titles until they came to a folder named Rick and Suzette in San Francisco. Anxiously, Lena double clicked on the file and it opened.

Michelle said, "I wish we had names and addresses for these people."

"We know how to find them if the Nances don't talk."

"Good! That way, we could rob them too. I can't wait to see the looks on their faces when we catch up to them."

Chapter 31

Suzette sat on the bathroom floor and watched the man wearing the Darth Maul mask as his head nodded. Sleep was almost upon him. He was lean and spectacularly cut. His biceps were thick—his chest deep with a Trident symbol tattooed over his heart. She wondered if he was a Navy SEAL. Her plan had worked so far. The masked man was now asleep, but his bodybuilder frame was also blocking the door. She wondered if he was as strong as he looked. But as his head bobbed from sexual fatigue, she started wondering if she could overpower him in his weakened state.

She wanted to know because her life depended on it. If she tried to overpower him too soon, he would most certainly kill her, she thought. From her perspective, she had made a deal, but she didn't know if the masked man planned to keep that deal. She wondered what were her chances of escaping from a SEAL who was probably trained to kill in his sleep. She decided it wasn't worth the risk and reached out and shook the masked man's foot. "Hey . . . hey?" The man's eyes opened and suddenly became alert. "Are you finished with me?"

The man cleared his throat. "Yeah . . . yeah. I'm finished."

"Are you sure? I can do it again if you want. I don't mind . . . really, I don't. Just say the word and we can do it as long as you want, okay? I want you to be satisfied so you can let us go, okay?"

"Again, huh?" He smiled.

"If you want . . . yes."

"Maybe later."

"You want me to get the money from the safe now?" Suzette asked.

"Yeah. Get the money while I get dressed."

The masked man opened the door and let Suzette walk through first. While she got the money from the safe, he sat on the side of the bed closest to the bedroom entrance. He pulled on his underwear, and then his pants. He reached for his socks and his boots and slid into them.

"Get—up," Suzette said quietly. She was aiming a .9mm Beretta at the man sitting on her bed. She would kill him if she had to.

"Huh?"

Suzette cocked the Beretta. "I have a gun and I know how to use it. Now . . . get up! Put your hands behind your head and face me."

"Thought we had a deal, Suzette. Half the money and a roll in the hay. Wasn't that the agreement?"

"It was, but I'm making sure—"

In a nanosecond, the masked man slipped an M37 SEAL pup knife from his boot as he rose to his feet, and threw it at Suzette before she had a chance to finish her sentence. She gasped and her head snapped back as the 5-ounce blade found its way into her right eye, then into her brain. She crumbled to the floor. Her body convulsed as she felt death invading her mind.

The man casually walked over to Suzette's still naked body. He was shaking his head like he couldn't believe she had tricked him. He was impressed. She was willing to die in order to live. Standing over her, he said, "Just so you know, I've never had a better blowjob in my life." He pulled the knife out of her eye and wiped it on her skin. He watched the light of life in her remaining eye dim more and more until she was gone. Then he walked into the closet, grabbed the money out of the open floor safe, and went downstairs.

Chapter 32

Michelle and Lena were printing out the information they found in the Nances' computer when the masked man walked in. Without saying a word, he went over to the printer and picked up a sheet of paper and began reading. He picked up page after page of the printouts and quickly read every word on the pages. Then he looked at Lena and said, "So . . . we were right. There are more thieves than we thought out there, huh?"

"Too bad we can't rob 'em all, Frank," Michelle said. "I think we need to get Rick to tell us how to find the others."

Lena looked at Frank and smiled. "Did you get the money, honey?"

"Got it." He showed them the bills, which were in a pillow-case.

Lena smiled when she saw all the greenbacks.

Frank said, "Let's do your thing with Ricky, Michelle. Then we can get outta here."

Moments later, Michelle, Lena, and Frank walked into the dining room, where Nancy, the woman wearing the black cat mask waited for them to return.

"Where's Suzette?" Rick demanded.

Frank said, "She's taking a much-needed shower, Ricky. Know what I mean?"

"You son-of-a-bitch!" Rick screamed. "You fucking bastard!"

Frank kind of laughed. "Hey, why blame me, pal? She offered. I took it. By the way, Suzette gives great head. But you know that, don't you, Ricky?" He paused and let it sink in. "Yeah, Ricky, your wife sure knows how to suck a dick. I mean shit, I never came like that in my life, man. What a fuckin' Hoover Suzette is, huh?" Rick's shoulders hunched as he wept. "I guess this'll teach you a lesson, won't it, Ricky?"

He nodded.

"Too bad the lesson isn't over, Rick," Michelle said. She picked up the double barrel and put it in Rick's face. "See, Rick . . . in life . . . you just can't fuck over people and expect to get away with it these days. People won't stand for that shit no more."

"Don't kill me!" Rick cried out. "Please don't kill me!"

"Sorry, Rick, ya gotta go." Michelle smiled in triumph. "Ya wanna live, Rick?"

"Yes, I wanna live. Please . . . I've learned my lesson. Don't kill us."

Lena said, "Okay, but we need the names and addresses for the others. And don't say you don't know what I'm talking about because two of your friends, Al Mundy and Filcher, just sent you an instant message. Give us everything you have on them and we'll let you two live."

After Rick wrote down all the names and addresses, Michelle put the shotgun a few inches from Rick's nose. She couldn't wait to see the look on his face when he realized the weapon wasn't loaded. "You have to answer for Bruce Michaels." She pulled the trigger. *Blam!* The gun discharged. It blew Rick's face clean off and knocked Michelle backward about five feet.

"Oh shit! Oh shit!" Michelle screamed. "What the fuck

just happened? I checked the gun myself. I checked it three times."

"I did it." Nancy laughed. "Fuck him. He got what he deserved. Did you take care of Suzette, Frank?"

"Yeah. Good piece of ass, though."

"You guys are fucking crazy!" Michelle screamed.

"Crazy is a relative term, Michelle," Nancy said, taking the shotgun from her and reloading it. "The question is do you really want to avenge Bruce's death?"

"Not like this! Not like this!" Michelle rattled off.

"Guys," Frank began. "Listen, we don't have time for this shit. Someone probably heard the shot. For all we know, the police are on their way. We gotta go! Now!"

"It's up to Michelle," Nancy said. She pointed the shotgun at her. "What's it gonna be? We're gonna get 'em all, with or without you. You've got three seconds to make up your mind."

"Might as well, Michelle," Lena finally said. "Who's going to believe you didn't kill Rick on purpose?"

Frank said, "More important, what are you going to tell the police about us?"

Blam! Nancy fired the shotgun.

The force of the pellets hit Michelle in the chest and blew her across the room and slammed her into a wall.

"Goddammit, Nancy!" Frank shouted. "What'd you do that for? Let's get the fuck outta here!"

Part Two

A Picture Within a Picture Behind a Picture

Chapter 33

Annapolis Marriott Waterfront Hotel
80 Compromise Street
Annapolis, Maryland

A man was sitting on the dock, relaxing, enjoying the cool breeze he felt snaking its way down the wharf, causing an assortment of flags to flap endlessly. There was an eighty-eight foot schooner docked a few feet from where he was sitting. The name, Woodwinds, was painted in large black Edwardian script against a stylish ethereal-white finish. Left of the name, near the anchor, was an intricately detailed painting of a flute and saxophone crisscrossed. Jazz music from somewhere inside the schooner tickled his ears. He was sitting at a table on the dock positioned in front of Pusser's Landing, listening to John Coltrane's "Bye Bye Blackbird." As the music filled the air, he sipped his decaf and enjoyed the spectacular view of the Chesapeake Bay. He was wearing a red muscle T-shirt, a bright white London Fog jacket, and a blue pair of Levi's.

He was dressed in patriot colors, but he wasn't the quintessential government contractor. He didn't bleed red, white, and blue. Nor did he believe in the oath he swore—not anymore—not after what the Agency asked him to do in the name of national security. Killing American citizens wasn't what he signed up for. However, he still followed orders. And he still maintained a certain measure of discipline. Contractors couldn't survive without it—not for very long anyway.

Several days after his birth, he was left on a pew in a catholic church, abandoned by his mother for reasons unknown. Father Reynolds of St. Mary's Cathedral took an active interest in his life and ensured that he received a top-notch education. With an intelligence quotient near genius level and being endowed with great physical gifts, he received academic and athletic scholarships from every Ivy League school in America. He had seriously considered going to Oxford, but Father Reynolds had other plans. Reynolds had attended Yale University, and guided the gifted young man to his alma mater.

The man was waiting for his immediate superior, Neil Yarborough, to arrive. Neil, after being contacted by his former college roommate, Father Reynolds, was introduced to the young man his first year at Yale. Neil was very impressed and took a keen interest in him, paying strict attention to his academic achievements and his athletic prowess on the gridiron. Due to Neil's influence, the young man was able to secure his admittance into the prestigious Skull and Bones secret society, better known as "The Order" by its distinguished members. Although the man wasn't the first African American accepted as a "bonesman," he was one of only precious few.

As he patiently waited for his mentor to arrive, he listened to more of Coltrane and sipped his Colombia Narino Supremo, savoring the smooth, nutty flavor as it slid down his welcoming throat. He'd gotten his first whiff of the tasty blend while vacationing in southwest Colombia, near the Province of Narino.

A satisfied smile emerged when he thought of Marilyn Mason, the young Navy lieutenant with whom he spent the previous night. She was asleep in the bed in his suite at the Marriott. He had met her the day before at Pusser's Landing. She was sitting in the same seat he now occupied, enjoying a tuna fish sandwich with a diet Coke. Every table had been taken, but he wanted to sit on the dock, breathe the air, and watch the sailboats as they navigated the Chesapeake.

Marilyn Mason, who was wearing her white Navy uniform, had been sitting at a table alone. When he approached her, her back was facing him; she was enjoying the breeze on a heated day and reading Phillip Thomas Duck's novel, *Playing with Destiny*. Politely, he interrupted her and explained why he wanted to sit at her table, promising not to interrupt her reading again. But when she turned around to address him, he was captivated by her good looks. Her chocolate skin, her big brown eyes, and that perfect heartbreaker smile won him over in an instant.

Before sitting down, he said, "Forgive me for lying to you before even learning your name."

She frowned. "What did you lie about?"

"I said I wouldn't interrupt you again. And now that I've seen the face that launched a thousand ships, I must interrupt you again."

"Thank you." She smiled, drawn to his confidence. Marilyn Mason was accustomed to men being intimidated by her beauty, but she could tell that this one was different. "Have a seat."

He pulled out the chair on her right. "I'm McAlister Sage." He extended his hand.

"Lieutenant Marilyn Mason." She placed her hand in his. "Military or civilian?"

"Government."

McAlister awakened from his brief lapse into the recesses of his mind when he saw fellow contractor, Carson Fletcher, approaching his table.

Chapter 34

Carson Fletcher eased into a chair next to McAlister Sage and tossed an unsealed manila envelope on the table. McAlister didn't say a word. His first thought was to ask Fletcher why he was in Annapolis, and more important, why he was in his space, disrupting the tranquility he was experiencing before Fletcher's untimely arrival. But the question was unnecessary. The unsealed manila envelope answered the question when it landed on the table. McAlister never said a word. He just sipped his Colombian Supremo again without acknowledging Fletcher. Then he picked up the envelope that would provide the answer, lifted the flap, and took out its contents. As he read the document, he occasionally cut his piercing eyes toward Fletcher, who looked like he was in pure heaven. Fletcher had already read the documents, and was very enthusiastic about carrying out the orders he had been given.

"Where's Neil?" McAlister finally said. "He was supposed to meet me here, not you."

Smiling, Fletcher said, "Couldn't make it. You know how it is."

"I work alone. Neil knows that," McAlister said and sipped his coffee again.

"Not this time, Mac. This one is too important. Besides, to be totally honest with you, the head honcho thinks you're losing your nerve."

"Losing—my—nerve?" McAlister's eyes narrowed, evidence that a volcano was not far from eruption. "You tell that bastard I don't need help—ever."

"I did. Told him the moment I got the orders. He told me to tell you that if you had been professional and followed orders when this whole thing began, it wouldn't be necessary to assign two contractors now." As the words spilled out of his mouth, Fletcher seemed to be relishing the reaction they caused. "Neil also said that five people are dead because you lost your nerve. I'm here to make sure this Scarecrow business never sees the light of day. He said to tell you in no uncertain terms that if you can't handle it, I'll have to."

McAlister looked up from the documents and shot a menacing gaze at Fletcher. "I can handle it."

"I sincerely hope so," Fletcher said with a satisfied grin.

McAlister read a little further and then looked at Fletcher. "What the hell is this shit?"

"You read it right, bubba."

"Phoenix Perry and Kelly McPherson? They're being sanctioned too?"

"If they get in the way, they're done too. Both of them." Fletcher smiled broadly. Against his mahogany skin, his teeth looked whiter than Alaskan snow. He would make sure Phoenix Perry got in the way. It was personal. If that meant McPherson had to die too—so be it.

"Neil musta lost his bunny rabbit mind. Why sanction our own?"

"You know why, Mac. Perry is like a dog on a bone. That's why!"

"And?" McAlister furrowed his brow, seeking more clarification.

"She handled Nimburu, didn't she? Took her head off with one blow. Who would have ever believed that shit? Besides all that, this is a personal case for her. She's related to Michelle Michaels and shouldn't even be involved in the first place. If she discovers certain information while she's trying to solve the case she's currently working, she won't stop digging until she finds oil. You know that, Mac."

"Shit!" McAlister shouted without thinking and slammed his fist on the table.

Customers stared at him when his profane outburst filled their ears.

"Uh-huh. You gettin' the picture now, huh, bubba?" Fletcher said.

McAlister rattled the documents in his hand. "Is this all we have on them?"

"We don't need much. The people we're looking for are headed east. They shouldn't be too hard to find. Their body count is through the roof with no signs of slowing down. With that kinda trail, we'll have them in less than forty-eight hours."

"Fine. We leave for Albuquerque first thing in the morning."

Fletcher folded his arms and exhaled hard. With rancor, he said, "Neil wants us on the next plane outta here, Mac. Lieutenant Dark and Lovely can wait until we finish this Scarecrow business."

McAlister ignored the comment about Marilyn Mason and stared into Fletcher's eyes. "We'll leave when I say we leave. You got that? Now . . . I suggest you get a room for the night."

"This is precisely why Neil wanted me with you. Our *orders* are to leave immediately. You can bang that chick anytime. We need to move on this thing—now!"

McAlister stood up. "Get a room, or sleep on the dock. I don't give a fuck. It's up to you. But know this. I'm not leaving until morning." Then he left, walking in the direction of the Marriott hotel.

When he saw McAlister enter the hotel and was sure he couldn't be heard, Carson Fletcher said, "Your days are numbered, too, Mac." Then he struck a match and lit the documents and watched them burn.

Chapter 35

Carson Fletcher could hear them making love through the open terrace door of their suite. He had gotten a room right next to theirs, and could hear the rhythmic bumping of the headboard. He sat quietly on his terrace, listening to Marilyn Mason's pulsating sighs, which sounded like a well-rehearsed symphony—the perfect blend of violins, harps, flutes, clarinets, piccolos, trumpets, trombones, and French horns coming together as one. Each time McAlister plucked her delicate instrument, a different musical began and the concert went on until the wee hours of the morning. Finally, there was quiet.

Carson listened to the hushed murmurings of the two lovers, though he could not understand their words. From time to time, their muted conversation became infectious laughter. Carson laughed too, even though he didn't know the punch line. He wanted to understand what was so important about Marilyn Mason. They had just met, he knew because he had been shadowing McAlister on the orders of Neil Yarborough. Was sex with the lieutenant better than sex with other women? To him, all women were the same—Coco

Nimburu being the only exception. They had a job to do, and yet McAlister put a woman ahead of their mission. This wasn't a run-of-the-mill assignment. This job involved national security, and McAlister was dousing the sausage instead of catching a plane to Albuquerque.

McAlister is definitely getting soft. Women have weakened him. It's really a shame too. He used to be revered as the best domestic operative ever. Now look at him. A fuckin' marshmallow! A goddamned cream puff! Living off his reputation instead of adding to his resume. What a fuckin' loser! I like to bang the goo from time to time myself. Hell, I need a piece every now and then too, but I don't let the shit tell me what to do. Killing him is going to be a piece of cake. I oughta kill him and the lieutenant right now and handle the mission myself. But that would be too easy. No challenge at all. I could just climb over this railing, sidestep on the wall over to their railing, and put a bullet in both their brains. But I want him to know that it was me who killed him. I want to look in his eyes as they fade to black.

Two hours later, Carson climbed over the railing and entered McAlister's room without making a sound. There they were. The happy Naval lieutenant and the government-sponsored killer. America's 007. Vulnerable. They were holding each other like they were lovers who had been apart for months. Their dark skin seemed to melt and blend together. They looked so happy—so relaxed—so satisfied. He pointed the silenced Makarov pistol Coco Nimburu once owned at McAlister. *See . . . a piece of cake! Chocolate cake!* Slowly, the corners of his mouth turned upward as a wide, sinister grin changed his appearance.

Then he left McAlister and the lieutenant alone in the quiet room. There would be plenty of opportunities to kill him later. But first, he was going to kill Phoenix Perry.

Chapter 36

1619 Buena Vista
Dallas, Texas
2 AM

"Where's the fuckin' money?" Lena shouted, her face hidden by the cat mask she wore.

Jack and Vicki Calhoun had been snatched from their bed in the middle of the night and duct taped to their living room chairs. The frightened couple looked at each other, wondering if the other knew what was going on. Neither did.

Confused, Jack said, "What money?"

"You mean to tell me you don't have any money?" Frank said calmly, his face hidden behind his Darth Maul mask.

"I've got a few bucks. That's all," Jack said desperately. "What's this all about? What do you think we did?"

"You've got a beautiful house here, Jackie-boy," Frank continued. "What did it cost you?"

"Two hundred and eighty-three thousand. We put everything we had into our business."

"Everything you own, huh, Jackie-boy?" Frank said.

"Every penny. I swear."

"Where's your checkbook?" Lena asked.

"It's in my car," Jack replied. "Just call the bank and see for yourself. It's an automated system. We don't have money. Not much anyway. I swear to God!"

"What's the number?" Lena said and picked up the phone. "You better not be lying."

Jack Calhoun recited the number and Lena hit the appropriate number on the handset. "What's your social security number?" She hit the numbers. "Security code?" She hit the numbers.

"Now all you gotta do is hit the pound symbol and it will tell you what we have in our checking and savings accounts. It will even tell you what we have available on our credit cards."

Lena listened to the automated voice system. She snatched off her mask. Slowly, a frown crept across her face and became a symbol of rage. "They're broke," she said and hit Jack in the head with the receiver. She continued to beat him with the phone. "You broke-ass son-of-a-bitches. We drove all the way to Dallas for nothing!" *Wham! Wham! Wham! Wham! Wham! Wham!*

"We've got a safety deposit box," Vicki offered desperately.

Lena stopped the beating and Jack kind of slumped over to the side, breathing deep breaths as lines of blood made their way down his battered face. She looked at the masked man to see what he thought about going inside a bank.

"Too fuckin' risky," Frank said. "They got cameras and shit. Bank could be crowded. They could try to escape. Cause a commotion. Anything to attract attention. We could possibly get away, but they would have descriptions and we would lose our advantage. As far as we know, they're still looking for the *real* Frank Howard. They probably don't even know Frank is dead. And they certainly don't know our real names. Besides, we can't go in a bank wearing these masks. It would seriously fuck up our program. As it stands, none of the thieves can call the police. We go into a bank . . . all that changes."

Aggravated, Lena said, "Well, let's kill 'em anyway for being broke."

"Yeah!" Nancy, the woman wearing the clown mask said and laughed a maniacal laugh. "Yeah, kill 'em dead."

"Please don't. That's no reason to kill a person," Vicki begged. "That's so senseless. If you're going to kill us, at least have a reason. You can leave right now and who would we tell? We get to live, and you guys can escape and remain anonymous. How about it? Let us live and we can call it even."

"She's got a point, girls," Frank said. "Okay, let's reason this shit out. Now, let's see . . . Vicki, you think people should be killed if there's a good reason?"

"No, but I could at least understand why."

"How 'bout a little game then?"

"What kind of game?"

"Let's see . . . what kind of game? Oh, I know. You'll love this. Let's call it You Can Bet Your Life. How's that for a title, huh?"

"No. Please . . . don't."

"Sorry, Vicki, you don't have a choice, but I'll tell ya what. If you can answer one question satisfactorily, I'll let you and Jackie-boy live. We'll untie you and be on our merry way. How 'bout that? Is that a deal or what?"

"What if we don't know the answer?"

"Ahh c'mon. You'll know the answer. You two can even confer and everything. Just like they do on *Who Wants to be a Millionaire?* Okay. Are ya ready? Here's the question. Who is Bruce Michaels?" He looked at Nancy and said, "How about a little music for our contestants, Nancy?"

Jack and Vicki Calhoun looked at each other as Nancy hummed Merv Griffin's thirty-second *Jeopardy!* theme. Neither one of them had any idea who Frank was talking about.

"Is that your final answer?" Frank said, mimicking Regis Philbin.

"We don't know a Bruce Michaels. There must be some mistake!" Jack pleaded. "You've got the wrong people."

"You're right. It is a mistake, and you made it, Jackie-boy! Now we've got a reason, girls."

"Nooooo!" Vicki screamed as the trio approached the doomed couple.

A loud *whoosh* sliced through Vicki's screams just before the golf club Nancy was holding hit Vicki in the face, shattering her nose. Blood spurted. Vicki cried out. But that was only the beginning. The savagery continued as blow after blow pulverized their faces and heads. While they were down, Frank caved in their skulls with a bat. Blood was everywhere. They continued beating the Calhouns until they were too tired to continue. All three assailants were doubled over, gasping for air.

After catching his breath, Frank panted, "I'm hungry. How 'bout you guys?"

"Me too," Nancy said, gasping. "Let's order a pizza when we get back to the hotel. I could eat a horse right now."

"Yeah. Me too," Lena said.

Chapter 37

Hasty Hills
12915 Secretariat Road
Toledo, Ohio

Twenty-four hours had passed since Michelle's death, and we were no closer to solving her murder. I was still on the case, still trying to figure out what had happened to my cousin and why. I needed to know why she murdered Rick Nance. We had finally learned something concrete. A computer tech called me on my cell and told me she had gone through the hard drives I had sent overnight. I gave her Michelle's fax number.

It turned out that Rick and Suzette Nance were posing as literary agents. They had over a million dollars in their safety deposit box. And Cody Mills was charging more than eight thousand dollars to edit manuscripts. I checked this critical information against what they reported on their tax returns. Neither reported any literary earnings to the Internal Revenue Service. I could hear another fax coming through.

Kelly grabbed it and started reading. A few seconds later, she said, "Read this."

I took it out of her hands and began reading the fax. "So, Bruce was keeping a journal?"

"Read on."

I did.

"Bruce was a writer?"

"Read on."

"Rick and Suzette Nance ripped him off?"

"That's what he thought. He's naming names, television shows, and movies that were stolen from him."

I read some more of the fax. "These are some of the hottest shows on television. I wonder if the producers know about this."

"It's going to be hard to prove without evidence, especially if he doesn't have the copyrights. If he didn't register his work, we won't be able to prove anything. The networks could say their writers wrote the storylines. It would be their copyright versus his journal entries. And let's not forget he killed himself. People are going to say he was a nut."

Another sheet came through the fax machine but slipped off the tray and floated under the desk. I pushed my chair back and looked for the sheet. I didn't see it, so I got on all fours to look. I crawled under the desk to get the sheet of paper. As I backed out, I bumped my head. I heard Kelly laugh, then say, "You okay?" She laughed again. I turned around to see what I had hit my head on and saw a key taped to the bottom of the drawer. I unpeeled it and crawled from underneath the desk.

"Look at this," I said.

"A safety deposit key."

"Yeah. Wonder what's in it."

"Do you know where they did their banking?" Kelly asked. "That's where this key most likely belongs."

"Yeah. Fifth/Third on Central. The whole family banks there."

"Better get a search warrant to open it," Kelly said. "I'll make the call."

Chapter 38

Two Albuquerque detectives were about to enter Audrey Jefferies' house when McAlister Sage and Carson Fletcher arrived in a rented almond-and-gray Chrysler 300. Fletcher parked the car and the two contractors got out.

"Gentlemen," McAlister called out. "Agents Warrick and Simmons."

They didn't work for the Bureau, but they flashed their authentic-looking FBI credentials as they opened the white picket fence and approached the men.

Both detectives were tall and slender, wearing dark-colored suits, rubber soled shoes, and mirrored sunglasses. One of the detectives had dark reddish color skin. He was probably Native American. The other detective was Caucasian and wore a thick mustache. As they approached the detectives, McAlister said, "We're investigating this murder in connection with a murder in Las Vegas and another in Tucson, Arizona."

The detective with the thick mustache spoke first. "I don't think so, pal. I'm Detective Malloy and this is my partner, Detective Morningstar. He's the primary on this case."

Morningstar said, "That badge don't mean shit to me. You're not going into the house. Not without proper authorization."

"Gentlemen," Fletcher began, flashing his FBI badge again. "Listen, this is proper authorization. You've seen our credentials. These are federal badges. You know that's more than enough authorization. Now . . . be a good sport and leave the premises."

"You fuckin' Feds think you can just come in here whenever you feel like it and show us poor ignorant locals how it's done, huh?" Morningstar said. "Well, we're not leaving until we hear it from our own people."

McAlister said, "Gentlemen, let's not bicker over this. This is a matter of national security." He looked at his watch. "Our superiors should have called your superiors by now. Call your department and see what they say. In the meantime, this is our house."

"You two wait here while I call this in," Malloy said, pulling his cell phone from a belt holder. He called the department. "Yeah, Malloy here. I got a couple of Feds trying to muscle me and Morningstar. Let me speak to the captain." He paused for a second and glared at Sage and Fletcher. "Yeah, Captain, this is . . . but . . . I know, but . . . yes, sir."

Fletcher laughed. *You dumb muthafucka. You just had to humiliate yourself, didn't you?* "Now that that's settled, what do you have on Audrey Jefferies?"

"Not much," Morningstar said. "We found her in a McDonald's parking lot, in the drivers' seat of her Jaguar, shot three times in the back of the head through the headrest. That's all we know so far."

"How much did they get?"

"I have no idea. But her safe was open when our people arrived. I'm betting there was plenty of money in it. I'm also betting Ms. Jefferies was up to no good, which is why they killed her."

"Thank you, Detective Morningstar," McAlister said. "You've been a huge help. I just need the keys."

The two government-sponsored contractors entered the Jefferies residence with the key given to them. They only wanted one thing—the computer disk drive. McAlister and Fletcher had a compact disk program that was capable of recovering deleted files. When finished, the program left no evidence of the files ever existing. They suspected Audrey Jefferies of ripping people off just as Rick and Suzette Nance and Cody Mills had. But the Agency wasn't interested in such a minute matter. They were interested in knowing what, if anything, Audrey Jefferies knew about Scarecrow. The police could handle the small stuff. But the existence of Scarecrow could not be discovered.

The operatives found Audrey Jefferies' office and turned on her computer. McAlister slid the compact disk into the computer and the program started searching the computer's filing system, looking for any programs that might have led to the existence of Scarecrow. The program didn't find anything suspicious. However, they did discover that Audrey Jefferies was working as a full-time editor. They found dozens of rewriteable compact disks with manuscripts on them. They also recovered emails sent to and from Rick and Suzette Nance, giving Audrey the details of several lucrative movie deals. Some of the deals were feature films, but most were straight to DVD films. The Nances were turning the manuscripts of the duped authors into screenplays and passing them off as their own, collecting a bundle. They were also rewriting the manuscripts, changing the titles, using a number of nom de plumes, and selling them to interested publishers, pocketing large advances and royalties that their clients should have collected.

"Let's take it all," McAlister said. "We'll be hurting Phoenix's chances of solving her case, but we can't risk missing anything. If Phoenix finds out about Scarecrow, we'll have to take her out."

Fletcher said, "McPherson too. I'd hate to have to kill such a sweet piece of ass, but that's how it goes."

"Phoenix is fine as hell too," McAlister said. "As a matter of fact, I'd rather have Phoenix than McPherson. Something about her defiant attitude makes me think she's probably a muthafucka in bed."

"That's right," Carson began to recollect. "You worked with her in the Homeland Security office for a while, didn't you?"

"Yeah. I was checkin' that out every day too. But she's happily married. I checked her and her husband out. The entire Homeland Security office staff, in fact. All of them were clean."

Fletcher smiled. "So, you didn't make a play for some of that?"

"No. I was there to do a job and to be invisible. I did that, and got outta there without any of them ever suspecting that I was investigating them and reporting everything to Neil."

"What's the deal with you and the lieutenant?" Fletcher asked, pretending to be ignorant of who she was. He knew her name and had personally checked her out already. He had even watched them meet yesterday from a surveillance yacht on the Chesapeake. He had listened to their conversation on a sophisticated infrared light, which was beamed against the stainless steel napkin holder on their table. Nevertheless, he played the dumb role like he was an Oscar winning actor.

"Marilyn Mason?"

"At least you remember her name."

McAlister stopped clicking keys and looked at Fletcher. "Unlike you . . . I remember them all."

"So, what's the deal with her, Mac?"

"The deal?"

"We should have been here last night, but you decided you wanted some poontang. Was she that good in bed? Or what?"

"Very sexy lady—a true sex-kitten."

"Sex-kitten, huh?"

"Yeah, she's got a very sexy laugh. Reminds me of Sybil Wilkes."

Fletcher frowned. "Who?"

McAlister rolled his eyes, thinking, *You don't know who Sybil Wilkes is?*

"Well, none of them measure up to Coco Nimburu, though. None of them."

"I almost thought you forgot about her, Mac."

"Never. I don't think any man would ever forget that woman."

"Remember that time she took us both on?" Fletcher shook his head involuntarily as that night materialized in his mind. He had relived his experiences with her many times. He had loved her, but could never possess her. Now he never would, and it was all Phoenix Perry's fault. That's why he was going to kill her. "Do you, McAlister. Do you remember that night?"

"You need to move on, Carson. Coco didn't love you, man. You were just a fuck. So was I. That's all. Why can't you accept that shit?"

"I've accepted it, Mac," Fletcher said defiantly.

"Any more irrelevant questions?"

"Nope."

"Good. Why don't you check the house for more computers so we can get the hell outta here?"

Chapter 39

The safety deposit key was registered to a box at the Fifth/Third Bank on Central Avenue in Toledo, Ohio. When I was in town for Bruce's funeral, we had gone to one so Michelle could get some quick cash. I called the bank and talked to a manager whose name escapes me and told her we needed to get into a box. She informed me of the need for a warrant, which had already been faxed to us.

We went into the bank and walked up to the first woman I saw sitting behind a desk. Her nameplate read: SANDY. We flashed our credentials and gave her the warrant, which she took to another woman sitting behind a desk in a glass-enclosed office. The woman was on the phone. Sandy handed the warrant to the woman. She looked at it briefly and handed it back to Sandy, gave her a quick nod, and continued talking on the phone.

Sandy came back and said, "I have to look up the box number and grab the bank's key. It'll just take a couple of seconds."

The computer keys clicked rapidly as Sandy typed. I presumed she had put in Bruce's name to find out what box he'd had.

"Hmmm." Sandy lifted her head from the computer screen and looked at me. "We don't show a box registered to a Bruce Michaels."

"Try Michelle Michaels," I said. "Both names are on the warrant."

Sandy looked at the warrant again. "Hmm, I guess I didn't read it thoroughly." She clicked the keys again. "Ahh, there it is. The box was originally in his name. We transferred it to Michelle a couple of years ago. I just need to grab the key. Follow me."

We followed Sandy into the vault, where the safety deposit boxes were. I don't know what we expected to find. Rare coins? Family heirlooms? A will, perhaps? Expensive jewelry? But we certainly didn't expect to find one unlabeled compact disk. I guess what bugged me was finding the key underneath the desk drawer in the first place. Whatever the disk contained had to be important to my cousin and her husband.

We drove back to Hasty Hills and slid the compact disk into the drive, and it opened. Kelly and I looked at each other when we realized that Bruce had transferred nearly sixty of his books and screenplays to the disk. I wondered how long it took him to write that many books because I had read somewhere that Louis L'Amour had written three hundred novels. I shook my head and Kelly sucked her teeth. Then it occurred to me that Michelle had taken possession of the box a few months after Bruce killed himself.

"Kelly . . . why do you suppose Michelle kept the box open if the disk only contained Bruce's work?"

"Maybe she put valuables in there from time to time. Maybe she never even looked at this disk. Maybe she kept it for sentimental reasons. Who knows?"

"How do you feel about reading his work? There could be something there."

"Phoenix, there are a billion books on that disk. Plus the screenplays."

"Half a billion for me and half a billion for you." I smiled. "I say we take the disk back to headquarters, get some paper and ink, and print these babies out."

Kelly laughed before saying, "We can get ink and paper here, Phoenix."

I knew why she was laughing. She knew I wanted to go home to see my husband. I needed to get laid. And I wanted to see my children. I figured I better watch the video Keyth sent me so I would know all about the tournament I missed.

I looked at Kelly and said, "Hey, you got yours with Sterling in the high rollers suite. Let me get mine. Who knows? Sterling might even be in DC."

"I'm gonna make sure." Kelly flipped open her cell and hit a button. A few seconds passed. "Sterling . . . where are you? Dallas?" She winked at me. "Got any business in DC? Yeah . . . we're in Toledo, Ohio, of all places. We're takin' the next plane home." She smiled and winked at me again. "Okay, give me a call and let me know what time you get to Reagan and I'll pick you up."

I looked at Kelly and shook my head.

Chapter 40

The media was all over the murders once it was revealed that people pretending to be in the publishing industry were being systematically killed. Frank Howard and his two accomplices, Nancy Newman and Lena Scarsdale, were in a Memphis hotel. The trio sat at the edge of their king-size bed, watching the story unfold on their television—all of them completely nude. Fox News was doing an in-depth report on all the murders, showing pictures of Rick and Suzette Nance, Cody Mills, Audrey Jefferies, and the latest victims, Jack and Vicki Calhoun.

"Jack and Vicki Calhoun were found in this quiet Dallas suburb yesterday evening by their daughter, Stacy Calhoun, who had just completed her junior year at Dartmouth," a young female reporter said. She was standing in front of the Calhoun residence. "The victim's neighbors describe the couple as the most unselfish people in the neighborhood. Vicki Calhoun served as surrogate mother of all the neighborhood children, headed the PTA, a women's social club, and many other charitable events. Jack Calhoun was a retired physical therapist, and was equally giving. It makes this reporter wonder why someone would not only murder them . . . but beat them savagely with a golf club, a baseball bat, and brass knuckles." The reporter shook her head slowly and said, "But we have learned from a credible source inside the Dallas Police Department that the Calhouns were moonlighting as scam artists. They were stealing the unpublished work of the authors they pretended to represent as literary agents. They then sold their work to interested parties in Hollywood."

"Hmmm . . . so the cops know there are three of us now," the man said.

"How, Frank?"

"The reporter mentioned three weapons. Believe me, the cops know."

"I wonder if they found your husband yet, Lena," he said, staying in character to ensure they never slipped up and used their real names in front of their victims. "Are you sure you got rid of all the pictures of you at his house?"

"Positive. They may know my name, but that's about it."

"Then we're in the clear," the man continued. "They don't know anything—nothing worthwhile anyway. But still . . . I say we get in a little rest and relaxation . . . maybe go to Graceland . . . see where The King lived."

"Whatever you say, lover," Lena said.

"I miss Michelle," Nancy said, almost whining.

Frank shot Nancy a stern look. "Then you shouldn't have killed her. She would have come around . . . especially when she realized that that was the only way to avenge Bruce's death."

"I didn't think she would ever see that," Nancy explained. "I could see it in her eyes. She was only willing to take their money. She would have never killed anybody willingly."

"That's why we tricked her into it," Lena said. "If you had given her time to let it settle in her mind, she would have made the choice and we'd all be together now."

"Oh, well. No use in crying over spilled milk," Nancy offered sarcastically. Then she stretched out her hand and massaged Frank's extremely long and very thick package until it was full grown and throbbing. She moved to the floor and positioned herself between his legs.

While Nancy kissed his inner thighs, Frank slowly eased backward until he was prostrate. With one of his hands, he beckoned Lena. She went to him and straddled his face, her bush already moist. As he teased her there, she began a slow, steady grind, moaning almost inaudibly at first.

The man was a rare breed indeed. Not only was he well built, he had the stamina of a pubescent teenager, able to have upwards of four orgasms before losing his erection, without the aid of Viagra. His refractory period was only two minutes, if he lost the erection at all. He was able to handle not only one woman, but several women in a single night—satisfying them all. Yes, the man who wore the Darth Maul mask was truly the envy of all men. With him, women made the kind of guttural sounds that would have been music to the Marquis de Sade's ears. The man took them both that night, over and over again, until they were all drenched in sweat.

Chapter 41

I heard a loud siren blare, and then what sounded like a couple of Braves chanting like they were on the war path, just before I heard the thunderous bass guitar on rappers Nelly, P Diddy, and Murphy Lee's "Shake Your Tail Feather." The music was coming from my daughter's room, and much louder than I allow. But I like the song and I had just gotten home, so I didn't want to come in yelling, since I had been gone for so long, especially since I missed Savannah's first martial arts tournament.

It was about 10:30 in the morning by the time I got home. I was on my way to the bedroom with my bags when Keyth came out of the den and spotted me. He took my bags and carried them into the bedroom for me. As I turned to leave, he grabbed my arm and said, "Where do you think you're going? I didn't take the day off for nothing."

He shut the door.

"Let me check on the kids first, baby," I teased.

He pulled me close to him and gripped my ass with both of his hands.

"So, I guess this means you missed me, huh?"

He didn't bother answering. He just plunged in with both lips, pressing his hardness against me. The sensation grew when I slipped him my tongue. I could feel myself losing control and pulled away. I needed to let my children know Mommy was home, and get those precious hugs they offered.

"What's wrong, baby?" Keyth asked, panting.

He looked desperate, like I was one of the spoils of war and he was ready to plunder his prize. Then he kissed me again and started unbuttoning my blouse.

"Just let me go upstairs for a minute and let Savannah and Sydney know I'm home."

"Come on, girl. It ain't gon' take long. Plus they're upstairs practicing their steps."

"Their steps? Steps for what."

"Savannah is teaching Sydney how to dance."

"Oh, I gotta see this," I said and pulled away and buttoned my blouse.

Keyth grabbed me again and kissed me. "You ain't goin' nowhere 'til we take care of a little business."

He unbuttoned my blouse again and skillfully unsnapped my red bra. Before I knew it, he had a nipple in his mouth. I don't know which one he had, and didn't much care. I just closed my eyes and gave in to the sensation he gave me. I could feel him unbuttoning my jeans, unzipping them, and pulling down my pants and panties at the same time. Then he touched me there, my sensitive area, moving his hand in a cadence that made my knees weak. I wanted to leave his mouth and hands for a few seconds and lock our bedroom door, but I couldn't move. I was in the moment and I went with it. Besides, I could still hear the music blaring from Savannah's room. I hoped they didn't come downstairs while I was doing the nasty with their father.

Chapter 42

Twenty minutes later, we had finished the satisfying quickie. I cleaned up in our adjacent bathroom and went upstairs to let our children know I was home—had to get my hugs. We climbed the stairs and tiptoed to Savannah's room. Annie Lennox's "Walkin' on Broken Glass" was playing. The door was cracked a little. I peered through the opening and looked at Savannah and Sydney. To my surprise, I saw my little girl dancing for the first time. I don't know what kind of dance she was doing, but she was doing it well. Dancing seemed to come natural to her. Sydney was doing his best to keep up. The duo pretended to tiptoe on broken glass each time Lennox sang the chorus of her hit single. I covered my mouth to keep them from hearing me laugh. We waited until the song ended before entering the room.

I was seriously disappointed when my daughter didn't run to me and throw her arms around me like she used to. Sydney ran to me and wrapped his arms around me, and held on for dear life. Rather than ask Savannah why she didn't hug me, I picked up my son and went over to where she was standing. I embraced her. When she realized I was going to

keep hugging her until she responded to the love I was of-
fering, she hugged me back.

"I missed you, Savannah," I said.

There was a long, silent pause. "Okay," she said.

"I missed you, Mommy!" Sydney said enthusiastically.

"I missed you too, Sydney." I pulled Savannah closer and
said, "I'm so sorry I missed your first tournament, honey. I
won't miss another one. I promise."

"Well, did you at least watch the video?" Savannah asked
skeptically.

"Yes. I watched three times. You were great."

"Better than Luther?"

"Of course."

I hated lying to my daughter and making promises I might
have to break because of my job, but my intentions were
good. Luther Pleasant was much better than she was, but I
wasn't going to tell her what she already knew.

"What do you guys want for dinner?" I said. "I'm cooking
tonight."

"Pizza!" Sydney yelled.

"Hamburgers and French fries!" Savannah yelled.

I looked at Keyth, who was laughing at me. I guess I
should've known that my children wouldn't appreciate having a real home-cooked meal by their mother. I said, "I'm
going to cook a good balanced meal for you two." They gave
me that *Awww, Mom look.*

"I'll let you two have pizza and burgers tomorrow, okay?" I
hated coming home and laying down the law, but that's all a
part of being a responsible mother.

Chapter 43

Michelle's funeral was held at the newly built Victory Life Worship Center in Toledo, Ohio, her church home, according to Aunt Ruth, who had made the arrangements. After debating whether we should take the children, Keyth and I decided we would. I told him how Aunt Ruth felt about seeing more of us, and we thought it would be a good idea to try to visit more often, or at least have my father's family come out to Arlington more often. Keyth wanted to drive our new Infinity Qx4 SUV and make it a family outing, but I told him that driving would take too much time if I had to leave on a moment's notice.

Keyth said, "If you have to go, go. But we're not going to live our lives around the Bureau's schedule. We're going to drive there with our children, sing songs, and play games like any other normal family. We're going to have lots of fun together for a change. Then, when we get to Toledo, if the case breaks, you get on a plane and do what you gotta do, all right?"

"I love you," I said. I got me another piece before we hit the road, and it was good, too.

It felt good to see my aunts, uncles, and cousins again, even if it was because of another untimely death in our family. Savannah and Sydney were able to see their family on my father's side again and I, being the FBI agent that I am, continued the investigation by asking family members if they knew Bruce was a prolific writer. Unfortunately, my investigation yielded absolutely nothing. No one knew Bruce was writing, and they certainly didn't know he was trying to get published. Bruce made his money in the haircare field and real estate. He owned three salons in Toledo and several in Detroit and Atlanta. The last time I was in town, Michelle had told me that Bruce was looking into opening some salons in Chicago and Washington before his death.

As much as I was enjoying the time off, I needed to get back home and continue the investigation, which meant reading Bruce's work. That's all we had to work with at the moment. Also, Savannah had to get back to Arlington for summer school and Keyth had to run Drew Perry Investigative Firm. But we did enjoy our time together as a family. The funny thing was that someone had to die before we took another trip together. The last time we went on vacation as a family, prior to Bruce's death (if you could call attending a funeral a vacation), was when Keyth and I took Savannah to San Francisco during that crazy summer back in 2001. Come to think of it, a lot of good people died that summer too.

Chapter 44

Nearly a week had passed since we'd gotten back to the District of Columbia. Strangely, there hadn't been any more murders—none that we knew about anyway. Perhaps all the media attention had caused the killers to stop the killings. I had mixed feelings about that. If they didn't kill another couple, I wasn't sure how we'd catch them unless we got really lucky. I hate to say this, but cops can't catch thieves or murders quickly unless they kill or rob someone they know or had some sort of known problem with. I guess that's why cop shows piss me off. They make it look so simple on television, when nothing could be further from the truth. The American public believes what they see on *Law and Order* and *CSI Miami* and the rest of those shows. But the truth of it is, it takes weeks, sometimes months, years even, to catch a smart criminal who carefully plans his crimes. That's why I had mixed emotions about catching the killers. If they stopped killing, we might never catch them. If they didn't stop, that meant more people would die.

Spending the week in the thick DC humidity reminded me of the heat in China and happier times with my deceased father. My father was a Naval intelligence officer assigned to the American Embassy, so I lived in China for twelve years. My father was murdered four years ago, and I still missed him. But it was good to be home—good to see my children, doubly good to ravage my husband every night for more than a week. I almost felt sorry for Keyth. I knew he was staying at the office longer and longer after the third straight night of me riding him. I'd hear him tiptoeing around the house after he eased in, probably hoping I was asleep. But I wasn't. I was up reading Bruce's novels, searching them for any information that might lead to the killers. Keyth wouldn't even come to the bedroom. He'd go straight downstairs to the basement and try to fall asleep on the couch with the television on.

I had just finished the prologue of the novel I was currently reading when I heard him come in. It was titled *Pay Day*. What I found interesting about this novel was that it seemed to be the blueprint for the Nance murders. According to the prologue, thieves had entered a house early in the morning, pulled a sleeping couple out of their bed, and robbed them, knowing the couple could not call the police. Unlike the people we were looking for, the thieves in the prologue did not kill the couple. I picked up the phone and called Kelly's cell.

"Hello, Phoenix," Kelly said after looking at her caller ID.

"Have you read *Pay Day*?" I was pretty sure Kelly wasn't reading much of anything while Sterling was in town.

"No. I've read a couple of books. Nothing special about any of them."

"Well, you gotta print it out."

"I haven't printed anything. I just used the copy of the disk we got from the bank and read the books from my laptop. What's so special about the book you're reading?"

"The Vegas murders are almost a carbon copy of the prologue in this book."

"Oh, really?"

"Yep. Our killers are following this novel step by step."

We stayed up until four reading and discussing *Pay Day*, which was only 366 double-spaced pages. Apparently Bruce's characters had planned several robberies, but the problem was that he had used fictitious names and places. The book we read never mentioned Las Vegas, Tucson, Saint Paul, or Dallas. According to the book, all the robberies took place in California, beginning in Sacramento and continuing on to San Francisco, Fresno, Bakersfield, Santa Barbara, Pasadena, Los Angeles, San Bernardino and San Diego in that order, but no one was killed.

Chapter 45

I met Kelly in the Quantico lab at about 11:00 the next morning. The techies had more information for us. A woman named Lena Scarsdale had sent Michelle a phone number, which meant nothing until were learned that the area code was in Saint Paul, where we found a tortured and very dead Frank Howard. We checked Michelle's home phone and cell records, but she never called the number. As a matter of fact, Michelle only called local Toledo numbers that belonged to members of our family.

"Phoenix," Kelly began. "What if Frank Howard was some-how involved with Lena Scarsdale?"

I said, "Why would you jump to that conclusion?"

"Howard's neighbors said he had recently divorced prior to moving into the neighborhood. What if Lena Scarsdale had something to do with it?"

"That's quite a leap, Kelly."

"Not really, Phoenix. Not when you consider that Frank Howard's house was a pig sty, and all the other victims were living in well-furnished homes in upscale neighborhoods. Maybe Scarsdale is his ex-wife or ex-girlfriend. Or she's somebody's wife and Howard was bangin' her. Either way, somebody shot the man in the nuts over sex. You can believe that shit. I don't think it's all that big of a leap. Let's say Frank Howard didn't know her at all. One of the few leads would still be a woman in Saint Paul. Where there's smoke, there's fire. We can't ignore what few clues we have."

"Who said I was ignoring Scarsdale, Kelly? I'm just trying to follow your logic on this one. That's all."

"All I'm saying is that Frank Howard was found murdered in Saint Paul and Michelle has this woman's number and she's from Saint Paul. Or she at least lives there."

"Hmmm. I looked at Frank Howard's phone records and I don't recall seeing any calls coming in or going out to anyone named Lena Scarsdale. For all we know, Scarsdale could be an Excalibur Foods employee like Michelle, or a client of theirs. We'll check that out too. Just to make sure."

Kelly and I went back to my office at the Bureau, where I kept Howard's phone records. It turned out that Howard was calling a woman named Liz Clayton every day for a week prior to his murder. Only one call lasted more than a minute. That call lasted nineteen minutes and thirteen seconds. It was the same number Lena Scarsdale had given to Michelle. We couldn't help but draw the obvious conclusion that the two women knew each other.

We went back to the lab and finished looking at the disk drives from the other murder victims' homes and learned that all the victims knew each other. We found email addresses and recovered instant messages which were sent nearly every day. They were all pretending to be in the publishing business, posing as either agents or editors. All the murder victims had made contact with major and minor publishing houses. They received numerous phone calls and emails from the editors, the royalties department, the cover designers, et cetera. They had duped industry professionals too.

As we dug deeper into the restored disk drives, we found

correspondence that mentioned Bruce Michaels' name. Fraudulent literary agents, Rick and Suzette Nance, had responded to an email Bruce sent them. It was starting to look like some disgruntled authors had plotted the deaths of the people who had swindled them. They appeared to be using Bruce Michaels' book to exact revenge, going from house to house, robbing and then killing their supposed agents and editors. According to the emails and instant messages, the victims were bragging about how much money they were stealing from desperate authors who were trying to break into the publishing business.

We went to Cody Mills' website, which stated that she was listed as a member of the prestigious Who's Who in America. I called the library and had them check to see if her name was actually there, and learned that she had never made the list. Apparently, she was using made-up credentials to earn a very nice living. I was blown away when Kelly and I saw what she charged—a minimum of $5000 per edit. That was the price if your manuscript was in good shape. She charged more depending on how much work she had to do. I was new to the business, so maybe that was a legitimate amount for someone with real credentials, but Cody Mills was a pretender.

I was totally dumbfounded when we examined the quality of her edits. The manuscripts were still in horrible condition when she finished working on them. Words were still misspelled, and the punctuation was almost nonexistent. Not only was she overcharging, but she was also doing a piss poor job of editing, yet somehow she had gotten a job teaching at the collegiate level before she was caught and subsequently fired.

Other e-mails revealed that counterfeit agents, like Rick and Suzette Nance, would call authors and tell them how great they were and how they just happened to be looking for the kind of material the author had sent them. But after all the sickening genuflection was done, they'd tell the author they could not represent them without first having the material edited. What made the con so sweet was that the Nances didn't solicit the authors for editorial fees, nor did they initially recommend an editor. We continued going through the emails and found that the authors—well over a thousand of them—would eventually ask their spurious agents to recommend a professional editor. Most of these con artists were patient enough to wait until the client sent a second email, asking for the name of a reputable editor. Only then would they send them the email address and website information of one of their partners in crime, adding that the prospective author would have to deal with the editor on his own and get the best deal he could because the Nances had nothing to do with what the editor charged. The author would then send their wonderful agents a great letter of thanks, never realizing they had seriously been screwed over.

The Nances tended to send their "clients" to Cody Mills. They then sent an email to Mills, letting her know to expect an email from a particular author, and they'd split the check when it came in.

"Phoenix," Kelly laughed.

"What, Kelly?" I asked, laughing with her, having read her mischievous mind.

"I say we let them kill all of them then take their asses down for doing so. What do you think?"

My laughter spilled out hard and loud. "You know we can't do that," I said, still laughing. "There's something going on at the Crystal Gateway Marriott in Arlington in a couple of weeks." We had read instant messages from two different people. One of the senders called himself Filcher, and other called himself Al Mundy. How brazen could these people be? I wondered. Filcher literally means "to steal." I used to watch the reruns of a show called *It Takes a Thief* when I lived in China, so I knew Al Mundy was a thief. Both senders had sent instant messages to the Nances the night of the Vegas murders. Our techies tried tracking the email addresses, but they were all fictitious, leading to overseas accounts that were also fakes. "There's a chance they're going to meet those two at the same hotel. If we don't catch them by then, we still may have one card left to play."

"Yeah," Kelly said. "It's probably a literary event of some kind. This may be how they get their suckers. The authors have no idea what's going on either." She chuckled a little. "No wonder they're called starving artists. What do you think?"

"Makes sense to me. In the meantime, we gotta try to hunt them down. We'll get the Marriott to fax us a list of everybody attending the event. They're probably coming in from all over the country. We're going to need help."

Chapter 46

After rifling through the hard drive, we learned that over one thousand authors had done business with counterfeit literary agents and editors. That meant a lot of leg-work, a lot of phone calls, and a lot of knocking on doors. That was way too many authors for me and Kelly to handle on our own. Most of the authors that we were interested in interviewing lived on the East Coast, but the rest were scattered throughout the country. Some of the states included Idaho, Montana, Wyoming, Nebraska, North and South Dakota, and Minnesota. Rick and Suzette were smart enough to only deal with people who not only did not live in Las Vegas, which was where they lived, but they didn't have any "clients" in the state of Nevada. When a Nevada resident sought them out for representation, they referred them to one of their friends in New Mexico, Arizona, or Dallas—anywhere but the state of Nevada. They told the authors they refused that they didn't know the agent personally, but had met him or her at a conference and that they seemed nice.

Cody Mills, who lived in Tucson, had no clients from Tucson and no clients in Arizona. The same was true for all the victims, which made con artist sense. No one was doing business in their own backyard, making it nearly impossible for an author, who was probably broke in the first place, to not only track them down, but, seek legal means of restitution for monies lost by the scam. If an author did hire an attorney, it would probably cost more to prosecute, and they probably still wouldn't get their money back. I guess those authors gave up and left the literary business altogether with a bitter taste in their mouth.

After I briefed Director Malone on our findings, she assigned the task of questioning the authors to the area field offices in the states or regions where the authors lived. They in turn were to report their findings to Kelly. The charade of Kelly being on point covered all our asses just in case something went wrong. Anyway, it was going to take a lot of legwork because the murder victims only gave the authors their post office box addresses, which meant our people would have to try to track them through the postal service. This was actually a good idea because we could get the Postal Inspectors involved. I was going to get them all. If it took ten years, I would get every last one of them. My cousin was dead because of these people and apparently, so was her husband.

I decided to check out Liz Clayton personally. We got her address from the phone company, and six hours later, we were on a commercial flight to Saint Paul, Minnesota. We rented a car, and as we drove over to Liz Clayton's place, I thought the time was right for a little girl talk. Sterling and Kelly had been seeing each other for several years, and I was wondering where it was going. So, I told Kelly how I felt when Savannah didn't run to me and give me one of those *I missed you* hugs. After I revealed some of my personal business, it was time to get into Kelly's.

"So, how's it going with Sterling?" I asked.

"Fine," Kelly said almost inaudibly, then reflexively looked in the rearview mirror.

Sensing she wasn't telling all, I looked at her and asked, "Hey, is everything all right between you two?"

"Yep."

"Are—you—sure?" I asked skeptically.

"The sex is still good, so why worry about the rest, right, Phoenix?"

"The sex is still good? That's your answer to my question, Kelly? The sex is still good?"

"What the hell more is there, Phoenix? Shit! Everybody can't find a man like yours, all right! So, ya just fuck 'em until you get enough, and then ya move the hell on to another piece, right?"

She wasn't laughing, which was a part of her internal make-up. I took her comments very seriously. I was about to respond, but she starting speaking again.

"What can ya do, Phoenix? I mean goddamn. A man has never told me he didn't want to get married because I was broke."

"What? He told you that? He said that to your face?"

"Yes. He's concerned about losing half his shit! Can't say I blame him, though."

"So, he loves you, but he doesn't trust you? Is that it?"

"In a nutshell—yes." She thought for a second. "Well . . . he never said he loved me either."

"Hmpf! But whenever he wants some pussy, he comes running to get it, huh? Flyin' his ass all over the country to get it, too. He's got a lotta nerve."

"Phoenix, I'm not a prostitute, okay? I'm not trying to marry him for his money, but he does have a lot of it."

"What does that have to do with prostitution, Kelly?"

"Listen, I would fuck Sterling broke or not, okay? The shit is the bomb, all right? But I wouldn't marry him—good dick notwithstanding. I guess what bothers me is I want him to do what I wouldn't do myself. Am I crazy or what?"

"What do you mean you want him to do what you wouldn't do?"

"I mean I wouldn't marry some broke-ass man, period."

I laughed. "I hear you. So, what are you going to do?"

"I don't know," Kelly said solemnly and parked the car. Then a wide smile blossomed. "It would be so much easier to leave his ass if he wasn't tappin' it just right."

We laughed and exited the vehicle.

"So, wait a minute. You're going to keep seeing him, knowing he has no plans to ever marry you?"

Kelly thought for a long minute before speaking. "I guess."

"You guess?"

"I don't know right now."

As we approached the steps of Liz Clayton's house, I said, "You've got some decisions to make. You know that, don't you?"

"Don't remind me."

We had been so busy talking about her relationship with Sterling we didn't notice that there were no curtains or blinds covering the windows. We looked inside. The house had been completely cleaned out. We were at a dead end again.

Chapter 47

Bruce Michaels' novel, *Pay Day,* explained how the victims were located, what each one did for a living, and how much money they had stolen. In the book, all the victims communicated online via computer. Using a victim's computer Internet Protocol address led them to the manufacturer's website. The victims had registered their newly purchased computers online, which required an address and phone number.

But the book never mentioned real names or addresses of the victims we had so far. It was possible that Bruce's book had more clues or answers for us. It was just a matter of figuring out what to look for and what to eliminate. It was 10 PM when we got back to Washington. I told Kelly we should reread the book several times if we had to, and discover some obscure details that would help us apprehend the killers.

By the time I got back to my Arlington, Virginia home, I was dead tired. I crawled into bed and closed my eyes for some much-needed sleep. Kelly had told me she was going by Sterling's hotel for the night. He was staying at the Willard Intercontinental, which is where he always stayed when he was in town. Suddenly, my eyes shot open. It occurred to me that the killers had used Frank Howard's credit card to pay for the room in Las Vegas. Could that be their MO? Is that what they were doing, using the credit cards of their murdered victims to pay for a night's stay at a plush hotel?

With renewed vigor, I swung my feet to the floor and looked back at Keyth to make sure I didn't wake him. He was out. Nothing was going to wake him up, it seemed. My first thought was to call Sterling's suite and wake Kelly so she could help. But then I thought, what if the hunch doesn't pay off? What if it's just a wild goose chase?

I went to my office and turned on my computer. Soon the desktop came up, which featured the latest picture of Wesley Snipes in an action scene from *Blade III: Trinity*. I clicked on the Homeland Security icon and typed in my password. Moments later, I was in the mainframe again. I clicked on the pull-down screen for hotel reservations and then typed in Embassy Suites. There were two ways to check guest information. I could simply type in a name, but since American names are so common, I might have to do more work than necessary. In all likelihood, I would probably end up chasing down people who just happened to have the same name as the victims. Frank Howard had registered at the Hotel on Paradise Road in Vegas, so I typed in Tucson, Arizona, which was where Cody Mills was murdered.

The Embassy Suites guests screen came up and asked me for a name. I already knew Frank Howard had registered at the Embassy on East Broadway, but just to check my theory, I typed in Cody Mills' name and hit enter. The computer searched for about five seconds and then read: No guest by that name. It occurred to me that Mills actually lived in Tucson, so the killers, if they were doing what I thought they were doing, wouldn't use her name until after they went to Albuquerque, New Mexico, where Audrey Jefferies was killed.

I typed in Albuquerque and then put in Cody Mills' name. After about five seconds, the cursor moved rapidly as the data materialized on my screen—including her credit card number, expiration date, and the last time it was used. *Yeah!* Now I knew the killers were using the credit cards of their victims. But to be sure, I typed in Dallas and Audrey Jefferies' name. *Yes!* We had them. The killers were definitely using the victims' credit cards after they killed them.

According to the printout, the killers used the victim's credit card for one day and never used it again. They were probably being careful in case a family member called the credit card company and canceled the card or something. If no one reported the deaths, the credit card companies wouldn't know the holder was dead. If no one bothered to tell the companies, or if I hadn't checked it out, they could quite possibly have used them for months. The good thing was that I now knew their *modus operandi*. And with that, we could figure out how to track them.

The computer keyboard clicked as I typed in the latest victims' names, Jack and Vicki Calhoun. Seconds later, the cursor began moving rapidly as data filled my screen, further confirming my theory. Even though they were dead, they were staying at an Embassy Suites Hotel on South Shady Grove Road in Memphis, Tennessee. But this time, there was no check-out date, which meant they could still be there. I paged down to see when they last ordered room service, which had been the previous night. After this, I searched the Westin, Marriott, Sheraton, Hilton, and a host of other hotels to see if the killers had ever deviated from their pattern. They hadn't, so I was reasonably sure they would continue staying at the Embassy Suites hotels.

I picked up the phone and called FBI Director Kortney Malone's home. I needed to use the jet the taxpayers provided for her. Normally, agents fly commercial like everyone else. In extraordinary instances like these and in the Coco

Nimburu case, we were allowed to use the "company" jet, which was loaded with state of the art electronics, such as global positioning tracking, access to satellite systems, color coded electronic map screens, satellite phones, and a host of other goodies. Besides that, the jet was luxurious and extremely comfortable.

"We could be in Memphis in less than two hours," I told Kortney. We had been quasi-friends since our initial training at the FBI Academy in Quantico, Virginia, so I could get away with calling her home and using her first name when addressing her—in private anyway.

As she lectured me about letting Kelly run the show, I looked at a map of the United States on my office wall. It occurred to me that the killers were steadily moving east. As far as we knew, the murders had started in Las Vegas. They then killed in Tucson, Albuquerque, and Dallas in that order. To my knowledge, no one had been killed in Memphis. Nevertheless, I was wondering why the killers only stayed at Embassy Suites hotels. I called Memphis PD and briefed them. They promised to cooperate.

Chapter 48

Agency operatives McAlister Sage and Carson Fletcher knew about Liz Clayton too. They had drawn the same conclusions as Phoenix and Kelly because they had gotten much of the same information from Audrey Jefferies' computer in Albuquerque. Not only did they need to find the killers and sanction them, but they had to make sure the existence of Scarecrow never became fodder for water cooler conversations. They had flown to Saint Paul and scoured the house, looking for any information that might lead to the whereabouts of Liz Clayton. Then they had an Agency cleaning team come to Clayton's home and remove everything, even the carpeting, so Phoenix and Kelly's investigation would come to a screeching halt. Having discovered the key to finding the killers, McAlister and Carson were on the next plane to the killers' location, so that they could tie up the loose ends.

When they arrived at the Embassy on South Shady Grove, Carson opened a silver briefcase with a sophisticated wireless computer and a satellite tracking system inside. He opened a program and checked for a specific reservation. After finding out that the killers were in room 1619, he programmed a key card so they could enter the room and surprise them. The computer terminal beeped, letting Fletcher know the card was ready. He pulled the card from the slot and stuck it in his pocket. Then both operatives pulled out their weapons, ejected the magazines, and made sure they were fully loaded. Next, they screwed on their sound suppressors, tightened them, returned the weapons to their shoulder holsters, and exited the vehicle.

After entering the hotel, the operatives walked over to the nearest courtesy telephone. McAlister called the room. A woman answered. He hung up and looked at Carson. "They're in the room."

Evil glee covered Carson's face. Killing the killers was going to feel so damned good. After all, they had put themselves in the jackpot by becoming murderers. They had become death brokers the moment they committed the Ridgeville Crest murders in China Lake, which no one but Carson knew so far. Now it was their turn to die. It didn't matter that they were getting even with Rick and Suzette Nance and the others. All that mattered to Carson was that they had killed. For that reason, it was okay to kill them—legal even. After all, he had a license to kill from the United States government—that's how he justified murder in his twisted mind.

McAlister and Carson walked over to the elevators and pressed the UP button. It illuminated. A bell sounded and the doors retracted a few seconds later. They entered the small glass-and-mirrored room that would ascend sixteen floors and let them out so they could make their kill. The elevator chimed again just before the doors retracted. They left the elevator and began the short trek to room 1619. Although their voices were very faint, the operatives could hear the killers talking through the door. They looked into each other eyes, making sure they would burst into the room and kill absolutely everything that moved. Carson pulled the electronic key card from his pocket and slid it into the door slot as quickly and as quietly as he could. The green light illuminated, letting the operatives know the door was no longer locked.

They burst in the room suddenly, weapons drawn. But nobody was home. The faint voices they had heard were coming from the television the killers had left on. Thoroughly disappointed he wasn't going to get to kill the murderers, Carson swore under his breath and then checked the bathroom to be sure no one was there. When he came out of the bathroom, he said, "We must have just missed them. Either they took the stairs or their elevator reached the lobby a second or two after we stepped into ours."

"They'll be back," McAlister said. "Their personal effects are still here. We'll come back at a more convenient time."

"I say we wait right here for them," Carson grumbled. "That way we can handle this piece of business as soon as they return."

"What if leaving the television on was intentional, which means we have to leave it on so they won't be suspicious and take off on us? What if Phoenix Perry and Kelly McPherson show up instead? What if they hear the same voices we heard, enter the room and find us here waiting? What then?"

The thought of killing Phoenix Perry brought back evil glee to Carson's face. "We ice them too. It's that simple."

"How many fuckin' times I gotta tell you, Carson? We're not going to kill our own soldiers unless it's absolutely necessary. Now, get your shit together, man! Let's go! We'll wait for our prey in the atrium."

Chapter 49

The killers had eaten dinner at Ruth's Chris Steak House. After dinner, they decided to see a two-hour film that started at 11 PM, and now they were only two miles from the hotel. Foxy's "Get Off" was blasting in the car's sound system. They were having a marvelous time, taking turns singing verses of the popular 70s tune, when a police cruiser flashed its red and blue lights and sounded the siren. Frank Howard had just passed a sign that read: SPEED LIMIT 30 MPH. He immediately looked at the speedometer and realized he was going 35 in a 30-mile per hour zone. He looked in his rearview mirror and cursed to himself.

"What are we gonna do?" Lena asked calmly.

"Nothin'," Frank answered. "They don't know nothin', believe me. The bastards don't have nothin' to do, so they sit around looking for people to bust for speeding. The sonofabitches!"

Frank pulled over and stopped, constantly looking in his driver's side mirror as the cop ran the plates on the car they had rented. He could see the cop looking down, like he was looking at the computer screen in his cruiser.

"Look at this motherfucker," Frank began again, "sitting in the goddamned car. Why doesn't he write the fuckin' ticket, which I won't be paying, and let us go on our merry way?"

"Let's kick his ass," said Nancy, who was sitting in the back-seat.

"Let's just be cool," Lena countered. "This kinda shit pisses me off too. But . . . we gotta let this go. We've got bigger fish to fry in Arlington, remember?"

"Yeah," Frank said. "Let's remember our objectives. The SOB isn't worth the risk. Let's just cooperate with the bastard and get on back to the hotel and take care of some serious business in the bedroom."

"I'm up for that, lover," Lena cooed.

"Me too," Nancy added. "But I'm gonna ask this bastard a few questions first."

The cop opened his door, got out of the cruiser, and walked to the driver's side of the car, ticket pad in hand.

Frank hit the power button when he saw the officer get out of his vehicle. The window hummed as it reclined.

The cop leaned forward and said, "License and registration."

Frank reached for his wallet and was pulling it out of his pocket, but Nancy retracted her window, leaned out, and said, "Why the fuck did you pull us over?"

The cop smelled liquor on her breath and frowned. "Ma'am, I suggest you keep your mouth shut before I run you in."

"For what?" Nancy yelled. "For asking a legitimate question?"

"No, for interfering with police business," the cop said through clenched teeth. "Now shut-your-fucking-mouth."

"Please excuse my friend, officer," Lena said. She leaned over so he could see her and forced an uncomfortable smile, attempting to defuse the situation before it blew up in their faces. "She's had a little too much to drink. You understand, I'm sure."

"Well, if she doesn't shut her hole," the cop began with rancor, "she'll be spending the weekend in County with the rest of the drunks."

"What the fuck for?" Nancy asked again, completely coherent. "For asking a legitimate question? Here's a suggestion, you simple-ass motherfucker. Instead of sitting around beating your meat, patrol the fuckin' neighborhoods, okay, *Dumbo*! See if you can do *that*!"

"Okay, that's enough outta you," the cop warned.

Nancy kept right on talking. "I'll bet you dumb fucks sit around all night jacking-off and shit, don't you? Meanwhile, people are being swindled out of their hard-earned cash, homes are being broken into, children are being kidnapped, women are being raped, and murders are being committed! All of these crimes being committed while you cops sit on your fat, doughnut-eating asses, lying in wait for someone to go one mile over the goddamn speed limit! Then when a taxpayer asks a question you don't wanna answer, you talk that shit about runnin' somebody into County! Well, I ain't goin' nowhere! None of us are! And if you don't shut *your* hole and *write* the stupid ticket so we can get back to our hotel room and get our fuck on, you'll be really sorry!"

"All right, goddammit! That's it! Outta the fuckin' car! Now! Everybody's goin' in tonight!"

The cop grabbed his handheld radio from its holster to call for a wagon, and was about to start talking when Frank forced his driver's side door open, hitting the cop with it and knocking him backward. The cop dropped the radio and was reaching for his Glock. As he was pulling the weapon out of its holster, Frank, who had gotten out of the car, grabbed the cops' wrist with his left hand and hit him in the face with his right. *Bing!* The cop dropped the weapon before he hit the ground. Nancy and Lena jumped out of the car and started kicking and stomping the officer's face, ribs, and groin.

Nancy screamed, "I bet you won't pull nobody else over, will you, ya lazy bastard!" Then she picked up the gun and pointed it in the cop's face. "Now what, huh? Now what?"

"Please . . . don't kill me!" the cop mumbled through a thoroughly bloodied mouth.

"Nancy!" Lena screamed. "Let him go! Don't do it!"

"Too late. He pissed me off." *Pow! Pow! Pow!* "How do you like that, cop? Huh? How do you like that?" She laughed maniacally. *Pow! Pow! Pow!* "You want me to close my hole?" *Pow! Pow! Pow!* "I'll tell you what. You close your holes and I'll close mine." Nancy laughed uncontrollably as she got into the car. She wiped her prints off the weapon and tossed it on the dead cop's chest.

Frank Howard and Lena Scarsdale were still looking at the murdered police officer's blood fill the street, stunned by what had happened so incredibly fast. Then Frank ran to the police cruiser and ejected the videotape. He checked the computer screen to see if the cop had run a check on their rented vehicle, but he couldn't tell one way or the other because he was running short on time and was afraid of someone seeing them or more cops showing up. He was sure that at the very least, someone had heard the shots. He went back to the cop and took his wallet, his cuffs, and the key.

Nancy stuck her head out the open car window. "Come on, guys! I'm wet! Let's go get our fuck on!"

Chapter 50

The Agency operatives were sitting in the hotel atrium, patiently waiting for their prey to return to their temporary domicile. Not far from where they were sitting was a small waterfall, which ran into a coin-filled aquarium where several fish species swam freely. Every thirty seconds or so, water would shoot up from several of the jets inside the aquarium. The atrium was located in the middle of the hotel and afforded the operatives an unobstructed view of suite 1619 and a view of the glass-enclosed elevators that ascended and descended constantly. Having no photographs of the people they were looking for, they studiously watched each couple that stepped off on the sixteenth floor, checking to see if they went to suite 1619—none did.

"I think we ought to call it a night," McAlister said. "I'm going to the restroom, and when I return, we're out of here."

"I say we wait it out, Mac."

"I say we we're out of here. Before long, security is going to want to know if we're guests here. That's the end of it, Carson."

After he turned the corner and was sure Carson couldn't
see him, McAlister Sage called Neil Yarborough again. He
had called several times and left messages for his mentor,
but the calls and messages had gone unanswered. He wanted
to give Neil a piece of his mind for sending a chaperone
along to watch him like it was his first sanction. As far as he
was concerned, Neil had a lot of nerve sending anyone to
help him take care of "company" business. If he ever needed
help, the last person he would want helping him was Carson
Fletcher, who was nearly burnt out. McAlister knew Carson
was no longer killing for the United States government. He
was killing because he loved killing. Killing for pleasure was
a strange phenomenon that happened to a lot of Agency operatives. Nevertheless, they had a plan, and they were running it step by step.

*Who does he think he's fooling? If he only knew that Neil wants
him dead. This is all an elaborate ruse to kill the great McAlister
Sage! The fool actually thinks he's in charge, when I'm running this
show. That's right! Me! Carson muthafuckin' Fletcher! It's going to
be so nice killing you, McAlister. After all, you deserve it after seriously fucking up the Scarecrow sanction in the first place. Soon, I'll
have everything. I'll even have his pretty little Naval lieutenant,
Marilyn Mason. I'm gonna have her singing a sweet concerto in A
minor.*

Carson felt one of his two cell phones vibrate. One was for
his personal calls, and the other was tied into McAlister's cell
phone. The transmitter on the phone was disabled, making
it possible to listen to calls without McAlister hearing the
background noise of Carson's location. It would give everything away if, for example, McAlister heard people speaking,
heels clicking, cars starting, doors opening, horns blowing,
et cetera.

*What do we have here? Mac is calling Neil behind my back
again.*

He put the earpiece in his ear and listened to their conversation.

Hmpf. Mac is seriously pissed at me.

"Where do you get off sending Carson here, giving *me* orders?" McAlister was saying. "I work alone. You know that, Neil."

"Calm down, my friend," Neil Yarborough said in a controlled monotone.

"Don't fuckin' tell me to calm down, Neil." McAlister raised his voice a few octaves. "And don't handle me either."

"Is this a secure line?"

"Yes, goddammit. Of course the line is fuckin' secure," McAlister said through clenched teeth as a hotel guest walked by. "Have you no confidence in me at all?"

Silence.

"Well, your silence says it all, Neil," McAlister continued. "This is it for me. You fuckin' hear me? After I finish this, I'm through. Do you hear me? I'm finished."

"Fine. I'll put you on extended leave after this. You've earned it, and you apparently need the time away. Go to the islands. Find a pretty girl and relax. You'll be back when you realize how boring life can be in the civilian world. And don't worry, McAlister, I won't hold anything you've said against you. Now, I really have to go. I'm late for a briefing on the North Korea situation. Ciao!"

And with that, the line disconnected.

Carson quickly put away his phone and watched for McAlister to come around the corner. "It's about time," he said. "I have to go too."

"I'll be waiting in the car," McAlister said. "We'll try calling them from the car every half hour until they answer the phone. I don't want the hotel people getting suspicious. Let's keep the body count to a minimum."

Chapter 51

Police cruisers pulled up to the front entrance of the hotel just as McAlister was getting into the car. Their red and blue lights bounced off the hotel and nearby vehicles. He called Carson and told him to slip out the back door before the cops surrounded the building. He adjusted his seat and drove around to the back of the hotel just as Carson was coming out of the building. After Carson got in, he pulled off and drove out of the back parking lot and went around to the front of the building, where he shut off the headlights and parked the vehicle on the dark street. Moments later, a huge black TACT truck stopped in front of the hotel. The TACT team members exited the back of the truck, wearing black uniforms and shiny black combat boots, carrying AR-15 rifles. They surrounded the building.

As the TACT team stood around talking, the Memphis Chief of Police pulled up and got out of his car. Apparently, he wanted to call all the shots on this one. He walked over to the two camouflaged officers who seemed to be in charge of the scene. One was wearing lieutenant bars on his collar. The other wore sergeant strips on his sleeves. He spoke to them briefly, and suddenly everyone went into action. The uniformed cops blocked the doors and detained the hotel guests attempting to enter the building. Soon, frightened guests were exiting the hotel, wearing gowns, pajamas, or robes. The guests had no idea what was going on. Some thought the police had trapped terrorists in the building.

Carson chuckled a bit. "Look at them. They're always *too* late. This is all a waste of time. No way they're coming back to this fiasco."

"If I remember correctly, we were a bit late too," McAlister said abruptly. "Let's get the hell outta here. They're not done. They'll kill again. And we'll be there to end it all."

McAlister turned on the police scanner and listened to police for a moment or two. Then he started the car and slowly drove away.

Chapter 52

Minutes after McAlister and Carson pulled off, Frank Howard, Lena Scarsdale, and Nancy Newman turned onto South Shady Grove Road, eagerly anticipating the wild sex they were about to have, until they saw what looked like a battalion of police officers and guests outside of their hotel. As they drove by, they saw a couple of satellite trucks and reporters interviewing guests and a few police officers. It took every ounce of strength Frank had not to press the gas pedal to the floor. Instead, he cruised by, making sure he was going no faster than the speed limit allowed. They held their breath as they eased past the hotel, and let out a collective sigh of relief when they were out of visual range. Suddenly, sirens rang out in the distance, increasing in volume as they continued on. Again, they held their breath as several police cruisers turned the corner and raced past them at incredible speeds.

Laughing, Nancy said, "I guess they found our friend with the radar gun."

"That was real smart, Nancy. Real fucking smart," Frank

replied, looking at her in the rearview mirror. "Now every cop in the country will be looking to blow us away."

"As long as we finish what we started first," Nancy said, returning Frank's glare in the mirror. "Now, let's get to Nashville so we can take care of another trickster agent, Ms. Juanita Lawrence."

"Well, one thing's for sure," Lena chimed in. "We can forget about staying at another Embassy. This is the second time the cops were there when we returned. This can't be a coincidence this time. They were looking for us."

Frank looked at Lena. "They know we're using the credit cards of the people we've killed."

"We can still go to the Embassy, guys," Nancy said with delightful glee. "They have no idea what we look like, and I'm certain they don't know our real names. I bet we could go right back to the hotel, check in under our real names, and they wouldn't know jack. Besides, I like getting my cooked-to-order breakfast every morning. And if we don't have to stay at another hotel, why should we?"

Lena said, "They've gotta know we know they know about the credit cards. The funny thing is, we can still use them, but not at a hotel. In fact, I say we continue to use them and throw them off the trail."

"What do you mean, Lena?" Frank asked.

"Well, they're going to think we aren't going to use the cards anymore, right? If we use them in a particular city, they have to follow the trail we give them. I mean that's what they've done so far, right? So, we let 'em think we're stupid, send them where we want, and then go in a completely different direction. It will take some driving on our part, but it will be worth it in the end."

"And Juanita Lawrence's cards will be the perfect decoy," Nancy said.

Lena said, "Yeah. Let's take care of that bitch once and for all."

Frank smiled broadly and said, "I've got a better idea, girls. You wanna handle this like we did in China Lake?"

"Yes, but I wanna drive," Nancy said. "I wanna be the one to run that bitch down, back over her, and run over her again. Or better yet, let's strip her naked, tie her to the rear bumper, and drag her good-for-nothing ass through Nashville."

Lena looked at her watch—2 AM Central Time. "Frank, do you think you can get us there by 4:30? If so, we can take care of her tonight, get a hotel and rest for a while. Then the next night, we can pay off Shirley Milgrove."

"I say we get outta town, get a hotel, and get some rest," Frank said. "Juanita Lawrence and Shirley Milgrove are luxuries that can wait. If we go in tired, we could make crucial mistakes. Let's stick to Bruce's book idea. Let's be thorough. We've got the rest of the summer to get these people—all of them. I've got the cop's wallet. Those bozos won't even put together that it was us that iced him. They'll think it was a robbery or something. But in case they do figure it out, we'll use the cop as bait. Let's take it easy for a day or so, and then take care of our enemies."

Chapter 53

The Memphis Police Department was crawling all over the Embassy by the time Kelly and I made it to the hotel. We exited our vehicle and slammed both doors violently. This was supposed to be an undercover operation, not an invitation to a presidential ball. If they had our suspects in custody, all would be forgiven. Having our suspects would be a good reason for being so visible, but if the suspects were out for the evening and had planned to return to the hotel, they would see an armada and simply disappear again. I was going to have somebody's ass if that was the case.

We approached the two uniforms guarding the entrance, flashed our credentials, and attempted to enter the premises. The two uniforms stepped in front of us.

One of the officers said, "Nobody goes in there without Chief Frost's permission."

I gave Kelly one of those *Can you believe this shit?* looks and then looked at the officer again. They wouldn't even know the suspects were at this hotel if I hadn't given them a heads up. "Where is he?" I asked politely. The badge I carried gave me every right to enter the hotel on my own authority, but I made nice because we would probably need those two boneheads later. Why piss them off and get next to no cooperation later?

The uniform on the left tilted his head to the right and said, "He's over there talking to the media."

Seeking to salvage something from the blown cover, I asked, "Do you have our suspects in custody?"

The uniform on the right offered a sarcastic chuckle and shook his head.

Kelly and I looked at each other incredulously and then looked over to where the officer had tilted his head. It looked like Chief Frost was doing a live interview with a young reporter. We walked over to where the interview was being conducted. They were just finishing up.

"Chief Frost?" I said in a questioning tone.

"Yes," he said. "And you are?"

"Agents Perry and McPherson," I said politely. We showed him our credentials. "I thought I told your people this was a federal investigation and to only stake out the hotel until we got here. What the hell happened?"

Chief Frost was African American, about fifty-five years old, and looked to be about six-foot four. He must have easily weighed three hundred solid pounds. His uniform fit him like a glove. The four stars on his shoulder twinkled when light hit them. He furrowed his thick brow. Age lines materialized on his forehead just before he opened his mouth.

"This is my goddamned town, and I'll do whatever I damn well please in it. The Memphis Police Department doesn't work for you, *Agent* Perry. We're law enforcement officers too. And I wasn't about to take orders from a woman who had her suspects trapped in a house and allowed them to shoot their way out, killing agents under her command and several locals in the process." He paused and glared at me, shaking his head. "Watched it all on television live. I remember you two well. By the way, didn't you almost get your acting director killed too, *Agent* Perry?"

Now that hurt, but I didn't let on. He was talking about a case Kelly and I had handled back in the summer of 2001, about five days before the World Trade Center towers came crashing down in Manhattan. Kelly wanted to surprise the killers, but there was another suspect on the loose, and I knew that if we went in, we could end up killing the two suspects in the house, and the other one could have gotten away clean. But I wasn't about to second-guess myself on that call, and I certainly wasn't going to let this cretin change the subject.

"Can't get it up, huh, Chief?" Kelly's sharp tongue was on the loose again. "That shit's gotta fuck with your mind after awhile. Is that why you're giving two female agents the only hard time you can give them? Is it because you can't get a *real* hard one anymore, little boy?"

Chief Frost whirled his big frame in Kelly's direction. "I heard about you too, McPherson. You are the talk of the town amongst your FBI brethren here in Memphis. With the kind of men you've chosen to sleep with, the last one in particular, I'd think a professional tramp like you would be more into, how shall I say . . . the female persuasion, munching carpet and whatnot."

Even though that zinger was directed at Kelly, it stung me too. It felt like collateral damage. Nevertheless, Frost wasn't referring to Sterling Wise. He was talking about one of Kelly's former boyfriends, who turned out to be a criminal.

My partner was about to respond, but I grabbed her arm and said, "Why didn't you wait for us before you brought in the Cavalry? More people are gonna die because you're a glory hound."

"As long as they don't die in Memphis," Chief Frost said,

smiling. "My job is to protect and serve the people of this city—not the country, *Agent* Perry."

I knew that last barb was a slap at the FBI, but before I could defuse the growing angst, Kelly said, "So, screw the rest of the country, huh?"

"You may not like my methods, but I can guarantee your suspects won't kill anyone in my city tonight. If they're here, they'll have to move on now, won't they?"

That's when I lost it and screamed, "So, you fucked up *our* stakeout in an obnoxious effort to get the killers to move on to the next city?"

"That and because you fuckin' Feds piss me off. Besides, turnabout is fair play since the FBI has always taken credit for crimes the Memphis Police Department solved. So, this time I decided to have my own people apprehend the killers before you Feds had a chance to take the credit. Good luck with your case." With that, he turned around and swaggered off, leaving us staring at his hind parts and shaking our heads.

Kelly yelled out, "You better walk away, ya broke dick bastard! Get some Cialis or some shit!"

Chief Frost stopped and glared at Kelly for a few seconds, and then turned around and continued on, swaggering all the way to his car.

"Kelly," I began. "I've figured out a way to get a photo of the suspects."

Chapter 54

The desk clerk was finishing an interview with the same young reporter who interviewed Chief Frost. We waited until she was on her way back to the front desk then approached her. She seemed to be excited by all the previous activity, TACT teams running around with flak jackets, fatigues, combat boots, and automatic weapons, guests being ushered out in pajamas, gowns, and robes. And to top all of that off, she was asked to do a live interview on television. She was now an official Memphis celebrity, right up there with Elvis! The desk clerk looked exhilarated, high from momentary fame. I thought now would be a good time to get her to cooperate without having to strong-arm her for vital information. It became clear to me that Frank Howard, or better yet, the man who was pretending to be Frank Howard, and Lena Scarsdale, who could be Liz Clayton, might have been surreptitiously photographed by the hotel's security cameras at the check-in desk. I told this to the clerk, whose nameplate read: ABBY, and she became even more energized. I liked dealing with this kind of citizen, who was always eager to help the police catch criminals and solve crimes, especially brutal murderers like Frank Howard and Lena Scarsdale.

The Abby's of the world were truly a scarce commodity, almost nonexistent. Most citizens didn't want to get involved. They were concerned for their own lives and livelihoods. Yet, those who refused to get involved were often angry when no witnesses would come forward to identify the person who robbed or assaulted them. They didn't understand that they couldn't have it both ways. They didn't understand that they had to get involved so that all of society would be safe. The "every man for himself" philosophy made it easier for criminals to get away with their crimes, and difficult for the judicial system to prosecute them. But Abby was a sparkling diamond, a rare jewel indeed.

"Abby," I began and flashed my credentials. "I'm Special Agent Phoenix Perry, and this is my partner, Kelly McPherson. We're going to need your help to solve this crime." I knew I was laying it on thick, but sometimes you have to stroke these kinds of witnesses a little to make it even easier to cooperate, though I suspected it wouldn't take much to get Abby to help us. "I need you to tell me what time Jack or Vicki Calhoun checked in."

"Sure," Abby said and hit the keys on her keyboard so quickly that it reminded me of the percussion section of the Florida A&M Marching Band. "Ahh, here we go, Agent Perry." The printer began.

I took the printout from her and looked at it. Jack and Vicki Calhoun checked in at 1:30 that afternoon, which was just over sixteen hours ago. I looked her in the eyes and said, "Where's the night manager?"

"He had an emergency and left me in charge," Abby said, smiling.

"Well, we need to see the security tapes. We're trying to get a visual on these guests. Do you have access to the security system?"

"I sure do. Follow me."

Abby opened the door for us and we entered the night manager's office. There were four monitors above the manager's desk. The monitors switched every few seconds from the front desk to the lobby to the back parking lot, and to the concierge station. I asked, "Where are today's tapes?"

Abby set up the VCR for us and showed us how to use the system. Then she gave us four tapes from the four cameras in the lobby and went back to the front desk. Fortunately for us, the tape was time indexed, and all we had to do was fast forward to 1:30. However, the tape wasn't in sync with the hotel's computer system. The security cameras and the computers were off by about 93 minutes. Thirty-two people checked in between 1:23 and 2:56 that afternoon. We had hoped to get photos and cross reference them with facial recognition software. If they were ever arrested and booked, we'd get a printout of who they were and the crimes they had committed.

This wasn't exactly what we were hoping for, but it was much better than what we had. Kelly and I believed Frank Howard and Lena Scarsdale were in the wind, having seen a police battalion waiting for them at the entrance of their provisional sanctuary. But to be sure, we checked each guest.

We got back on the Director's plane and headed back to Washington. I called the Tucson Police Department from the plane to ask a favor of Detective Santana. She wasn't on duty, so they patched me through to her home. I asked Santana to go over to the Embassy and get the security tapes and overnight them to Washington. If they had the budget we had since the September 11 attacks, they could have bought state of the art computers, uploaded the information and emailed it to me. But the locals were still handicapped by outdated technology, and it cost us precious time.

I could've asked a detective in the Tucson Police Department to run the errand, but this was an opportunity to ask

Maria Santana what she thought about becoming an FBI agent. She told me she'd think about it. I gave her my office and home numbers and told her to call me when she'd made up her mind.

After that, I called the Embassy hotels where our suspects registered, and had them overnight me the same information. We were going to use our computers to get photos of all the people who checked in during the hours the suspects did. It was going to take a lot of leg-work, but we were going to find out who they were. Eventually, something was going to break and lead us to the killers.

Chapter 55

It took several days for the managers to comply with my request. Needless to say, I wasn't happy about their lackadaisical response to an official FBI request, but that's John Q Public for you. When Kelly and I walked into my office, all the tapes were sitting on my desk. We immediately began sifting through the tapes after cross-referencing the check-in times of the victims. I guess I shouldn't have been surprised that the check-in time and the camera times at all the hotels were out of sync. They probably bought all their equipment from the same companies. Nevertheless, it didn't take very long to narrow down our suspects because only one man appeared to be deliberately avoiding having his picture taken. The man we suspected of being the counterfeit Frank Howard was smart enough to wear slight disguises to hide his face from the clerks. He wore an assortment of cheap-looking fedoras and dark sunglasses, and he never looked into the camera.

The check-in desk cameras never got a clear picture of his face, but there would be no mistaking him because he was a tall man, at least six-four or five, and very well built. He looked like he could play linebacker for the Redskins or be a

Navy SEAL. A guy his size and build couldn't hide who he was no matter what kind of disguise he used. I figured that he might feel comfortable once he checked in, and wouldn't bother to wear the disguises, not that it mattered with a guy his size.

We wanted a clean photo of his face. It's easy to ignore cameras after a while, especially if a dark glass bubble covers them. With that in mind, we checked all the security tapes, including the lobby, the parking lot, all of them. This bit of detective work, though it was time consuming, yielded us clean photos of not one woman, but two. The same two women showed up at the same hotels around the same time the man pretending to be Frank Howard did. That could only mean one thing. They were all in it together.

After further investigation, we saw the two women with a man. Assuming one of the women was Lena Scarsdale, was the other one Liz Clayton? Even though the women didn't look like sisters, they reminded me of the tennis pros, Serena and Venus Williams. Both women were black, tall, around five-ten or eleven and solid, like they could whip any man that even thought about taking sexual liberties. One even had blond hair like Serena wears. The other had black hair. They were casually dressed, but sharp; hoop earrings, gold chains around their delicate necks.

The man with them was black also, and was no longer wearing a disguise, just as I suspected. He must have thought he was in the clear. He looked young, maybe twenty-four or twenty-five. All of our suspects looked as if they were in their twenties.

We ran their pictures through the Homeland Security facial recognition software, hoping for a match. Nothing. While I didn't say anything to Kelly, it bothered me that these young, intelligent people were going from city to city, brutally murdering people. I felt the same way when I learned that the Beltway Snipers were black. To be totally honest, I always felt better when white folks cornered the market on serial killers. Oh, well, as they say, nothing lasts forever.

After printing out pictures of our suspects, we checked the lobby and parking lot video again, hoping to see what kind of car they were driving at the time, but we came up empty.

Even though we thought we had the right people, we still had four obstacles to overcome. First, we had absolutely no idea where they were. Second, we didn't know their real names. Third, we didn't know where they were from. Fourth, we didn't know what kind of car they were driving. All of this meant we had to wait until we got a fresh stiff again. All of the problems notwithstanding, we put their pictures on the wire anyway. It would be like trying to find a needle in a haystack. If they all started wearing disguises all of sudden, registered under their real names, using their real driver's licenses, or changed their MO, we'd be thwarted again.

Or worse, what if the women were wearing disguises in the photos we had? What if they were conscious of the covered cameras and dressed accordingly to hide who they really were? And didn't they know they would stick out like sore thumbs if they resembled the Williams sisters? I was starting to wonder if we had anything thing on them at all. I decided to concentrate on the two *real* names we had: Frank Howard and Liz Clayton. We didn't know if Lena Scarsdale was a real name, since we only knew it from an email.

I pulled Frank Howard's jacket and began reading it again. He was born August 31, 1963. He joined the Navy February 5, 1981 under the delayed entry program. His actual induction date was September 5, 1981. After basic training and tech school, he was assigned to the USS Nimitz, where he first met Lieutenant Driver, a SEAL who later recommended he join up and do some *real* fighting. He served under Driver's command for two years before being severely wounded in the 1993 Mogadishu incident during Operation Gothic Serpent.

The assault force was made up of Delta Force, Ranger Teams, and Navy SEALs. During the fierce battle, Lieutenant Driver and several members of the assault force were killed.

After serving an additional eight years, Howard retired from the Navy on September 5, 2001. The Navy paid for a plane ticket back to Saint Paul, Minnesota, and shipped all of his belongings to the same address where we found Liz Clayton's empty residence. The house looked as if it had been empty for a while. According to the telephone records, Liz had lived at the address since May 1998—at least that was the earliest bill on record. After further examination of the phone records, we learned that Clayton's phone was disconnected only hours before we arrived. Then I saw: HLSP, which stood for Homeland Security Priority.

"Kelly," I yelled out. "Come and take a look at this."

"So, Homeland Security is in on this?" Kelly said after looking at the computer screen.

"That's how it looks. The question is why would Homeland Security even care about Liz Clayton and Frank Howard?"

"Why is Homeland Security watching them?"

I shrugged my shoulders. "Beats the hell outta me."

"Are they suspects in a terrorist network?"

"I don't know, Kelly. Who knows what we're going to unearth? Check with our Saint Paul people and see if they've turned anything up on Liz Clayton."

Chapter 56

I called Naima Marinelli, an Italian African-American woman, affectionately known as Lady Mob Boss at the office of Homeland Security. I worked with Naima while I was pregnant with Sydney and riding a desk. Naima was thirty-two, very attractive, heterosexual, and had never been married, nor was she even thinking about it. She was a cool woman to know, and we got along great. We had lunch together regularly and chatted, so I felt she would look into the Liz Clayton thing and keep it quiet.

The phone was ringing.

"Naima Marinelli."

"Aren't you supposed to say, 'Lady Mob Boss' when you answer your line?"

"Phoenix?"

"Yeah. How are things over there?"

"Well, you know, things could be better and they could be worse. How are things at the Bureau? I hear you're back on the street."

I didn't bother asking how she knew I was back doing what I do, because there is no such thing as a secret in the

government. Everybody knows your business. Agents take
pride in finding out what's going on with other agents and
passing it along to everybody else. One time, the whole Homeland Security office knew of an agent getting served with divorce papers before she did.

"Listen. Can you check something out for me?"

"Sure."

"I'm trying to find out why Liz Clayton is being investigated by Homeland Security."

"Hmmm, never heard of her." I heard her fingers rapidly
tapping the keyboard. "I see the order came from this office,
but I have no idea what it's about. Let me look into it and get
back to you, okay?"

"I need everything Homeland has on her, okay? Everything." I laughed and added, "It's a matter of national security."

Naima laughed. "Isn't it always?"

I hung up the phone and pulled up all telephone records
for Elizabeth Clayton in the Saint Paul area code. There
were a number of people with names that could be our suspect. There were three E. Claytons, two Liz Claytons, and
seven Elizabeth Claytons. There was only one at the home
we had personally checked out.

It turned out that Liz Clayton had called Michelle regularly. Most of the calls lasted for over an hour. We knew another woman was involved, so I checked the log again, looking
for frequently dialed numbers. Besides Michelle, there were
three other frequently called numbers.

I picked up my phone and hit the star button then the appropriate numbers to block the caller ID of the number I
had dialed from. I dialed one of Liz Clayton's frequently called
numbers. A woman's voice answered, saying, "Hi, you've reach
Liz Clayton. Sorry I can't take your call right now. Leave your
name and number and I promise to call you back soon."

I thought it strange that she would call her own cell so

many times. I immediately thought of two possibilities. One, she was checking her voicemail a lot, which didn't make sense since she could do that from her cell. Or two, someone was calling Liz from Liz's home phone.

I called the second number, but it was disconnected. It had belonged to a Naomi Weir. Then I called the last number. I got a recording stating that the line was no longer in service or something like that. I did a search on the number and discovered that the disconnected number had belonged to Frank Howard.

Kelly hung up the phone. "Liz Clayton is a teacher at Humboldt Senior School in Saint Paul. Our people are faxing us Clayton's photo."

The fax machine started, and a detailed report with a photo of Liz Clayton printed out, along with a copy of the divorce decree. I looked at the photo first. There could be no doubt now. The photo matched the stills we had of one of the women the hotel security camera's picked up. I looked at the divorce decree again and handed it to Kelly. "You were partially right. Frank wasn't married to Lena Scarsdale. He was married to Liz Clayton."

Kelly said, "So, now we know who Clayton is and what her relationship to Frank Howard was."

"Yep."

Later, in the lab, we dug further into the contents of Bruce's hard drive and discovered that he was visiting a members only chatroom, Pissed Writers United. Strangely, not long after Bruce's funeral, Michelle started visiting the same chat room. And what we discovered in there blew us away.

Snapshot Sequence 2:

The Death of Bruce Michaels

Chapter 57

Hasty Hills
12915 Secretariat Road
Toledo, Ohio 43615
May 11, 2002

Michelle Michaels pulled into the circular driveway and parked her sparkling pearl white Escalade. A few hours earlier, her doctor confirmed her suspicions that she was pregnant. She had an afternoon appointment, but her doctor's office called her office and told her they'd had a cancellation and that she could come in earlier if she wanted. She was so excited that she called her mother from the doctor's office and told her the good news. Her mother had been hinting at grandchildren, and she wanted her to know right away. On the way home, she scrupulously planned a romantic dinner with the intent of surprising Bruce. To celebrate, she stopped by Kroger grocery store and picked up a couple of steaks, some red wine, and a Sara Lee cheesecake for dessert. She was planning to charbroil the steaks, smother them in gravy and sautéed onions, and serve them to Bruce with a baked potato filled with chives, bacon bits, cheese, and sour cream. But she had forgotten the sour cream and had returned to the store. There was no way the meal was going to be less than perfect. The news she was about to share with the love of her life demanded it.

Blam!

What the hell was that?

Her body jerked violently as the echo of what sounded like a shotgun blast suddenly reverberated from inside her home. The suddenness of the blast, the sheer power of it, caused her upper lip to quiver uncontrollably. She jumped out of the Escalade and hurried to their two-story red brick home, praying that her husband was okay. With the exception of Jodeci's "Love You for Life" playing softly in the distance, the house was quiet—deathly quiet.

"Bruce!" She called out from the arched foyer.

Hearing no response, she looked to the left, where the living room was, then to the right, where the music lingered in the air. Tentatively, she crept down the hallway toward the music, which was coming from Bruce's office.

Of course Bruce was in his office, Michelle thought. *Where else would he be?*

Bruce was always in his office writing, which she hated because it took time away from her. That's why she never read a word of any of the books he had written. What bothered her most was that he spent hour upon hour in that office writing, and not one book had been published. He wanted to self-publish, but Michelle quickly vetoed that option. He was spending their hard-earned money going to conferences, supposedly to network, yet he hadn't made a single contact in six years—none that led to publication anyway. If he couldn't get published in six years, he wasn't ever going to get published, and she didn't see any reason to keep funding a dream that would never be realized. As far as Michelle was concerned, it was a miracle she was pregnant because they barely had time for sex with all the traveling they both did because of their professions. Michelle was a food broker for Excalibur Foods, and Bruce was a cosmetologist who owned beauty and barber shops in multiple cities. His businesses made money, but they were far from being independently wealthy. Bruce had a dream. He wanted to become a *New York Times* bestselling author. The fame and fortune of making the list had no appeal to him; it was all about the love of writing and knowing that people enjoyed his work enough to purchase copies of his novels in droves.

Just a couple of feet away from Bruce's office now, Michelle could hear the Jodeci song, which was close to ending, much clearer, even though the door was closed. She knocked and listened for her husband's response. She didn't dare open the door while he was writing, "interrupting his flow," as he called it, and incur his wrath.

"Bruce?" she said tentatively. "Are you okay, honey? I thought I heard your shotgun go off." The music stopped, and then began playing the same song. She knocked on the door again. "Bruce?"

Hearing no response, Michelle opened the door and walked into the room. She gasped when she saw her husband sitting at his desk, lying face down in front of his computer, with half his face blown off. Fresh blood ran off the desk onto the newly laid navy carpet. The one eye still left in his head was staring at her vacantly. Suddenly, the room spun and Michelle collapsed.

Chapter 58

Michelle Michaels opened her eyes slowly and scanned the unfamiliar room. *Where am I? A hospital room? Why? Is my baby okay?* She turned her head to the right and saw her mother sleeping in a chair next to her bed. Suddenly, she began to remember. Like flashes of light, she remembered getting out of her car and rushing to her home. She heard the awful sound of that shotgun blast, and jerked much like she did when she heard it in her driveway. She saw his face, her husband's face; the face of the only man she would ever love—what was left of it anyway, and realized that her husband was dead.

"Mama," she said in a dry, raspy voice.

Her mother opened her eyes and stretched as if by reflex and yawned.

She cleared her throat before speaking. "How do you feel, honey?"

"Is Bruce dead?" Michelle asked, hoping it was all a dream, hoping the images invading her mind were just that—images.

Her mother's eyes looked away, which confirmed what she

was thinking, what she knew in her heart. From deep within, a guttural wail found its way out of her mouth and filled the room, snaked down the hallway, and echoed throughout the entire floor. Tear after tear slid down her face. "Why, God? Why Bruce?"

Ruth rushed to her daughter's side to comfort her. She embraced her and rocked her as only a mother could. She knew what she was feeling because she had lost her brother and Phoenix's father, Sydney Drew, during the summer of 2001. She knew what it was like to learn of the unexpected death of someone you loved and had never expected to die as suddenly as they had.

Nurses left their other patients and rushed into her room. After they realized that Michelle was only grief stricken, they exited the room, leaving only Ruth and one nurse, who was taking her vitals. After injecting a sedative into Michelle's IV, the nurse left quietly.

Ruth stroked her daughter's head gently as tears formed in her own eyes. Bruce's death was only part of the bad news. Sooner or later she would have to tell her that not only had she lost the baby, there was a chance that she would never be able to have children. But that bit of news could wait, she thought.

Michelle rubbed her stomach slowly and asked in a drug-induced state, "Is my baby okay?"

Silence.

Michelle looked at her mother and frowned. Ruth looked away. And with that, Michelle knew the baby she had desperately wanted was no more. As the reality of losing her husband and baby washed over her, she wept again.

"Did he leave a note, Mama?" Michelle asked, almost pleading.

"No, he didn't."

Desperately searching her mind for answers and finding none, she looked at her mother and pleadingly asked, "He didn't even say goodbye to me? He just left me? Why, Mama? What did I do . . . what did I do?"

"You can drive yourself crazy trying to figure out why he did it, Michelle. But no matter what, you can't blame yourself for what Bruce did to himself. He must have been going through something terrible to have done this. Were things okay between you two?"

"Yes, of course."

"Everything okay financially?" Ruth asked skeptically.

"Yes. As far as I know they are. I do the bills," Michelle offered, tears still flowing.

"Well, there had to be something bothering the man."

"We had the best of everything, Mama—beautiful home, nice cars, money. The only thing missing was a baby."

When Michelle heard herself say "baby," she cried all the more, knowing even that was now gone.

Chapter 59

After being pampered at her mother's house for a little less than three weeks, Michelle, still shaken by what had happened, hid her devastation and moved back to her Hasty Hills home. For some reason, she had an unnatural desire to see where her husband had died. Tentatively, she walked down the hall where Bruce's office was. The house still had the aura of his powerful presence. It was as if he was still in the house—at least that's how Michelle felt as she approached his office.

The door was closed, and she was about to knock before entering, remembering how Bruce hated when she barged in while he was creating one of his fictitious worlds. She turned the doorknob and entered the room slowly, as if she expected to see Bruce still sitting in his chair with what was left of his head still on the desk, that one brown eye staring at her. In the room now, she looked at the desk, and then the floor where his dark red blood had covered the carpet. There were no stains—no blood at all. Ruth had the carpet replaced and the walls painted so Michelle wouldn't have to see the mess the gunshot blast had made of Bruce's face.

She inhaled the fresh paint as she walked over to his desk
and sat in his chair. She turned on his computer. Now that
he was dead, Michelle had a burning desire to read Bruce's
books. Perhaps by reading them, they would provide the answers she desperately needed to get past the guilt that plagued
her mind during her waking hours and often invaded her
dreams. The computer's desktop was visible now, and she
scoured every inch of it, looking for something that might
explain all the madness in her life, but found nothing. One
by one, she opened his documents and found nothing there
either.

She opened drawer after drawer, looking for his compact
disks. Having found them, she put in disk after disk looking
for something, anything that might provide clues to Bruce's
demise. But they were all blank, as if someone had erased
them. *Did Bruce erase the disks? If so, why? He spent a lot of time
writing his books and screenplays. Why would he erase them? Maybe
he no longer saw any value in having them. Is that why he killed
himself? Was it because he couldn't get anyone to take him seriously?
Hmmm, I'll take the disks to a computer store and see if they can re-
cover anything.*

She looked at his filing cabinet and decided to check
those for some of his manuscripts. That's where they'd be,
since they were not in any of the desk drawers, she thought.
Just as she started rifling through his papers, she heard the
chime of an instant message. She frowned, wondering how
she could be receiving an instant message when she hadn't
signed on.

It occurred to her that Bruce was connected to Buckeye
Cable, which meant his computer was always connected to
the Internet. She walked over to the computer and looked at
the computer screen. Bruce had more than fifty messages,
dating back to the day he died. The earliest messages were
from his family. He had heard from his brother Bernard,
who lived in New York City. He'd also gotten one from his

sister, Daisy. Nothing surprising about that. Bruce's family were a close-knit bunch.

She continued sifting through the messages, which were from people with strange names. Most of the messages were very short. The sender typed: BRUCE? or HELLO? IS YOUR SCREEN FROZEN? There were lots of those, and they came primarily from three people. Their names were The Clown, Catwoman, and Darth Maul. Those three had sent the most messages, and they sent them at various times nearly every day.

She heard the chime again, but she didn't get a new box, which meant that it was from someone who had already sent a message. She went through each one, looking for who had sent her husband a message. Having found it, she read the name the message came from. It was from Darth Maul. He even had the famed Star Wars character's likeness on his Yahoo! messenger box.

The message read: "WHERE'VE YOU BEEN, SCARECROW? WE THOUGHT YOU WERE DEAD. LOL!"

Two tears raced down Michelle's cheeks. She rested her chin on her palm and contemplated whether she should respond. She had no idea who Darth Maul was, but he was calling Bruce Scarecrow.

Why? Does he have Bruce mixed up with someone else? Maybe this Darth Maul person is a woman, looking for my husband. I've heard about Internet affairs. With all the traveling he did, he could've met some chick in a city where he has some of his shops. Maybe that's the real reason we didn't have more sex. Maybe he was getting what he needed elsewhere. But why would a woman call herself by that name? To throw off a suspicious wife, that's why. I'll play along for a while and find out what the hell is going on.

A private chatroom invitation box opened. The title of the room was Pissed Writers United. Overwhelmed with curiosity, she entered the room, hoping someone in there could tell her something she didn't know about Bruce.

Chapter 60

The room was filled with other chatters, all talking at the same time, none of it making much sense. This was Michelle's first time in a chatroom, and she had no idea what to expect. On the right side of the private chat frame was a smaller box containing the names of the twelve chatters, all of them colorful. She continued reading the messages that went back and forth between the chatters, and they started making sense. All the messages were an expression of the chatter's anger with specific people in the publishing industry. The room was appropriately named Pissed Writers United. Everyone in the room had to be writers—just like Bruce, she thought. *These people must be Bruce's friends.* She decided to stick around and find out what the writers were so angry about. Just then, she heard the familiar chime of an instant message. It was coming from Catwoman.

HEY, BRUCE! WHERE YA BEEN? the message read.

Michelle didn't respond. She just sat there, waiting, hoping she would continue talking. Maybe Catwoman had the answers she sought. Maybe she was Bruce's lover when he was on the road, she thought. Maybe she was only one of fifty women Bruce was seeing. Maybe he got one of them pregnant or something. Michelle's mind rambled on and on, conjuring up all sorts of scenarios to explain why her beloved husband had blown his brains out. Anger began to mount when she thought of her own fidelity. She traveled from city to city too. And yes, there were a myriad of offers for sex in hotel rooms—several of them very tempting—but she had never accepted any invitations or room keys from her drunken colleagues, and returned to the peace and security of her room. *Why couldn't Bruce do the same? Men are such dogs! You can't trust any of them!*

Another private chat invitation filled Michelle's screen. She clicked OKAY and entered the private chat. But this time, there were only three people in the room. Darth Maul, Catwoman, and The Clown.

BRUCE! WHERE YA BEEN, BUDDY? Catwoman asked again.

Michelle didn't respond. She was waiting to see what they would do if she remained silent.

Meanwhile, Maul, Catwoman, and The Clown were sending private messages to each other.

DARTH MAUL: I THINK BRUCE'S WIFE IS ONLINE WITH HIS SCREEN NAME. DO WE LET HER KNOW WE KNOW, OR DO WE LEAVE THE ROOM?

CATWOMAN: WELL, I THINK WE SHOULD FIND OUT IF IT'S HER. IT'S NOT LIKE HE'S DOING SOMETHING WRONG. IF WE LEAVE, SHE'S GOING TO READ HIM THE RIOT ACT. SHE'LL BELIEVE HE'S HAVING AN AFFAIR OR SOMETHING.

THE CLOWN: IF IT'S MICHELLE, WHERE'S BRUCE? IS HE OKAY? HE TOLD US THAT SHE NEVER USES HIS COMPUTER, REMEMBER? WE BETTER FIND OUT WHAT'S GOING ON WITH HIM.

DARTH MAUL: I AGREE. WE DON'T WANT TO GET BRUCE INTO ANY TROUBLE WITH HIS WIFE SINCE HE HASN'T DONE ANYTHING WRONG. JUST FOLLOW MY LEAD IN THE ROOM.

HELLO, MICHELLE. Maul said in the private chat room.

A chill surged through Michelle's body. *They know who I am?*

Maul continued. WE'RE BRUCE'S WRITING PARTNERS. WE KNOW IT'S YOU, MICHELLE. YOU MIGHT AS WELL CONFESS. BUT IN CASE WE'RE WRONG, AND YOUR COMPUTER IS FROZEN, RESTART YOUR COMPUTER AND COME BACK TO THE ROOM. OR JUST GIVE US THE PASSWORD.

Michelle stared at her computer screen, trying to decide if she should tell them Bruce was dead. Finally, she typed: WHO ARE YOU GUYS?"

WE'RE BRUCE'S FRIENDS. Maul offered.

Relieved, Michelle responded, OH, OKAY. I DON'T KNOW HOW TO TELL YOU THIS, BUT BRUCE COMMITTED SUICIDE.

Chapter 61

Three days after Michelle moved back into her home, she still had not found any of Bruce's work. She had taken the disks to Computer World, but a clerk told her the disks were brand new. Nothing had ever been on them. That fact puzzled her, and she became obsessed with finding something he had written. She convinced herself that his manuscripts contained all the answers to the questions that nagged her daily. She felt a tremendous amount of guilt because she hadn't read any of his work while he was among the living, and that drove her to ask his online friends about his novels and screenplays. Since they were writing partners, they had to have something, she thought. If so, maybe they would send something to her.

Later that evening, when she got home from work, she entered Bruce's office and turned on his computer and signed on to his Yahoo! account. Bruce's buddy list appeared, and she saw her deceased husband's online friends, Darth Maul, Catwoman, and The Clown. A split second before she double clicked on Maul's screen name, which was a shortcut to opening an instant message box, all three of Bruce's friends sent her an instant message, saying, HELLO, MICHELLE. HOW ARE YOU FEELING? HOW ARE THINGS IN YOUR LIFE THESE DAYS? Bruce had made some great friends, she thought. They cared enough about their dead friend to check on his wife in his absence. She answered each of them and asked them if they could get a private room together to talk about Bruce. They all agreed and entered a private chat. She looked at the names in the corner and realized that she was Scarecrow, Bruce's online persona. She said, "Scarecrow. I like the sound of it. I wonder what it meant to Bruce." Then she began to type.

SCARECROW: HI GUYS. I WAS WONDERING IF ANY OF YOU HAVE ANY OF MY HUSBAND'S MANUSCRIPTS. I CAN'T SEEM TO FIND THEM ANYWHERE.

DARTH MAUL: HE KEEPS THEM ON CD IN A CASE ON HIS DESK.

SCARECROW: I CHECKED THOSE, AND THERE'S NOTHING ON THE DISKS.

CATWOMAN: THAT'S STRANGE. WHY WOULD HE ERASE THEM?

SCARECROW: THEY HAVEN'T BEEN ERASED. THE DISKS ARE BRAND NEW. I THOUGHT YOU GUYS COULD SEND ME SOMETHING HE HAD WRITTEN. I WAS THINKING HE MAY HAVE TOLD YOU GUYS SOME-THING THAT HE COULDN'T TELL ME. ANY GUESSES ANYBODY?

For about thirty seconds, no one said anything.

SCARECROW: NO GUESSES???

No one responded.

SCARECROW: COULD ONE OF YOU PLEASE TELL ME WHAT HE TOLD YOU, OR WHAT HE WAS WORKING ON? AT LEAST TELL ME WHAT YOU WERE WORKING ON TOGETHER.

DARTH MAUL: SURE YOU WANNA KNOW, MICHELLE?

SCARECROW: VERY SURE.

DARTH MAUL: SHALL WE TELL HER, GIRLS?

THE CLOWN: WHY NOT? SHE DESERVES TO KNOW. SHE MAY WANT TO HELP US GET THOSE RESPONSIBLE FOR HIS DEATH.

When Michelle read that last message, her heart pounded. This was the first time there was ever any mention that Bruce's death could have been something other than suicide. In a way, what she'd read made her feel a whole lot better. At least he hadn't left her without a message. At least she wasn't at fault. Her fingers moved quickly as she clicked the keys on the keyboard.

SCARECROW: SOMEONE IS RESPONSIBLE FOR BRUCE'S DEATH? WHO? WHY?

The trio ignored her questions and continued talking to each other as if Michelle wasn't in the room with them.

DARTH MAUL: CATWOMAN? ARE YOU OKAY WITH THIS? IT HAS TO BE UNANIMOUS.

CATWOMAN: I DON'T SEE WHY NOT. SHE MIGHT AS WELL KNOW.

DARTH MAUL: JUST SO I'M CLEAR. LET'S TAKE A VOTE. I VOTE YES.

CATWOMAN: YES.

THE CLOWN: YES.

SCARECROW: IF BRUCE WERE ALIVE, HE'D VOTE, SO I SAY YES TOO.

DARTH MAUL: MICHELLE, WE'RE GOING TO CALL YOU IN ABOUT TEN MINUTES. WILL YOU BE AVAILABLE?

SCARECROW: YES. WHAT ARE YOUR REAL NAMES?

DARTH MAUL: IF WE EVER TELL YOU OUR NAMES, IT'LL BE OVER THE LANDLINE.

And with that, each of them exited the private room one by one. Exactly ten minutes later, Michelle's phone rang. She looked at the ID box. Whoever Bruce's friends were, they had their number blocked.

"Hello," Michelle said.

"Hi, Michelle," a man said. "For now, just use our screen names. What we have to tell you could send all of us to jail for a very long time. And if you're not interested in what we're going to do, you won't know who we are to tell the police. But you should know up front that it was Bruce's idea. We'll have to get to know you, Michelle, before we can trust you with who we really are. And that's going to take some time, so be patient. That's why the phone number is blocked on your caller ID. When we know we can trust you, we'll tell you everything. Agreed?"

"Agreed," Michelle said.

"I'll tell you this much for now, and don't say anything to anyone—nobody!"

"Okay, I won't."

"We were turning one of Bruce's novels into a screenplay. It's a thriller like nothing else out there. It's called *PAY DAY*."

Part Three

Scarecrow

Chapter 62

We had them! The tap I put on Liz Clayton's cell phone worked perfectly. Edward Doherty used Clayton's phone to make hotel reservations. The people we were looking for had seriously screwed up. Edward Doherty was the dead Memphis police officer who was shot down in the middle of the street. That cold-blooded murder made the national news. Now, local, state, and national police officers were looking for suspects driving the make, model, and vehicle license plate Doherty called into dispatch. While that might sound like a good thing on the surface, this new development was going to cause more problems than it solved. Yes, we'd have more men on the job, but when you've got this much testosterone on one case, there's always problems because everybody wants to be in charge.

For example, a few years back, for weeks, two African American males were shooting pedestrians with deadly accuracy on the Beltway from the trunk of their vehicle. Dealing with the media and the cops was a nightmare. Every precinct commander thought he should be running the show. Nobody seemed to have confidence in the chief in charge of the case. As the story mushroomed, civilians who knew nothing about the suspects were giving the cops false reports and then repeating this to national news correspondents. This ridiculous scenario would have been hilarious if the events taking place were in a movie spoof. But this was happening for real, and a lot of innocent people had been shot in the head at random.

All the cops in Tennessee were looking to blow away the suspects on sight. This was personal, and they had to get even immediately because they couldn't have criminals thinking they could kill a cop and live. If the cops didn't put down the fool that killed one of their brothers of the shield, criminals would think it was open season on cops. Being a law enforcement officer, I understood that kind of thinking. Once a perp killed a cop, it was like killing the law. And if the law was dead, no real deterrent would exist, which put all of society at risk because anarchy would reign—at least until the law found and killed the perp.

The locals didn't know they were looking for our suspects, and I wasn't about to tell them, which is one of the main reasons cops and Feds don't get along. If we told the cops our suspects had in all likelihood killed one of their brothers, there would be an incredible show of force at the hotel, and that was the last thing we wanted, given the fiasco in Memphis. Plus, our friend, Memphis Police Chief Frost hung Kelly and me out to dry. He told everyone he could that I had gotten police officers killed a few summers ago due to negligence. I knew we were going to have a hard time dealing with the locals because of it. Why bother? I thought it best to follow the leads Kelly and I had acquired and apprehend the murderous trio alone.

Director Malone offered to come along and use the weight of her office to get maximum cooperation, but I said no. Reluctantly, she let us go, reminding me that I had already agreed to let Kelly run the show. We both knew that was a charade,

but we had to do it to cover everybody's ass on this one. If it
got out that one of the robbers in Vegas was my cousin, all
hell would break loose, and all three of us would most certainly lose our jobs. The system loves to screw women because
a lot of the men don't think we belong in law enforcement
in the first place. So one could imagine what they thought of
me once Chief Frost let it be known that I supposedly screwed
up and had gotten good law enforcement officers killed.
Anyway, I didn't trust the locals to bring the suspects in alive,
especially since one of their own had been shot down like a
rabid dog and left in the street. We needed the suspects to
enter the hotel like they had done so many times in the past.
I didn't want them to walk into what they probably saw in
Memphis and flee again. Suddenly, Chief Frost's words echoed
in my mind: *You may not like my methods, but I can guarantee
your suspects won't kill anyone in my city tonight. Tell that to Edward Doherty's widow, Chief of Police Frost!* I thought.

Instead of coordinating with the cops, we headed over to
the Embassy Cool Springs location at 820 Crescent Center
Drive in Franklin, Tennessee. We thought about posing as
desk clerks, but our pictures had been splashed all over the
news when the story broke. There was a chance the killers
didn't see us, and perhaps they wouldn't even recognize us if
they had, but why take the chance, we concluded.

We entered the premises, hoping our suspects hadn't
checked in. If they had, they could be anywhere in the hotel.
Or they could be at one of their victims' houses, which
meant that if they came back to the hotel, another couple
might be dead by the time they returned. We flashed our
credentials and asked the desk clerk if our suspects had
checked in. She hit a few keys on her computer terminal and
said, "No. Not yet."

Kelly and I looked at each other and smiled. We had
them! I was sure of it.

"When they arrive," I said to the clerk, "put them in a

room nearest to the elevators so we can see them from the atrium."

I handed the desk clerks photos of our suspects and told them they were dangerous, warning them not to be heroes. Before we left, I gave both clerks our FBI business cards, which had our cell numbers on them. I didn't want there to be any chance of missing them because of a bathroom break or reading a magazine while we waited.

Chapter 63

McAlister Sage and Carson Fletcher were at the Cool Springs Embassy too. While listening to their police radio, they had heard a Memphis 911 operator say a police officer had been found in the street. When she gave the location, the two operatives realized it was only a couple miles from the South Shady Grove location, and paid strict attention to what was being said. They learned that Officer Doherty had been shot a minimum of nine times at point blank range. By the time they got him to the emergency room, he was dead. The cops' initial thoughts were that it was aggravated robbery, since he had pulled over a car. But McAlister and Carson decided to monitor the Embassy Suites central reservations database on a hunch.

When they saw that someone with the same name had made reservations at the Cool Springs location, they thought it was more than a coincidence since Doherty's wallet was missing. They went to the police station, posing as FBI agents again, and learned Doherty's widow's name, where the couple lived, and where they banked. Using the information they had acquired, they went into the bank, still posing as FBI agents, and told the manager their suspicions that someone was using the dead officer's credit cards. Eager to help, the manager gave them full discretionary access to Doherty's records and anything else they needed. It was a long shot, but they played it and it paid off.

Now they were sitting in a rented car, waiting on their un-witting prey to enter the trap, having drawn the same conclusions as their FBI counterparts. Then, as if by magic, they saw Phoenix Perry and Kelly McPherson enter the hotel.

"Fuck!" McAlister shouted when he recognized them.

He knew it would be difficult to avoid killing the agents now because the people he was looking for were definitely going to die shortly after they checked into the hotel.

But when Fletcher saw them, he could hardly contain himself. A malevolent grin crept across his thick lips. He was positively beaming because he knew they were going to show up sooner or later. He was finally going to kill Phoenix Perry. She had it coming. It was just a matter of time now. As soon as their targets arrived, the killing would begin. He wanted this so incredibly bad he could almost taste it. He had carefully constructed it all, and now the time was approaching, just as he knew it would. Phoenix Perry had to answer for Coco Nimburu's death. Fletcher loved Coco as he had loved no other woman.

Nevertheless, the whole thing was twisted because the Asian beauty, who Fletcher thought was his woman, had treated him like foul-smelling offal. She had opened her exquisite legs and offered her tantalizing nectar to lots of men who wanted nothing more than to enter her hot folds of flesh; men who only wanted to pump her hard and fast like a rabbit in heat and then expel their life-creating seeds into her tight, inviting sheath.

She even told the fool to his face that she didn't love him. Unrequited love notwithstanding, Fletcher somehow mangled her truth in his twisted mind and made himself believe that all Coco needed was to sow her wild oats for a while. Then she would come to her senses and return to him, the only man on the planet who truly loved her unconditionally. What Fletcher didn't know was that lots of men—and women, for that matter—felt the same way he did about the dangerously seductive coquette.

In addition to being a private contractor, Nimburu had been an operative too, using her extraordinary martial arts and linguistic skills for the United States government. Fletcher first met her at "The Farm," another name for the training facility at Camp Peary, near Williamsburg, Virginia, where several government and military agencies trained. They were often paired together on training exercises, and as their relationship as recruits developed, nature took its course. After graduation, Fletcher was assigned to Berlin, where he found comfort in the arms of a young fraulein. Coco Nimburu was assigned to Singapore, her country of origin, where she found comfort in the arms of McAlister Sage, who was there to supposedly "observe" her first mission for the Agency—at least that's what she was told.

The truth, however, was a bit more diabolical. McAlister was supposed to seduce Nimburu and ensure that whatever ties she had to Fletcher were severed—permanently. Fletcher and Nimburu would travel the world, and the Agency wanted them unencumbered by the entanglements and drama personal relationships often offered. Nevertheless, McAlister soon found out there were no ties to Fletcher as Nimburu sweetly ravaged him two hours after they met. When Fletcher found out about it, he was devastated. That was the real reason he was going to kill McAlister too.

Chapter 64

I had gotten a call from Lady Mob Boss, Naima Marinelli, as we waited patiently in the atrium of the hotel for the rats to enter our trap. Naima told me she couldn't track down who at Homeland Security was assigned to a case that involved Liz Clayton, which meant the orders came from the top—perhaps the White House. I found it strange that our killers, one of whom was a schoolteacher, were being investigated by Homeland Security and that it was so secret that Naima didn't have clearance to view the files. She was stonewalled by her superiors when she made inquiries. That meant that someone or a group of people knew a whole lot more than we had discovered about our killers. I wondered if Clayton was on the terrorist watch list. Was she somehow working with an Islamic cell? Whatever the reason, someone was running serious interference for her.

Where were Liz Clayton and the other two suspects? I wondered. It was approaching midnight, and they hadn't shown up at the hotel. Kelly and I gave each other that familiar look; the kind of look that basically said, "They know we're onto them." Given what Naima told me, I wondered if Clayton was of such importance that someone was feeding her information, making it possible to elude us again.

"How much longer do you want to wait?" Kelly said and yawned a long, relaxing yawn, stretching at the same time like a feline.

"Just a little bit longer," I said, unwilling to give up yet. "They could still show up. And if they do, I don't want to miss them."

Kelly kind of laughed and said, "There's no chance of them coming through here tonight and you know it. I say we get on the first thing smokin' back to DC and get some sleep." She yawned again, covering her mouth.

"Let's give them one more hour, Kelly. Just to be sure, okay?"

Kelly yawned again and gave me a sarcastic, "Sure, okay. Whatever."

"Like you got something better to do," I said and rolled my eyes.

"I do. I could be getting laid. So could you."

I laughed. "That doesn't sound like a bad idea now that you mention it. I've been wearing Keyth out regularly. I know he needs some rest to let the fluid build back up again." We laughed. "So . . . what's going to happen with you and Sterling? I mean he did pretty much tell you the relationship isn't going anywhere. Are you okay with that?"

"Not really, Phoenix. But what can I do?"

"Are you in love with him, or what?"

Kelly remained quiet for a long minute, carefully considering her answer before saying, "I don't know, Phoenix. I just don't know. We've been foolin' around for a few years now, but does that mean we should take the next step?"

Her response really got under my skin. Women can be incredibly gullible sheep for a ruthless wolf. It was so obvious Sterling was using my best friend that a blind man could see it. And while Kelly was totally oblivious to it, I knew he would toss her away as soon as he'd had enough. If it weren't for the distance between them, if he could see her every day, have sex with her as much as he wanted, the relationship would have been over by now. I'm sure of it. But the distance between them, him living in Muir Woods (a suburb of San Francisco), and Kelly living on the East Coast, gave them something to look forward to, I guess.

With a bit of rancor, I said, "So, you're willing to accept what he's dishing out then? You're willing to suck him off whenever he wants and everything, huh? Why would he, or any other man, for that matter, make a commitment to a woman if he's getting seriously blown whenever the mood hits him?"

"Phoenix, it's a little more complicated than that. I mean we've been—"

"Fucking," I said, interrupting the bullshit that was about to come out of her mouth. "That's all you've been doing. Now . . . as your friend . . . I'm asking you, is that all you're interested in? If so, keep doing it. But . . . I get the feeling you feel a bit used by him. Am I right or what?"

Kelly remained quiet for a long time again, looking straight ahead, thinking about the penetrating question I posed. At least she was thinking now. That was a good thing.

"So, you're saying I should break it off because I want more from him than an occasional romp? Is that it?"

I looked into her eyes before speaking the troubling words that occupied my disturbed heart. "Do you want more than an occasional romp, Kelly? If you do, you should let him know now and either move forward with him or cut him loose. That is, if you can. Can you, Kelly? Can you cut him loose? The Kelly I know could drop any man without thinking twice about it and have another man before nightfall. Where's she? Is she still alive? What happened to her?"

The blood drained from her face when the questions reg-

istered, awakening her from the emotional coma she was in.
She looked as if this was the first time she had thought about
whether she could walk away from the relationship. I stared
at her, patiently waiting for her to come to the conclusion on
her own. I liked Sterling, but from what Kelly had told me
during numerous conversations, it sounded like Sterling was
in it for Sterling. I guess if I'm being fair, Kelly used to do the
same thing to guys. Love 'em and leave 'em. The difference,
fair or unfair, I guess, was that Kelly was my best friend; Sterling was a distant acquaintance in comparison.

Angrily, Kelly said, "You don't know what it's like to find a
man who really knows how to please a woman. You've only
had the one man; the man you married, and—"

"Maybe there's something to chastity, huh? Maybe chastity
keeps a person from forming habits that blind them to bad
relationships, huh? I guess my father knew what he was talking about after all. I would sure hate to be in your position,
knowing a man isn't good for me, but being totally powerless
to leave him."

Kelly was about to say something, but I kept on talking.
"Passion that consumes you can't be good for you, my friend.
That's almost like being a crack addict, I'll bet."

"Listen, Phoenix," Kelly said, almost shouting. "Not everyone can be a goody two-shoes like you."

Her words wounded me. They felt like someone close to
me, someone I trusted implicitly, walked up to me, and then
slid a sword into my ribcage, smiling the entire time. Viru-
lently I said, "You know, Kelly, I expect that from other women,
but not you. Lots of women have chided me for living by a
higher standard. Instead of applauding me for making good
decisions, I'm belittled. You wanna know what's really sad,
Kelly? Women of my hue, black women, would be more ac-
cepting of me if I was more of a whore, what they call a
hoochie mama."

"C'mon, Phoenix, you're being melodramatic. Not all black women feel that way."

"Maybe not all of them, but too many. I'm not going to apologize for going to college and choosing a good black man instead of one of them fools running around pretending to be good black men. One segment of them consciously choose men with baby mama drama; men who have babies with four or five different women. Another segment loves the thug; men who have a history . . . a history, Kelly, of breaking the law, committing violent crimes. That's what they want. And then these simple-minded women are surprised when the criminal goes upside her head."

"Yeah, I see a lot of that, but I never said anything about it."

"Why, Kelly? Why did you never say anything about it?"

She offered an insincere, "No reason."

"Please, Kelly. You're the liaison agent with DC Metro. You see this every damn day, and the only reason you never said anything about it is because I'm black. If I were white, I'm sure you would have said something about this insanity a long time ago." Kelly shamefully looked away. "Now here you are using your biting sarcasm as a weapon much like they do. I'm not going to apologize because I wasn't defeminized."

Kelly found me with her eyes again. "Defeminized, Phoenix? Don't you think you're exaggerating a teeny weenie bit?"

"No. The defeminization of women has been going on for decades. Women have been and are being socialized to be more like males and less like females. We've been brainwashed to think that being a whore is en vogue."

"See, that's what I mean, Phoenix. When you say shit like that, you act like a woman who should be living in the nineteenth century."

"Imagine that. A black woman with morals. Well . . . stop . . . the fucking presses."

"Women can have it all now, just like men."

"Can we, Kelly? Can we really? That's the kinda thinking that's making Maury Povich rich. Women think they can have it all, and yet they don't know whose baby they're carrying, so they go on Maury's show to find out? Now what kinda shit is that?"

"See, Phoenix, that's why women don't like you. Besides, most pregnant women know who fathered their children. You make people feel bad for having a little fun. Jesus! What's wrong with a woman getting her swerve on every now and then? Men started it. They've been doing it for thousands of years. It's our turn."

"That's what I mean, Kelly. You see being like a man as a good thing. I see it as a concerted effort to destroy all things feminine; the exchanging of virtue for that which will one day bring about the destruction of America, much like it destroyed the Roman Empire. You ever wonder why popping out babies wasn't tolerated fifty, even forty years ago? Ever wonder why it's tolerated now?"

"Well, at least Sterling hasn't popped out any babies that he doesn't take care of."

"That's something, I guess. He doesn't go upside your head either. Might as well add that to his stellar resume too."

Again Kelly remained quiet, seemingly contemplating my blunt words. "I guess I should let him go, huh, Phoenix?"

Frustrated, I exhaled hard. "You guess?"

"I guess," Kelly said almost inaudibly, as if letting Sterling go was the smart thing to do, but not the thing she wanted or could do.

Even more frustrated, loudly, I repeated, "You guess? Damn, Kelly! Is it that good?"

Without changing her expression, shaking her head as if complete resignation consumed her, she said in a matter-of-fact, but very dry voice, "Yes, Phoenix. It is."

I laughed hard and doubled over.

"What? What's funny, Phoenix?" Kelly said, laughing with me.

Still laughing, I looked at my watch, shook my head, and said, "Let's get on the first thing smokin' then. I think we both need to get tightened up. We'll pick up their trail when they kill again."

Chapter 65

Carson Fletcher was positively seething when he saw Phoenix and Kelly come out of the hotel. He looked at McAlister, who responded with a slight smile, which upset him even more. This was Carson's chance to sanction all of them at the same time. His plan, while not completely predictable, had worked marvelously so far. He had anticipated their every move. After all, he was the one who started the group chat, Pissed Writers United. Carson had even recruited most of the writers in the room, including Bruce Michaels. He had picked Bruce Michaels specifically because he was related, albeit by marriage, to Phoenix. It was a simple task to recruit angry authors because most of them belonged to Yahoo! online writing groups. Many of the authors had never met each other, and had no idea what the others looked like. To develop online relationships, all he had to do was join one or two online writing groups and send a few angry instant messages to an author who had expressed any kind of anger about being ripped off by a supposed editor or agent.

Led by Carson, Pissed Writers United toyed with ways to get back at the people who had done them wrong. Most of the authors and screenwriters thought it was fun to vent about the industry a little, but some were dangerous. A few were real psychopaths. They were quite serious about tracking down certain people and killing them. Some people left the group when they realized how crazy some of the authors were. Carson, who belonged in an asylum himself, relished the idea, pushed the right buttons at the right time, which he believed would one day lead his unbalanced band of lunatics to actually carry out real murders. He had started it all for one reason only—to kill Phoenix Perry with the blessing of the Agency. That way, none of it came back to him. He needed the blessing of the Agency because of Phoenix's close ties to former President Davidson, who still wielded power, even after leaving the Oval Office.

After gaining the confidence of authors who were hostile, desperate, extremely gullible, with a stipend of lunacy, he formed a Pissed Writers United inner circle, where writers used nom de plumes to hide who they were so they could share damaging information, using the names of real agents, editors, publishers, screenwriters, producers—charlatans pretending to be in the publishing and motion picture industries, who had either spurned them or screwed them over without fear of reprisals.

Most people outside the publishing industry have no idea what really goes on inside its hallowed halls. They have no idea that it is just as cutthroat as the music industry, if not more. Most people outside the industry think authors write books and they magically hit the shelves two months later, which is far from the truth. Most people think authors are rich, when only four, possibly five percent have lucrative careers and no longer need a day job. Most people believe that once an author has a book out, he or she will soon be Oprah Winfrey's Book of the Month and somehow become an overnight sensation. Most people don't know it usually takes years, dozens of books that failed, to finally hit the jackpot like Dan Brown did with *The Da Vinci Code*. That's why the death penalty for theft of their prized manuscripts and screenplays was the only course of action—in their minds anyway.

He had almost given up because none of his recruits were crazy enough to actually kill someone. He kept telling himself to be patient; it would all come together sooner or later. However, patience was not one of his strengths, especially not now; not when he was so close to having what he had wanted, what he had planned for—not after coming to the edge of killing Phoenix. Not after actually seeing her, knowing she was within striking distance. Not after he had waited four years for this moment and now he had to back off? He wasn't about to back off. The time was ripe, and Phoenix was about to die. He was going to shoot her right in that lovely face of hers—Kelly too. He pulled on the door handle to exit the vehicle, but when he heard the hammer on McAlister's gun cock, he hesitated.

Eerily calm, McAlister said, "If your foot touches the pavement, the sensation traveling up your leg will never register in your infantile brain." He paused for a moment. "Now . . . close the door. We're not going to kill our own soldiers."

"I was just going to the bathroom, Mac. Damn!"

"When they pull off, you can go to the bathroom—not before."

Fletcher thought for a long moment before pulling his hovering foot back into the car and slamming the door. He forced himself to smile when he looked at McAlister, who was staring at him menacingly, like he would love the opportunity to put a large, gaping hole in his head. "You know, Mac, these two can be sanctioned if they get in the way. We've got orders to kill them. You know that, don't you?"

McAlister ignored the question and asked one of his own. "Why are you in such a hurry to kill them?"

"In a hurry? Listen, my friend, I'll say it again. We've been ordered to kill them both if they get too close. You read your orders, Mac! This is precisely why Neil wanted me with you. You fucked up the Scarecrow sanction and you know it. You killed the first target, but for whatever reason, you let the second target live. I don't get it, Mac. You know better than that. If you hadn't fucked up, Phoenix Perry and Kelly McPherson wouldn't even be on the fucking list. Yet you ask me why I'm in such a hurry to kill them? This is your mess, not mine! I suggest you follow the orders you have in hand or I'll—"

Quietly, coolly, McAlister said, "Or you'll what, Carson? You'll what?"

Silence filled the vehicle.

"Or you'll kill me, Carson? Is that it? You'll kill me, too?"

"Look, man, I'm not trying to step on any toes, okay? Let's complete our fucking assignment and get the hell outta here, okay, Mac? Damn, man. Shit!"

"Last warning, Carson!" McAlister said, shouting. "This is the last fucking warning! The next time you even think about killing either one of them, I'll filet you and leave your carcass in the street for homeless dogs. You got that shit?"

Carson laughed under his breath as the night that McAlister and the young Naval lieutenant slept in each other's arms at the Marriott after their marathon-like romp flooded his wicked mind. He'd had them both in his sights, his weapon cocked and ready to fire, but it was too easy; way too easy for a slick operator like him. Besides, when he killed the great McAlister Sage, Carson wanted to see his eyes so he would know what McAlister was thinking as the life-giving blood oozed out of his bullet-riddled body.

Full of himself, arrogantly, Fletcher said, "Sure, Mac, sure. You have no problem popping me, but Phoenix Perry, you won't pop. I wonder why that is. Did you fuck her while you both were at Homeland Security, or what? You got up in that? Is that what it's about? I don't blame you or anything. I mean look at her. She's fucking beautiful. I would fuck her too, but I would pop her right after. The shit wouldn't bother me either. But you can't do that anymore, can you, Mac? You can't fuck 'em and pop anymore, can you? That's why I'm here . . . to do what you can no longer do. Don't worry, when the time comes, I'll do 'em both. But . . . if I were you, I'd seriously consider retirement. The game has passed you by."

"I won't warn you again," McAlister said and started the car.

Snapshot Sequence 3

McAlister Sage: The Scarecrow Sanction

Chapter 66

Hasty Hills
12915 Secretariat Road
Toledo, Ohio 43615
May 11, 2002

McAlister Sage had gotten orders to sanction Bruce Michaels because he had stumbled onto Operation Scarecrow. Bruce didn't know it, but he had been writing a fictional book about an actual CIA plot. The Patriot Act had given the Office of Homeland Security carte blanche as far as surveillance was concerned, and they were looking into everything, particularly authors, published and unpublished, who might be able to think of a plot that might topple the United States government. Bruce Michaels had unwittingly done this with a novel titled *Scarecrow*. Homeland Security agents meticulously scoured the country, listening to personal phone calls flagged by the Agency's sophisticated computer system.

To be flagged, specific words had to be mentioned singularly or in combination. Some of the words were "President,"

"Islam," "9/11," "The Capitol," "White House," "planes," "bombs," "nuclear device," "nerve gas," "anthrax," explosives of any kind, et cetera. Bruce Michaels was targeted because he had been in an online chat room that was discussing ways to blow up Monuments in Washington, DC. Although Bruce was only seeking ideas for a novel, Homeland Security tapped the phones of everyone in the chat room and monitored them closely to assess the possibility of a real threat. Agents heard Bruce discussing fictional plots with several people and dismissed him as an American author trying to come up with a plausible novel and submit it to a publishing house. The plot was too ridiculous to take seriously as far as they were concerned. However, to cover themselves, Homeland Security sent reports about Bruce and his book to the FBI, the CIA, the National Security Agency, and the White House.

When the report reached Neil Yarborough, he saw Bruce's novel as a serious threat. He had information that the agents who submitted the report didn't have, as it was far above their pay grade. He immediately dispatched McAlister to Toledo, Ohio to steal the book and silence Bruce and Michelle Michaels forever. First he was supposed to kill Michelle and then Bruce. It was supposed to look like the happy couple had a fight that ended in a murder/suicide. Yarborough expected the papers to turn their murders into a national tragedy; another loving couple dead due to domestic violence. Everyone would get coverage out of it and then, like the rest of the human interest stories, it would go away.

McAlister had no problem killing Bruce, but he refused to kill Michelle. Bruce and Bruce alone was the real threat to national security, not his lovely wife. He didn't see much sense in killing a woman just to cover his murderous tracks. He was a government-sponsored killer, but he didn't believe in killing for the sake of killing. There had to be an important reason to kill someone—especially a woman.

He had watched the couple closely and listened to all their phone calls. He knew when it would be safe enough to enter their premises. After watching the couple leave their home, he surreptitiously entered their house using an electronic lock pick and planted state of the art listening devices and cameras to watch the couple. Once he was sure that Michelle didn't have to die, he was ready to sanction his target. Now all he needed was patience. McAlister learned early in his career to never rush a job.

When he was in his early twenties, on his third "mission," he grew restless waiting for his target to return. He had been waiting for two hours in the target's home because he didn't know the man had decided to have a one-night stand at an out of the way hotel with a woman he'd met at a bar. Using the target's own global positioning system, he found the guy and went to the hotel and waited for him to come out. The man realized he was being followed and made a run for it. Fortunately for McAlister, his target lost control of his Cadillac and wrapped it around a tree. The target had died instantly. It could have gone the other way too, though. The target could have gotten away or somehow gotten others to help him, maybe even the police, which meant McAlister would have had to kill more than the one person he was sent to kill. That's when he realized that patience was the key to being a government-sponsored hit man.

He called Bruce's office and watched him pick up the phone through his monitor. Posing as a new chimneysweep company in the area, he offered to sweep two of their three chimneys free of charge if they hired him to sweep the third for an affordable price. He could tell by Bruce's reaction that he thought he'd gotten a great deal. After setting up the appointment, he watched Bruce hang up the phone. McAlister continued watching him, wanting to see if he'd write down the appointment. He didn't. If Bruce had, McAlister would have had to make sure he retrieved that bit of evidence. He watched Bruce slide his keyboard back out and continue writing his latest novel.

Now, sitting in a van just a few blocks from where Michelle and Bruce lived, he watched them from a remote location and listened to their phone conversations. When he heard Michelle tell her husband she was leaving, he knew from his surveillance that she was going to the doctor for a pregnancy test. He also knew the time had come to end Bruce's life. McAlister watched Michelle leave in her Escalade. (What he didn't know was that Michelle had changed her appointment when her doctor's office called Excalibur Foods and offered her an earlier appointment that very morning.) He hit a few buttons on his sophisticated laptop, tapping into the Onstar system. In seconds, a global positioning map came up. Michelle was on Central Avenue, heading toward Sylvania, where her doctor's office was. When he was sure she was long gone, he drove down the alley behind their house and parked. He opened the gate and walked around to the front of the house, up to the front door, and rang the door bell. The two men exchanged pleasantries when Bruce saw the name of his chimneysweep company stenciled on his overalls.

As Bruce showed him where the chimneys were, McAlister said, "Wow. This is a really nice home, Mr. Michaels. May I ask what you do for a living?"

"I own a string of beauty salons and barber shops."

"Must be a long string, man. That's all I can say."

Bruce looked at him, smiled, and said, "Do you like your job?"

"It's okay, I guess. Cleaning chimneys can get old, ya know? I only do the job so I can write without my wife nagging me all the damn time."

Excited, Bruce said, "You're a writer?"

"Yeah, man."

"I write too. You got an agent?"

"Yeah. She just got me a two-book deal with Kensington under the Dafina line. I've been writing for ten years, man, and I'm finally getting somewhere. What about you? You got an agent?"

"Not yet," Bruce said in a dejected tone. "I got scammed by a so-called agent and editor, though."

"Are you serious?"

"Do you hear me laughing? I know several people who've been scammed too."

"Well, just hang in there and you'll get a break too."

"Man, I'm at the point of giving up on publication. I'm seriously considering self-publishing. My wife doesn't want me to, but hey, I've got all these books just sitting in the drawer, and I can't get one reputable person to take a look at them."

"I know what you mean. I've been there too. My wife wouldn't even read my work, man. She's happy as hell that I finally got a deal now, though."

"That sounds just like my wife, man. Michelle thinks I'm wasting my time. But I love writing, man. I love it! Hey . . . would it be asking too much to take a look at my work?"

"I'd love to, man."

"You would?"

"Yeah, man. I love reading. When my books take off, I'll be leaving this chimneysweep gig behind for good."

"If you like it, maybe you can hook me up with your agent. You know what they say. It's who you know."

"Sure, man. Brothas gotta stick together."

"I hear you." The two men gave each other the universal soul brother handshake. "Okay, come into my office. I've got a thriller called *Scarecrow*. I think you'll love it."

"Lead the way," McAlister said, smiling.

Jodeci's "Love You for Life" was playing softly when they entered the room.

"It's right in here, man," Bruce said, opening the door for

his new author friend and following him into his office.
Bruce sat at his desk, hit a few buttons, and pulled up *Scarecrow* for the man who had promised to mention his work to
his agent.

McAlister positioned himself behind Bruce, watching
him, waiting for him to relax, which was when he planned to
snap his neck.

Having found the document, Bruce leaned back and said,
"Here it is, man . . . my masterpiece."

Bruce heard a loud, crunching sound—the snapping of
his neck—just before he breathed his last breath.

As quickly as he could, McAlister went to the master bedroom and retrieved Bruce's shotgun. He knew where it was
because he had been in the house to plant the surveillance
devices and found it. He hurried back to the office. When
he looked at Bruce, he almost looked as if he was alive because his eyes seemed to be watching his every move. But he
was quite dead.

He reached into his pocket and pulled out a pair of earplugs, a clear shower cap, and surgical gloves. He wiped his
prints off the shotgun and positioned it under Bruce's chin.
Using Bruce's index finger, he pulled the trigger. Even with
the earplugs, the sound of the discharge was loud. Because
people probably heard the shot, he knew he had to get out
of there as soon as possible. He removed the earplugs and
pulled off the shower cap and put them back into his pocket.
Seconds later, he heard the front door open.

"Bruce!" He heard Michelle shout.

He looked at his watch, wondering why she was back so
soon. There was no way she could have gotten her pregnancy
test in less than thirty minutes. It would take thirty minutes
to get there and back, he knew, because he had timed it himself. Something had happened. What, he didn't know, but
he knew he had to hide. After all his careful planning, the
unexpected had happened. He had wanted to avoid killing

Michelle, but now he knew he had to kill her too. Quickly, he stepped into the closet across the room and kept the door cracked so he could see her if she entered the office. He heard Michelle knock on the door and call out to her husband. He pulled out his silenced weapon and eased back the chamber, regretting what he was about to do. He saw Michelle walk into the room. She took one look at her deceased husband and fainted.

McAlister released a sigh of relief and quickly exited the closet. He stepped over Michelle and walked out the back door. He checked to see if anyone had seen him. To the best of his knowledge, no one had. He made his way to the alley, taking his time, but moving at a steady pace. He got into his van, took another look around and drove off.

He stayed in town for a few days, watching the police, making sure they didn't rule Bruce's death a homicide. A few days later, he read Bruce's obituary in the *Toledo Blade* newspaper. His death had been ruled a suicide. Michelle was staying with her mother, which gave McAlister ample time to get back into the house to retrieve the surveillance devices and Bruce's compact disks.

Chapter 67

Literary agent Juanita Lawrence was found near her Nashville, Tennessee home. Unlike the rest of our victims who had been bludgeoned to death, Juanita had been stripped naked, tied to the back of a car, and dragged through the streets. By the time she was found, she was a heap of raw flesh. I cringed when I saw her autopsy photos. She reminded me of a creature from a bad horror film. She no longer looked human. This time we didn't bother going to the crime scene. We knew they were long gone.

They had completely outfoxed us, leaving us a clue they knew we'd bite on. They deliberately sent us to a hotel they knew we'd stake out and come up empty, giving them plenty of time to find and kill their next victim. The killers had obviously been paying attention to the media coverage and knew we had figured out their pattern of behavior. I called the Nashville office and requested that the assigned agents fax me a copy of all their findings, which I knew wouldn't be much. But as they say, every little bit helps.

It turns out that Ms. Lawrence was another so-called English professor, posing as a literary agent, ripping off would-be authors and screenwriters. Much like Mr. and Mrs. Nance, she, too, was in cahoots with a so-called editor, and selling good storylines to interested Hollywood producers, collecting hefty sums for movie options. The difference between her and the Nance's was that she was greedy enough to create an editorial service called the Best Editors Agency.

I went to the website to take a look around. I wanted to see how they sucked in so many writers. The site was professional-looking and impressive enough to make the neophyte hire the Best Editors Agency. I positioned my cursor over Ms. Lawrence's biography and clicked on the link provided. I kept shaking my head while reading her resume, which read like she was the reincarnate of Jesus Christ himself—able to walk on water, at least when it came to editing.

Her biography purported her as one who'd gone to a couple of the most prestigious schools in the nation, graduating Magna Cum Laude with a 4.0 GPA, and being a Phi Beta Kappa member. Young writers, like most of America, probably thought that if it's in print, particularly on the Internet, hey . . . it must be the gospel. With those "credentials," I wondered why she wasn't on staff at a legitimate publishing house.

I moved the cursor over to the link that read: WE HAVE HIGH STANDARDS, while inwardly saying, "Brazen." I clicked on the link that opened a new page that read: FIVE PROMISES WE KEEP. First, they promised to read the manuscript before making any corrections to get a feel for the author's style and voice. Second, they promised to edit the manuscript three times by three different editors. Third, they promised to find and correct all typographical errors and misspellings. Fourth, they promised to meticulously check punctuation, syntax, et cetera. And fifth, they promised to make content suggestions to ensure the authors' manuscript would be top notch and get the attention of the publishers they sought. The Best Editors Agency never guaranteed they could get an author published, but their motto was "We can get you published." I bet they thought a statement like that was not only their legal caveat, but it was their ethical duty as well.

The Best Editors sales pitch sounded good to me and thousands of other would-be authors, I'm sure, but nothing could've been further from the truth. According to the report an agent from the Nashville office sent me, Ms. Lawrence was the only employee of Best Editors. She had a post office box at a Nashville post office, where she collected manuscripts, screenplays, and hefty checks from the fool hardy and unlearned. I laughed a little when I remembered what Kelly had said at Michelle's house; something about letting the killers find and kill all these charlatans and then take them down when they finished what I'm sure they thought was justifiable vigilantism.

At the same time, though, I felt for the authors because they had no idea what they were getting into and how ruthless their supposed editors and agents were. The good news, however, was that we had learned from Bruce's computer that our suspects and several more of their intended victims would probably be at the Crystal Gateway Marriott in a few days, and this whole episode would come to an abrupt end. I would see to it. Truth be told, I was very tempted to allow the killers to finish what they started, but if I did that, I couldn't justify arresting them for crimes I wanted them to commit.

Chapter 68

Even though we knew about the conference at the Crystal Gateway Marriott, which would offer a lengthy list of potential victims, the killers had the upper hand again because we had no idea where they were or who their next victims were. After speaking with hotel management, we learned that more than three hundred people registered for the conference. The list we had only told us who could be next, but it didn't give us a schedule, and we certainly couldn't protect them all. I thought it would be a good idea to let the locals know what was going on.

Kelly brought the Arlington Police Department up to speed. She also asked the cooperative chief to position a few detectives at all the Embassy Suites in the Arlington area, just in case they didn't know we were on to them. We considered warning the victims, but if we did that, our killers—if they were planning to show up, and we fully expected them to—would simply disappear and kill again somewhere else if they so desired. We decided to let the conference go on as planned and to stake out the place with plain-clothes law enforcement officers, FBI, and locals.

In the meantime, I took advantage of the time I suddenly had and spent nearly all of it with my precious daughter, Savannah. She was twelve years old now, and for the life of me, I didn't know where all the years went. It seemed as if I just gave birth to her yesterday. Now she was a year from being a know-it-all teenager. Soon she would be into boys too. That scared me because kids experiment with sex and other grown-up things long before they're ready. After talking to Kelly about her jacked-up relationship with Sterling, I knew I had to do something before my daughter ended up just like her. For too long, I had expected my husband to do what my father had done for me.

My father had taught me about the birds and the bees because my mother died giving birth to me. I was reared by strong, law-abiding, good men, beginning with my dad, who as far as I knew, only made one mistake in his life. He had been linked to Coco Nimburu, but that's another story. The other man who helped rear me was my Kung Fu instructor, Master Ying Ming Lo, a disciplinarian, but also big on hugs and kisses when I did the right thing. Sue Ling, my master's wife, was the closet thing I had to a mother, but for some reason, we were never very close. I was closer to the men in my life for whatever reason, and honestly, I think it served me well. But at the same time, I had never really known what it was like to have a mother, so perhaps that's why I was lacking in that department. Nevertheless, I knew I needed to get more involved with Savannah, and I would. It wasn't my mother-in-law's responsibility. It was *mine*.

Kelly and Blaze, her daughter, had a different kind of mother/daughter relationship. Their "relationship" was another reminder to do something and quick because Blaze, who was sixteen, blonde, pretty, and well put together, was already acting like her salacious mother. She was having sex with boys while her mother was working. Kelly was doing the best she could to put food in her daughter's mouth and keep a roof over her head. While I was pregnant with Sydney and working over at the Office of Homeland Security, Kelly took me out to lunch one afternoon and told me she had come home and caught her daughter having sex with two teenaged boys at the same time. Blaze was only twelve years old when this happened. According to Kelly, one of the boys was taking her from behind, doggy style, while she performed fellatio on the other. I couldn't imagine Savannah doing something like that—ever, let alone being a preadolescent when it happened.

Savannah was so excited when I told her we were going to the Owings Mills Mall to shop all by ourselves with no little brother tagging along. This was going to be a girl's only afternoon outing, and we were going to have some fun shopping until we dropped. After four hours, we happened past a bookstore called Urban Knowledge. I'd never been in there before, so we stopped in and took a look around. I ended up buying a couple of books written by black men. One was titled *God in the Image of Woman*, by some dude named, DV Bernard. And the other was titled *The Badness*, by Nane Quartay. While Savannah looked around for the latest J.K. Rowling novel, I overheard a couple of the clerks talking to the owner of the store, who happened to be a publisher. They were asking him questions about shipments and other innocuous bookstore business.

I thought I could pick his brain a little about the publishing game. He was quite accommodating and unguarded, even though he had never seen me before. He told me that approximately a million and a half manuscripts were submitted for publication every year, and of that number, only sixty to seventy thousand were going to make it to publication by traditional publishers. He went on to say that most authors don't make a lot of money, and they know next to nothing about the business end of publishing.

I learned that most published books only sell about three

to five thousand copies, if they're lucky. If they're unlucky, well, they sell a couple hundred, if that, and those are sold to friends and relatives. I was blown away by this new information. I had no idea how many people were submitting manuscripts every year. I would wager that most new authors don't know this; otherwise, they wouldn't have been so easily scammed. With that many submissions and so few making it to publication, those numbers may have spawned the literary crook. There was money to be made—serious money. The crooks were like stockbrokers. They made money whether the book was published or not. As someone who works for the Bureau, I know there are no gatekeepers who watch the publishing industry, which gives the crooks in it free reign.

After purchasing our books, we took the escalator to the upper level and had a light lunch at Chick-fil-A and chatted. We had a marvelous time. For a few hours, I had forgotten about our puzzling case and enjoyed life with my daughter. When we finished eating, we went over to the AMC Theater to see *Sahara*. We both had a jones for some of the buttered popcorn we smelled wafting throughout the mall. Savannah had a thing for Matthew McConaughey. I did, too, but I would never admit it to my daughter. As far as she knew, her dad was the only man on the planet that I would ever find attractive.

Chapter 69

Owings Mills, Maryland is only about a hour or so from my home in Arlington, Virginia, but the traffic was horrendous that evening, and I had promised to watch the fight with Keyth. I enjoyed the day with Savannah, but I wanted to *really* enjoy my night with my husband. By the time we got home, it was 10:30. Fortunately for me, the main event wasn't going to start until about eleven. I enjoyed boxing and I was geeked up about the fight. Two of my favorite boxers were fighting on Pay Per View. Arturo Gatti, a real crowd pleaser, was fighting pretty boy Floyd Mayweather Jr., in Atlantic City.

I rushed into the house, a billion bags in tow. I put the bags in our bedroom and rushed into the family room, where I knew Keyth and Sydney would be. I was about to say something, but Keyth shushed me and pointed at Sydney. My son was in my husband's lap, sound asleep. I walked over to him and looked down at what used to be my little bundle of joy and smiled. I reached out for him and whispered, "I'll put him in his bed." Sydney wrapped his arms around me and held on, but he was still in a deep sleep.

"Okay," Keyth said without looking at me.

I looked at the screen and saw a couple of unknowns mixing it up. "Do you think I have time to take a bath before the main event?"

"Yeah, they probably won't even get into the ring before eleven."

"You'll come get me if it starts before then, right?"

"Uh-huh. How'd you two enjoy your trip to the mall?"

"We had a great time together. We talked about my job and stuff. She seems to be okay, but I plan to try and spend more time with her, ya know?"

"That would be wise."

"I think she'll be asleep before long. We've been gone all day. She was nodding out in the car."

Keyth looked at me, picking up on my hint for some hot sex. The way I was feeling, I wanted to do it all tonight. I wondered if other "respectable" women ever got like that—you know, horny as hell. I do. More and more these days.

Keyth smiled at me and whispered, "If you hurry up, we might be able to get a quickie off before the fight even starts. After Mayweather whips Arturo's ass, we can go upstairs. I bought some whipped cream."

"You did, huh?"

"Yep, sho' did."

"So, you were expecting to get busy tonight, huh?"

"Yep. So do whatcha gotta do and come on back."

Forty minutes later, I checked on the children to make sure they were sleeping while their mom and dad had a little fun playing grown-up games and doing grown-up things to each other. Having done my duty as a mother, I was about to do my duty, with pleasure, mind you, as a wife. *Sigh.*

Back in the family room now, I was wearing one of the many kimonos I'd made over the years. I made a few more after seeing the trailers of *Memoirs of a Geisha*. I had read Arthur Golden's book and couldn't wait until December when it would be in theaters. Anyway, the kimono I was wearing was made of black and gold silk. Two miniature dragons, which symbolized supernatural power and wisdom, were on the upper portion of the garment, a few inches above my supple breasts.

I anointed my body with Egyptian Musk. The aroma made me feel sexy and desirable. My hair was hugging my slender shoulders; my nails were painted black and gold and beautiful to behold. I walked up to the big screen TV, my back to Keyth. The fight was about to start. I could see Arturo Gatti and his trainer, Buddy McGirt, entering the ring, which meant if I wanted to see this fight, I had to put on my little show a little quicker than I had planned. I turned and looked at Keyth. He had kicked off his boxers, and his constant companion was full grown, reminding me of the Washington Monument, albeit a much darker shade. I opened the kimono, holding the silk garment in both hands, exposing my nakedness to him.

But when I heard Michael Buffer, the perennial announcer for big fights, introducing the fighters, I closed the kimono and rushed to my seat as if a strong wind from the North had blown me across the room and onto the couch next to my husband. As we watched the fight . . . well . . . massacre, I stroked my husband's monument, teasing him, but also warming up my pleasure palace. I shook my head as blow after stinging blow landed upside Gatti's head and face. He was really getting tattooed in there. I felt sorry for him because Floyd was too much that night. Finally, mercifully, Buddy McGirt stopped the fight. It was the right thing to do, and McGirt was also protecting Gatti so he could fight another night. Now that the fight was over, I eased down on Keyth's "Arlington Monument" and begin a slow, steady grind.

Chapter 70

We were on our way home from church the following day when my cell rang out "Stranger" by the 70s musical group LTD. I had downloaded that particular song because not only did I enjoy Jeffrey Osborne's smooth vocals, it was apropos in that it let me know when someone other than a family member or a close personal friend called me. In this case, it was a text message from an agent in the Billings, Montana office. The text message read: CALL JACK ROBINSON. HE'S AN AUTHOR AND A MATERIAL WITNESS TO YOUR CASE. LADY MOB BOSS SAYS HELLO. A smile emerged when I realized that my friend Naima from Homeland Security was still helping with the case. I immediately looked at my watch. It was 1:45 PM, making it 10:45 AM in Billings. I hit the appropriate buttons to reach Mr. Robinson, hoping he'd answer. He did.

"Mr. Robinson . . . Special Agent in Charge, Phoenix Perry . . . I understand you have some information for me."

My daughter said, "There she goes again. Working on the Sabbath."

I ignored her.

"Well, it's about time!" Robinson said excitedly.

"Really?"

"I've been trying to get one of you Feds to take me seriously for over four years now."

"Well, you've got my attention now. What do you have for me, Mr. Robinson?"

"I've got an extensive list of cheats, snakes, and flimflam men and women; so-called publishing industry people. I've even got a website listing their names and addresses, warning authors, screenwriters, and any other writer to stay away from these blood-sucking vipers."

I began to lose confidence in this "material witness" because he seemed too good to be true. And in my business, it wasn't often an agent ran into this kind of witness. As a matter of fact, law enforcement officers always get calls from "concerned" citizens on big cases, but most are a complete waste of time. I immediately began to believe this guy had an axe to grind or something, like he had received a thousand rejection letters for his "masterpiece."

"Okay, pal, you've had your fifteen minutes of fame," I said, somewhat testing him to see how he responded.

"Hey, you guys called me this time. I gave up on you FBI types two years ago. Goodbye!"

He hung up.

I looked at Keyth.

"What was that about?" he asked.

"I'm not sure. Could be something. Could be nothing. But I'm sure I don't have time to waste with some impatient crackpot who wasn't committed enough, and couldn't, for whatever reason, break into the publishing business."

"Sounds like you've got nothing but time to me. Your suspects are still on the loose, probably about to kill someone else, and you have no idea where they are or even who they are at this point, right?"

I remained quiet, contemplating the veracity of what Keyth had said. He was definitely on point. I guess I was a bit confused as to why Naima sent Robinson my way if he couldn't help my case.

"Call him back," Keyth commanded. "Question him. See if he's legit."

I hit the TALK button and my cell automatically redialed Mr. Robinson.

"Yeah," Robinson said with rancor.

"I apologize, sir. Please, tell me your story. I promise to give it all due consideration, okay?"

Dead silence dominated the space between us.

"Are you there, Mr. Robinson?"

"Yeah, I'm here," he said hesitantly.

More dead silence.

I knew I had to be patient with this guy. He was seriously pissed because he was attempting to be a good citizen and from his point of view, the FBI wasn't interested in what he had to say. I had to show him I was different. I had to hold on to the phone and wait him out. I've learned over the years that people want to tell you things, but they need to see if you're willing to listen. One way of knowing if you're going to listen to their story is being silent. But I wanted Mr. Robinson to get to the friggin' point. I probably wouldn't have been as patient if it hadn't been a Sunday. Holding a cell phone while my minutes diminished would have pissed me off after about twenty seconds of silence. After about a minute or so, he opened up to me.

"Agent Perry, do you have any idea, I mean any fuckin' idea how many authors try to get their work published every single year?"

"Yes."

Silence again, but only brief silence this time.

I had gotten the information from the owner of the Urban Knowledge bookstore, so I was a certified expert on the publishing business. *Right!* Sure, I was green, but this guy already had a low opinion of the Bureau's agents; I didn't want him to know I knew next to nothing about the ins and outs of publishing. From the American public's point of view, as an FBI agent, I was supposed to be omniscient. *Right!* That's why we didn't catch those Islamic fundamentalists taking flying lessons in Florida, who were brazen enough to tell their instructors they didn't need to know how to land the planes. That's how friggin' omniscient we agents are.

"How many?" Robinson asked.

"I'd say about a million and a half or more."

"And, Agent Perry, how many actually make it to publication?"

"About sixty to seventy thousand."

"Hmmm, so you've done your homework. That's good. Most of you FBI types don't know shit. Ya gotcha little badges and ya run around in circles like a dog chasing its tail."

I took a deep breath to keep from ripping this guy a new one. "Mr. Robinson, do you have anything for this FBI type who's giving you the floor?" As an afterthought, I decided to lighten up a bit by saying, "Speak now or forever hold your peace."

"Okay, Agent Perry, let me start by telling you that one of your victims, Cody Mills, was my agent."

That was a jaw-dropper. Calmly, I said, "Go on."

"I also had dealings with all of your victims so far, and I could probably tell you who's next, or at least tell you who's on the list."

"Explain how you've had dealings with all the victims, Mr. Robinson."

"I submitted to them after I learned that Cody Mills was a flimflam artist. I have been compiling a list of these crooks for years, doing my own investigation. I figured that if my agent, Cody Mills was involved, maybe there were others, and boy, was I right. I called the FBI I don't know how many times, and nobody seemed to be interested until people started dying. To be honest with you, if I wasn't restricted to a wheelchair, I may have joined the secret group in the Pissed Writers United chat room.

"If I had to guess, I'd say they're the ones running around killing these . . . these . . . well . . . I call 'em human debris. I'd gotten an email invitation from someone who had visited my website, so I joined the group. The first day I went into the chat room, the people in there were seriously talking about killing people. I said we should go to the police with this, and the next thing I knew, I no longer had access to the group. All I can say is that I'm glad I wasn't in the group long enough to trust them with what I knew."

Chapter 71

Mr. Robinson went on and on and on, naming names, dates, places, addresses, the whole kit and caboodle. He even told me about a murder in the Mojave Desert that had gone completely without notice. I later found out who the murder victims were. Their names were George and Angela Steels, two more would-be agents and editors, murdered by our suspects, we believed, judging by the way they were killed—vehicular homicide. George had been found in the living room, tied to a chair, beaten severely about the head and neck, while Angela was found on North China Lake Boulevard. She had been run over, backed over, and run over again. The autopsy photos were gruesome. Her face had been bashed in. According to the medical examiner's notes, the damage was done by the rear bumper as it backed over her.

I alerted all the police departments in the hometowns of the people we suspected of being literary phonies. I asked them to patrol their neighborhoods if they could, but not to question anybody. I wanted to arrest everyone involved, but it was going to be a very complicated procedure because every state had different laws for what constituted a felony. It was going to be a big mess, and the defendants would still walk away virtually scot-free. Michelle and Bruce deserved better. They deserved justice, and as far as I was concerned, justice for what these swindlers did demanded serious jail time. So I called the Postal Inspectors.

Most of the "commerce" was being done via US mail, which meant it was mail fraud, and postal attorneys are an aggressive bunch. When it comes to the US mail, when the Postal Inspectors come after you, they're going to get you. After speaking with an inspector, I learned that the scam artists were in violation of Title 18, Section 1341 of the United States Code, which says that if you intend to deceive someone via US mail, you could get a maximum of five years in prison for each count. The inspector went on to say that under the 1984 Criminal Fine Enhancement Act, they could be fined up to $100,000 per offense, but only up to two offenses. I wish we could get them on more, but $200,000, plus five years in prison for each count was what I called justice, and I was going to see to it that they did every single day, if I could. Even though the Postal Inspectors had to pursue the case, the Justice Department had to approve. And I knew enough people in the Bureau to make sure our people approved.

Kelly picked me up in her shiny black Stingray and drove us over to the Crystal Gateway Marriott hotel, which was only a few miles from where I live. The Great Mystery Escape 2005 Conference was being held there, and we wanted to bring the staff up to speed. However, at the same time, we didn't want them to know how dangerous our suspects were. If we told all, they'd probably cancel the event and our killers would scurry away like frightened vermin, free to continue their vicious rampage.

The conference didn't start until Thursday, which gave us plenty of time to set the trap. We gave pictures of our suspects to the managers, who in turn gave them to the desk clerks and told them to check the suspects in as they normally would. If they spotted our suspects, they were to alert one of the FBI agents we had stationed in the hotel. We planned to have all the exits covered, but there was still a problem. On Thursday, there would be a sudden influx of people, and in all likelihood, a mass exodus of guests checking out.

Kelly and I were going to be stationed in the manager's office, watching the monitors, hoping to spot the killers, in case the agents and the desk clerks missed them. I didn't know if the suspects were going to check in. They knew we had tracked them down two times already, and they had barely escaped. They had to know we knew about The Great Mystery Escape Conference. Besides, with Washington, DC being an incredible international tourist attraction, hotels were plentiful. They could choose any one of them.

The Gateway Marriott offered 697 guestrooms, twenty-five meeting rooms, capable of seating 2100 people. Making matters worse, three conventions were being held the same weekend; one of them was a college cheerleading conference. All we needed was a slew of beautiful young women running around in their skimpy little cheerleading uniforms, distracting the men I had stationed in the lobby and various other parts of the hotel.

I also invited our friends from the Postal Inspection Service to collect those individuals on our list if they showed up at the conference. However, with so many conventions going on and so many ways to get in and out, considering the underground shopping center beneath the hotel and the Metro subway system bringing more people in every fifteen minutes, covering the hotel was going to be a logistical nightmare, which is why I believed the killers were going to show despite knowing that we would probably have the hotel covered.

We only had a few days left to prepare for their arrival. We started by checking the reservations against our list of victims and their credit card numbers, in case the killers were dumb enough to try using them again. That turned out to be a fruitless endeavor, but it had to be done. We even checked to see if Frank Howard's ex-wife, Liz Clayton, was registered. She wasn't. After that, we phoned the contact people for each convention, and acquired their lists of people who planned to attend. I thought all of this was a serious waste of time. I thought our killers were too smart to be on their lists, but again, it had to be done. The good thing about cross-referencing the list was that Postal Inspectors would be making arrests even if our suspects somehow got away, or never even showed up for the dance.

The suspects had picked the perfect area and the perfect time of the year for their homicidal finale. I had a feeling that no matter what precautions we took, they were going to get in the hotel, kill whoever they wanted, and be in the wind before their victims were cold. If that happened, we had one last card to play. We still had Liz Clayton's cell phone number. If they were somehow able to get in the hotel and kill whomever they wanted to kill, I'd have to try calling that cell. I'd have to try to keep Clayton on the phone as long as I could.

The problem with calling Clayton, however, was that once she answered and I identified myself as an FBI agent, she could simply toss the phone out of the window. If she just turned it off and kept it in her possession, we could still track the phone. To shut off the signal, she would have to separate the battery from the phone. Hopefully our suspects weren't cell phone aficionados. By waiting to make the call only in the event that they escaped from the Marriott, even if she tossed the phone out of the window, we'd have helicopter coverage and plenty of cops in the area. Hopefully, they wouldn't get far before we apprehended them.

Chapter 72

I looked at Kelly, who had been conspicuously quiet. At first I thought it was because we were coming to the end of the case. I thought she was gearing up for a firefight if it came to that, but when I looked at her, she seemed to be intentionally hiding her eyes from me. We had been best friends for almost fifteen years, so I knew something was bothering her. It wasn't the case or the suspects. It was Sterling Wise. At least that's what I believed. Their relationship bothered me, but it wasn't my business. If she wanted to see a man who wasn't serious about her and let her know he wasn't from the beginning, who was I to keep talking about it? But I opened my big mouth anyway and said, "Have you made up your mind yet?"

Kelly was looking at the computer screen. She frowned before saying, "About what, Phoenix?"

Compassionately, I said, "You wanna talk about it?"

Still looking at the screen, she said, "Talk about what?"

"You know what," I said forcefully. "We're about to take down these killers and for the first time, you're not with me. You're with Sterling Wise, aren't you?"

"Not anymore."

I stared at her for a few seconds, waiting for her to clarify the morsel of information she'd offered, waiting for the details of the break-up. I wanted to know when it happened and what triggered it.

"Well," I said.

"Well, what?" Kelly said without looking at me.

I reached out for the arm of her chair and turned it toward me so I could look at her. When our eyes met and locked, I knew she was torn up inside, which meant she had fallen in love with Sterling even though she had told me she wasn't serious about him. As we looked at each other, I saw tears forming. She turned away from me, but I still felt what she was feeling. I still felt the agony of separation, the withdrawal of love rejected. I slid my chair over and embraced her. Slowly, she wrapped her arms around me, and released all that she was feeling. Her body shook uncontrollably as she cried out like an infant. I had been with her through a divorce and many break-ups, but this was different. I wasn't sure why, but it was. Perhaps this was the first time she had broken off a relationship and was still in love. I wasn't sure, but I knew not to say anything, and held her while the cleansing took place.

After a while, she said, "Why, Phoenix?"

Unsure of what she was asking, I said, "What do you mean, *why*? I'm not following you. Tell me what happened."

She sniffed a few times before saying, "Well, you know he was in town, right?"

"Right."

"Well, I met him at his hotel, the Intercontinental, like always, and we did our thing together, like usual." *Sniff!* "Well, afterwards, I told him how I felt about him, and he told me that he didn't feel the same way about me." *Sniff!* "And when I told him I wasn't going to meet him again, no matter what."

She paused for a moment of reflection, shaking her head slowly, like she couldn't believe his response. After taking a deep breath, she said, "And he didn't even care, Phoenix." *Sniff!* "He could have cared less that I loved him."

Angrily, I said, "He said he didn't care? He told you that to your face?"

"No, he didn't, but when I put my clothes back on and walked out, he didn't even bother to stop me, Phoenix. He just let me leave like I was a one-night stand, like I was a streetwalker; someone he could pay, fuck, and get rid of."

With each word, it seemed like her heart broke a little more. The pain she was in was difficult to measure.

"You wanna know what hurt most, Phoenix?"

"What, Kelly?"

"As I drove home, I realized that I was a one-night stand. I realized that I was just a whore with FBI credentials, Phoenix. I realized that he wouldn't marry me because men don't marry women like me. But they love to fuck us, though. They can't wait to bust a nut in us, though. And when all the fucking's done, they leave. No commitment. No nothing. Not even a fucking 'Thank you for the blowjobs.' It's just 'Get the fuck out, bitch!' He never said that, but that's how I felt." *Sniff!*

The first thing that came to mind was, "I told you so." But thankfully, I kept my big mouth shut for a change and just listened to her bare her soul. As I held her, I thought about my marriage and how truly lucky I was. What happened between Kelly and Sterling could very easily happen to me and my husband. Who knows how many women tried to push up on my man? Men were always making passes at me, and they knew I was married. Marriage never stopped any dog from sniffing privates that didn't belong to him. As a matter of fact, from my experience, marriage seems to make the dogs more persistent; female dogs included, I suppose. I wanted my marriage to last even though temptation was everywhere.

I knew I had to make sure I stayed on top of my game because I knew there were plenty of women who'd love to take my man from me.

I was satisfied that we had done all we could do at the hotel. There were agents everywhere in case the killers showed a few days early. But I didn't think they would. I thought it would be best to slip in when the lobby was full of people. Perhaps they would have disguises or something. At any rate, on my way home, I called Keyth on his cell and asked him out to dinner—just me and him, no kids.

Chapter 73

Seventy-two hours later, Kelly and I were sitting in the manager's office watching the monitors, waiting for our prey to enter the trap we'd set. Kelly seemed more focused, ready to do what we did best. I almost opened my big mouth to ask if she had talked to Sterling. I hoped she hadn't. I hoped it was finally and permanently over. That way, she could move on with someone who truly appreciated her. Deep down, though, I think Kelly went back to Sterling's hotel and they ended up making love again, and that's why she was in a better mood. He probably apologized, which made her feel better, and then they hopped in bed and did the nasty again. Oh, well. Live and learn, I guess.

Anyway, back to the FBI stuff. The monitor in the manager's office had four screens. I could see the front desk, the lobby, inside the elevators, and the valet area. My focus, however, was the lobby, which was full of people, mainly cheerleaders who, it seemed, were quite proud of their schools. I could hear them cheering loudly even though the door was closed. We had been at the hotel since noon. Check-in time was three. It was eight o'clock, and there was no sign of the killers—none that we detected anyway. I told our guys via radio that we were going to take a quick break and to pay strict attention to the desk while we were gone. We decided to get a quick bite to eat and some coffee over at Bin1700, the hotel's trendy wine bar, which boasted forty-five different beverages we couldn't drink from the sweet vine.

We heard more cheering and turned to see. I looked at one of our guys. His eyes were glued to the scantily clad collegians, no doubt hoping for the chance to bed several of the Texas Longhorn cheerleaders. Dressed in yellow-and-white uniforms, they belted out a loud, "Everywhere we go-oh . . . people wanna know-oh . . . who we are, and we tell them! Go-oh Longhorns!" They pumped their fists and did splits. A few did summersaults.

This was then answered by the well-built, sultry-looking leader of the Florida A&M Rattlers, who happened to be standing there watching the Longhorns like a number of other cheerleading teams. The Florida squad was wearing orange-and-green uniforms. The leader belted out a loud, "Are you ready, girls?" In unison, they shouted, "Sho' ya right!" The leader had a cooler-than-a-fan way about her, and shouted, "Hit it!" All of a sudden, they began to step a sexy, synchronized dance routine, stomping their feet to a smooth cadence—no cheering. They finished the electrifying number by chatting the *Batman* theme, singing, "Nahna nahna nahna nahna, nah, RATTLERS!" When they finished, they all made the sound of a rattlesnake. Then they high-fived each other and pranced off toward the elevators.

I smiled as we made our way over to Bin1700, thinking, *Black folk sure know how to put on a show.* The bar was filled to near capacity when we arrived, yet we were able to navigate our way through the residual happy-hour crowd that remained an hour longer than the time allotted. I noticed the flat screen plasma TV mounted on the wall over the wines when we walked up to the bar and sat in the tall lounge chairs. Before the bartender had a chance to greet us and take our order, I heard an anchor on Fox News mention a brutal slaying that took place in Fort Lauderdale. The news crawler at the bottom of the screen read: MAN WALKS IN AND SEES KILLER FLEEING 90 MINUTES AGO. The anchor was speaking to a reporter in Fort Lauderdale who had promised an interview of the man who had seen the killer.

The bartender was still gawking at the cheerleaders, but finally spotted us and came down to take my chef's salad and tea order. Kelly wanted wingdings and coffee. She tried to order wine, but I reminded her that we were still on duty. I knew she was only kidding, and saw it as a good sign. She was definitely in a better mood. Perhaps she had changed Sterling's mind. Or maybe she let it go like she'd said three days ago, and was starting to move forward. I guess after three days, she knew how to handle her business, which was why I hadn't planned on saying a word this time. If she wanted to talk about whatever happened to change her mood, that was up to her.

When I saw her flash a smile at the bartender, I changed my mind and said, "Somebody's feeling a lot better, huh?"

"Yeah, I am," she said in a ho-hum sort of way. "And from this moment forward, I'll be doing things a whole lot differently. There's a good man out there for me. I know it. I just gotta be patient until we meet. I'm gonna change some other things too. I'm gonna stop—"

Kelly cut her words short when she heard Fox News come back on. The studio anchor made a few comments and then switched to the reporter on the scene.

"Thank you for granting me this interview in your time of grief, Mr. Devlin," the young woman said. "In your own words, could you tell us what you saw when you entered your home?"

Devlin was remarkably calm when he spoke. "I saw a black man beating my wife over the head with a club or something. I couldn't believe what I was seeing at first. It was like a dream or something. I guess I froze for a second or two because I just stood there in shock. Then I screamed something like, 'What are you doing?' I can't really remember. It happened so fast. The man then turned and fired a pistol at me and I took cover. I heard another shot and the back door opened. I heard him run out and down the stairs."

"I called out to my wife, but she didn't answer. I stood up and looked at her. The man had fired the second shot into Judith's head before running out of the house." After those last words, the man broke down and wept uncontrollably. "We were supposed to catch a flight to Washington, DC tonight," he continued after gathering himself. "We were going to the Great Escape Mystery Convention in Arlington."

Chapter 74

When we heard Devlin mention Arlington and the convention, Kelly and I looked at each other. I knew we were thinking the same thing. The Devlins were part of what was happening. We grabbed our food and beverages and hustled back to the manager's office. As we ate, we reviewed the extensive list that our friend Mr. Robinson from Billings, Montana had faxed me. We search carefully, but we couldn't find their names on the list.

There was a television in the manager's office. Kelly turned it on and we saw the crawler scrolling again, which reminded us that the murder had taken place an hour and a half ago.

Kelly said, "Our killers are in Florida, Phoenix. They knew we'd be here looking for them and decided to play it safe. Now we know for sure they saw the cops at the hotels in Tucson and Memphis."

I said, "It appears that at least one of the killers is in Fort Lauderdale, but what about the other two? Is it possible that the women slipped in and we didn't catch them? Is that why the Fort Lauderdale murder was so flagrant? Is it because he wanted to make sure it made the national news this evening? He had to know it would if he let the husband live. I mean he did have the gun. Why didn't he kill him too? Either way, something's not right."

"Maybe they're trying to lead us away from this hotel," Kelly said. "If we think they're in Florida, why wouldn't we pull our guys out? Why else would they break their MO and not kill the husband and the wife together? That's what they've been doing from the beginning, right? Why change now? No reason to. They know we're here, so they have all the time in the world to kill the Devlins, steal their identities, and use their charge cards like they've been doing all along."

"That's bothering me too, Kelly. Why change tactics that have been working perfectly for the most part? It makes no sense. Something is really wrong here." I paused for a moment, contemplating whether I wanted to tell my partner what was going through my mind.

"Let's hear it, Phoenix. You're holding back something. Might as well put it on the table with the rest of the theories."

I laughed a little and said, "What if they're already here?"

She said, "You think the two women are here and we somehow missed them?"

"Yep. The Fort Lauderdale murder was supposed to pull us out of here. Let's give them what they want. Let's pull our guys out. What's it going to hurt? Kortney'll be happy that we're saving her a ton of overtime."

After looking at the monitor again, Kelly said, "Phoenix, look at this shit."

I looked. The staff was so busy with a line that never seemed to diminish that they clearly weren't cross checking the customers' driver's licenses with the photos we provided like we asked them to. They were following normal procedures, swiping credit cards, and then handing out electronic key cards to the coaches, I presumed. I got the feeling that the morning shift didn't brief the afternoon shift on the procedures. Besides the miscommunication problem between desk clerks, it appeared that the coaches were checking in their cheerleading teams, which meant we weren't getting their team members on film.

I unclipped my radio from my belt and keyed the mike. "It's a wrap, ladies and gentlemen. Let's call it a night. Acknowledge."

"What's going on, Agent Perry?" I heard one of our people say over the air.

Looking at Kelly, I keyed the mike and said, "The killers struck in Florida less than two hours ago. They're not even in Arlington."

Someone keyed their mike for a long time without saying a word. I knew exactly what they were feeling. They had gotten geared up for a fight, and now nothing was going to happen. Finally, a female agent spoke, "We G-men aren't gonna go lookin' for 'em, are we?" She said it sarcastically, like she had something better to do.

"For what?" I said. "The woman's dead. The killers are in the wind again. I'll keep you informed. Thanks, everyone. We'll get 'em next time. Goodnight."

Chapter 75

After cleaning several wingding bones, Kelly said, "Okay, Phoenix, assuming they're here, how do you wanna track 'em down?"

"It's real simple," I replied, pouring the house salad dressing on my light dinner.

Kelly curled her lips, put another wingding in her mouth and said, "Phoenix, there are two wings, eighteen floors, and 697 guestrooms. And there are at least twenty-five meeting rooms. We just let the hired help go home to their families. How do you figure it's so simple, assuming, of course, that we're right and they're in the hotel already? We don't even know what names they're using."

"We don't need their names," I said confidently. I had worked it out in my head—at least I thought I had.

Skeptically, she said, "Let's hear it, Sherlock."

"Think about it for a second, Kelly. If you could stay in a nice hotel at someone else's expense, what kind of room would you get? Would it be a regular room or would it be a *really* nice room?"

Kelly smiled. "A *really* nice room, of course, because that's what they are accustomed to."

"Exactly."

"But there are eighty-two suites in this hotel."

I put a fork full of salad in my mouth and said, "Yeah, but there's only one presidential suite. I say we start there. I say we find out who's in the room and check it out. If we're wrong, you know what we gotta do, right?"

"Check eighty-two fuckin' rooms. Phoenix, you do realize that they could be anywhere in the hotel, right? And that's if they're even here in the first place. They could be in Fort Lauderdale for all we know. I mean, if they changed their MO by killing Judith Devlin and not her husband, they could change again by getting a regular room, knowing it would be much more difficult to find them. Why would they choose the suites anyway? Wouldn't that make it easier to track them?"

"They'd stick with the suites because that's what they like. The murder in Fort Lauderdale was supposed to make us think they were in Florida, not Arlington. But if I'm wrong and they're not in a suite, I still think they're here. I don't think they could pass up the opportunity."

Rolling her eyes, Kelly said, "Fine, let's check it out."

I smiled and said, "Like you've got something else to do."

"I might. The bartender wasn't too hard on the eyes."

"You wanna stop at the bar and get his number before we take the elevator to the presidential suite?"

"No need."

Kelly pulled out a napkin and opened it. The bartender had obviously slipped her his number.

I shook my head and hit a few keys on the manager's keyboard, checking to see who was in the presidential suite. In microseconds, the computer screen told us that a man named Bryan Singer had checked in a week ago. The reservation was made six months ago. He was scheduled to check out in the morning.

I continued eating my salad and said, "We don't have a Bryan Singer on the list, do we?"

Kelly licked the spicy juice off her fingers and then wiped them with a paper towel before picking up our list of literary phonies. "I don't see his name here."

I took a sip of my tea and said, "Let's check him out."

Chapter 76

McAlister Sage and Carson Fletcher were in the Crystal Gateway Marriott too. They had been monitoring the FBI frequency and had heard Phoenix call it a night. Like their FBI counterparts, McAlister and Carson believed the killers were already in the hotel. They were on their way to the killers' suite to put an end to the deadly game they had been playing with the cops who pursued them. They were making their way over to the hotel elevators when they heard, "FBI! Freeze!" They turned to see what had happened in the crowed lobby.

Phoenix and Kelly had drawn their weapons on their suspects. The agents spotted the murderous trio when they left the manager's office. They had just walked into the hotel, as if they, too, were monitoring the FBI radio frequency; almost as if they knew that the men and women tracking them had been pulled off the job. The male suspect and the two women with him stood still, shocked they had been caught. They were dressed in Minnesota Gophers gear. They apparently were going to try to blend into the cheerleader crowd.

When Phoenix and Kelly moved in to cuff them, two actual Gopher cheerleaders, listening to music on their iPods through headphones, walked in front of the suspects.

The man took advantage of the situation, probably trusting that the two FBI agents holding guns on them would not shoot while the cheerleaders were between them. He pushed the young women into the agents. Screams filled the crowded lobby. Phoenix and Kelly lowered their weapons when the girls fell against them. By the time they raised their weapons to take aim again, all three suspects had fled. One ran through the glass lobby doors, which led to Jefferson Davis Highway. The other two ran past the coffee stand and around the corner toward the mall. They were heading for the Metro railway system. But Phoenix and Kelly had no idea McAlister and Carson were chasing them while they chased their suspects.

The man and woman ran like Olympic track stars. They blasted through a set of glass doors as they ran downhill, heading for the underground mall. In a matter of seconds, they were running uphill through another set of glass doors.

Shots rang out. *Pow! Pow! Pow! Pow!*

Phoenix and Kelly had fired a couple of rounds each at the first set of glass doors, shattering the glass, which allowed them to keep running at full speed through the now empty doorframes. By the time they got through the second set of glass doors, they could only see the man running. Apparently, the two suspects had split up.

Phoenix yelled, "You go after him, Kelly. I'm going after her. She's probably heading for the trains."

Chapter 77

The underground mall was a ghost town at night. Most of the shops were closed for the evening. Everything was working out perfectly as far as Carson Fletcher was concerned. Kelly had continued chasing the male suspect, while he and McAlister chased Phoenix and Liz Clayton. He knew McAlister wouldn't dare let him chase down Phoenix by himself, which was exactly what he wanted. He wanted to keep McAlister close because he was going to kill all three of them in the next few minutes or so. And then he'd find Kelly and the man she was chasing, who had posed as Frank Howard, and kill both of them too.

Later, he'd find Natasha Weir, better known as Nancy Newman (The Clown), who had run out the lobby doors. Carson had known who they were all along; after all, he had recruited them. He could have stopped the killings a long time ago, but it was all necessary to get Phoenix Perry on the case. Besides, being a person who enjoyed killing people, he thought the people who had scammed naïve authors deserved to die for what they did.

* * *

Phoenix was gaining on the suspect. They had both run down a short flight of steps and through another set of glass doors leading to the Metro system escalators. Downward, both women ran at full speed; one running for her life, the other trying to catch and arrest her for a long list of murders she had committed. When they reached the bottom of the escalator, they ran through a hall leading to the turnstiles, which led to the train. The suspect leaped over the turnstiles like a deer leaping a fence. Phoenix, in hot pursuit, leaped over, too, and continued giving chase.

Just before the suspect ran down another escalator leading to the waiting area, Phoenix pulled out her weapon and yelled, "Freeze, Clayton! FBI!"

The suspect stopped and turned around. Breathing heavily, she bent over and placed both hands on her knees, sucking an enormous amount of oxygen, desperately trying to catch her breath.

"Hands behind your head," Phoenix yelled. "You're under arrest!"

Still breathing heavily, the woman panted, "They . . . got . . . *Gasp*! "what . . . they . . . deserved!" *Gasp!* I . . . don't . . . regret . . . a thing! I'd . . . do . . . it . . . again!" *Gasp!*

Suddenly, shots rang out. *Pow! Pow! Pow!*

All three shots hit Liz Clayton, who had stood erect when she saw someone behind the FBI agent who had captured her. Two in the chest, and the final shot pierced her forehead and exited out the back. Her body jerked violently as each bullet ripped through her. She fell backward over the balcony, bounced on the pavement beneath, and onto the train tracks, right in front of an oncoming train. The train mangled everything as it ran over her and stopped as scheduled.

Phoenix holstered her weapon. As she was turning, she was saying, "Why'd you do that, Kelly? I had her cold."

Instead of seeing Kelly, she saw two black men coming toward her. They both had cocked semiautomatic pistols aimed at her chest. She went for her Glock.

"Don't do it," Carson shouted. "You'll be dead before your weapon clears the holster."

Chapter 78

"Freeze!" Kelly shouted to the man she was chasing.

"I ain't goin' easy!" the man yelled. He reached inside his boots and pulled out two long knives. "You gon' have to kill me right here. Go ahead and shoot. I'm ready to die." He threw a knife, which Kelly skillfully dodged. The knife hit a stone column and clanged to the cement floor. "You gon' have to kill me, bitch!" he yelled and ran at her like she was a tackling dummy.

Stunned by his sudden offensive, Kelly was slow to react, and by the time she got her Glock out to point it, her attacker had grabbed her wrist and punched her in the face, which separated her from her weapon. The gun hit the ground and Kelly hit the wall.

As he reached for the gun, he said, "If I had time, I'd get a piece. I've never had a lady cop, and you look good enough to eat."

This was the moment Phoenix had warned her about, Kelly realized. A few short weeks ago, her best friend, after giving her a fierce whipping in her martial arts school, had told her a day would come when she would have to rely on the skills she had acquired over the years. As her assailant edged closer to her pistol, she knew he planned to kill her. She'd seen it in his eyes prior to running at her. Although she couldn't explain it, she could always tell a person's intentions by looking deep into their eyes. And his eyes told her that the man she had chased believed he was in a life or death situation. She quickly realized that she might have to kill him in self-defense.

Her first thought was to get her Glock 23 before he did and peel his scalp with a few rounds, but having lost her gun, that was no longer an option. She was a trained martial artist facing a deadly criminal who had told her he was ready to die. Mace came to mind, but she decided against it. She might end up choking too. Other than her hands and feet, the only other weapon she had was the expandable tactical baton. She pulled the baton from its holder, which was attached to her belt, and snapped out its 21-inch steel arm.

"It's a shame that I'ma hav'ta mess up a pretty thang like you to make my escape," the man said and smiled. "Damn shame. We oughta be makin' love, not war."

Nervous, Kelly's normal sarcasm abandoned her for the first time in a long while. She ran at the man the same way he'd run at her. Because he was bending over to pick up her weapon, he was off balance when her body slammed into his. He stumbled backward, attempting to regain his balance, and fell to the hard ground. In the process of running at the man, her feet accidentally kicked the Glock, and it slid far across the cement.

They both looked at the gun and then at each other, each wondering if they could reach it before the other.

"You want that gun, don't you, bitch? Go on. Try tuh get it. I'll give you a chance. Go on! Try!"

Kelly remained quiet, cool even, ready for any movement the man in front of her made.

Suddenly, he lunged forward with his knife. Using her baton, she blocked the thrust with ease. The sound of two steel objects coming together rang out in the quiet underground mall and bounced off its beige walls. Just before he lunged at her again, she sidestepped the thrust. Using the twenty-one inches the baton added to her reach, she hit him on the side of his left knee. The powerful blow caused him to grimace and lift the leg a bit. Having moved forward a little while striking the blow, she was in perfect position to knock the knife from his left hand. While pain impulses bombarded his mind, she brought the baton up and hit his left wrist. The knife flew high up in the air and spun. While he tried to shake the pain out of the wrist, she hit him in the forehead, which immediately began to swell.

He reacted to the blow by grabbing his forehead with his throbbing left hand. In one smooth motion, Kelly hit his right fist, which was rapidly moving toward her face, and then backhanded him in the face with the baton. As the knife in the air started its downward trajectory, the man tried to punch Kelly with his left, but she hit him in the head with the baton again, which dazed him momentarily. As he was starting to swing again, in one smooth motion, Kelly caught the blade and stooped as the punch harmlessly went over her head. Being in a stooped position, she immediately plunged the knife into his left foot. She put the baton between his legs and stood up quickly, which made his eyes bulge out of his head. He doubled over and clutched himself.

"Had enough?" she asked, feeling good about herself and what she had accomplished. It had happened just like Phoenix had told her. With all his skills, he was no match for her. Disarming him and punishing him was a lot easier than she imagined.

"You better kill me, bitch!" he forced himself to say as blood ran down his forehead.

As she cuffed him, she said, "Oh, you're going to live. You're going to be electrocuted, and then you're going to burn in hell, and you'll still be alive."

"At least pull the knife outta my foot!" he demanded.

"Let's leave it in there for the time being, shall we?" Kelly said, smiling, relishing every minute of what she had done to a man much taller, who outweighed her by at least sixty pounds. "That okay with you?"

"You fuckin' bitch! I'm gonna sue you! I'm a minor! You can't touch me! That's the law!"

Kelly laughed. "That's the first time I've heard that one."

"I'm not kiddin'! I'm sixteen years old. And you can't do this to me."

Kelly frowned, realizing he was serious. She reached into his back pocket and grabbed his wallet. She found his Minnesota driver's license. His name was Jonathan Lambert, and he was sixteen years old, just as he had claimed. Flabbergasted that a serial killer was a minor, she shook her head. He looked like a man, easily six foot four and built like an NFL linebacker.

Still stunned by the revelation, she said, "What happened to you to turn you into a murderer, Jonathan?"

"I don't have to tell you shit! I know my rights! I want my lawyer!"

Kelly looked to the left and to the right. Seeing no one, she hit him in the head several more times with her baton. In case the judicial system let him go with a slap on the wrist, she wanted him to feel the weight of steel upside his head. And then she made him limp with the knife still in his foot all the way back to the shoeshine stand positioned at the mall entrance. She cuffed him to the stand and ran down the hall toward the trains.

Chapter 79

"I'm FBI! Don't shoot! I'm going for my ID!" Phoenix shouted, putting her hand into her pocket.

"No need. We know who you are, Agent Perry," Carson said, smiling, unable to contain the bubbling glee.

"Drop the weapon, Phoenix," McAlister added.

"What's this about, gentlemen?" Phoenix asked, gingerly pulling her Glock from its holster and dropping it as ordered. The gun clanked loudly when it hit the hard floor.

"You drop yours too, Mac," Carson said, suddenly aiming his weapon at his former friend. "Both of you are finished."

McAlister cut his eyes to the right and looked at Carson, who had a smile on his face that could only be rivaled by a boy who, after opening his presents, discovered that he'd gotten everything he'd wanted on Christmas morning.

"I know what you're thinking, Mac," Carson began. "I know what you're thinking too, Phoenix. Both of you losers are thinking that I can't take both of you down without either of you getting a shot off. But I can. The moment you flinch, Mac, you're all done. Then I take out the bitch who killed my Coco. Now, drop the weapon, Mac. Now!"

McAlister's weapon clanked when it hit the ground. "So, you and Neil were in on it all along, huh?"

Totally confused, Phoenix said, "What the hell is going on? What does Coco Nimburu have to do with this?"

"You wanna tell her, Mac?" Carson said. "Or shall I?"

"Why don't you tell her? You're on a roll, it seems."

Carson laughed. "It seems? I got you 007. You didn't even see it coming, did you? Neil wanted you out of the game. You've gotten old. You've gotten sloppy. You can't hack it anymore, can you? That's why you couldn't sanction Michelle Michaels when you did her husband. Isn't that right?"

Phoenix frowned and said, "You killed Bruce? My cousin's husband?"

"I'm afraid so, Agent Perry," Carson said, relishing every moment. He still had his weapon on McAlister. "But don't blame him. It was me. I did it. I set Bruce up a few years ago."

Stunned, Phoenix said, "But Bruce killed himself . . . didn't he?"

"That's what you were supposed to think, right, Mac? You couldn't kill Michelle, so you improvised, didn't you? I wanted to kill you when I found out you had fucked up my plans. But when Michelle got involved, I knew Phoenix would have to investigate, being the renegade agent she is. I knew you'd get involved the moment you found out your cousin had been shot in Las Vegas. And when you did, good ol' Mac here would have to get involved again. That way, I could take both of you out at the same time."

"Wait a minute," Phoenix interrupted. "Are you saying you set up the victims?"

"No. The victims got what was coming to them. I just

found a few crazies to do the job, knowing you would eventually get involved."

"All of this because I killed Coco Nimburu?"

Carson swung the gun to the right and pointed it at Phoenix. "Be careful what you say about her. I loved the ground she walked on."

McAlister laughed and said, "He thinks he loved her. He loved the kinky sex she provided. That's all."

"You shut your mouth, Mac!" Carson shouted and swung the gun back to the left as he spoke.

"Or what?" McAlister said, suddenly unafraid.

"You don't think I'll do it, do you, Mac?"

McAlister laughed and said, "I know you won't, Carson. You're all done. Finished . . . as you said."

And with that, shots rang out. *Pow! Pow! Pow! Pow! Pow! Pow!*

Carson dropped the gun when he felt six bullets rip through his vital organs. He could feel life leaving his well-toned body, but he had to see who had killed him. He had to know how McAlister Sage had outfoxed him. It took all of his remaining strength to turn around, and when he saw who had shot him, he said, "Lieutenant Dark and Lovely?" He took a few steps toward her, totally shocked by who had taken his life. He would have never guessed that Marilyn Mason, the woman McAlister had supposedly just met, had killed him—especially since he had checked her out himself.

McAlister walked over to Carson and smiled as he looked into his dying eyes. "I recruited her. This was her first job. It wasn't me who'd gotten old, Carson. It was you. You couldn't hack it anymore. That's why Neil pretended to go along with you, when we were setting you up all along."

"But . . . I heard . . . what you said to . . . Neil at . . . the hotel."

"We know. It was all staged to make you over-confident."

Carson was bitterly disappointed and dejected that Marilyn Mason was his executioner. With a mouth full of blood, his final words were, "Killed by a fuckin' rookie. It wasn't supposed to happen like this. Damn."

Chapter 80

"Drop the weapon!" Kelly shouted, pointing her gun at the back of Lieutenant Mason's head.

Marilyn Mason's weapon clanked on the hard pavement.

"Hands behind your head," Kelly ordered.

Mason raised her hands and laced them behind her head.

"You okay, Phoenix?" Kelly asked.

"I'm okay, but I'm confused as hell," she said as she picked up her firearm and put it into its holster.

"Me too, Phoenix."

"What about?"

"Who these two and the one on the floor are. And what they're doing here."

McAlister said, "Agent Perry, I need to call a cleaning crew immediately. Otherwise, you're going to have a lot of explaining to do when the cops show up."

"A cleaning crew?" Phoenix repeated. "What are you guys? CIA or what? Let see some ID,"

"We'll show you identification, but you gotta let me call my people immediately, okay?"

"Let's see the ID," Phoenix repeated.

McAlister and Lieutenant Mason handed Phoenix their official CIA badges. She took their small leather folds and opened them. After looking at their pictures and their badges, she said, "Make your call. But you need to explain how all of this fits together and why the CIA is openly violating its charter not to conduct clandestine operations on American soil."

McAlister flipped open his cell and hit a few buttons. "Neil. It's done. Yes, sir, Fletcher's dead too. No, sir. He had no idea. Your plan worked perfectly, sir. And Lieutenant Mason performed her duties admirably, sir. Thank you, sir." He hit another couple of buttons and said, "Come down to the Metro Marriott stop immediately. We've only got a few minutes. One body." He looked at Lieutenant Mason. "Marilyn, do you have the evidence?"

"Yes, sir. I copied it to my iPod," she said and handed it to him.

McAlister said, "Go down to the train and stop anybody who tries to come up here. Tell them they're material witnesses or something. This won't take long."

Before following the orders she'd been given, Lieutenant Mason put her hand to her ear, which contained an earpiece. Then she said, "Mac, our people picked up the chick that ran out the lobby entrance. Her name is Natasha Weir—sixteen." She looked at Phoenix. "My badge, please." Phoenix handed it to her. Then she made her way down the escalator and over to the train.

Kelly said, "That's interesting. How old would you say our male suspect is?"

"I only got a glance at him," Phoenix said, "but I'd say twenty-five or twenty-six. Why?"

"Try sixteen, same age as the girl their friends picked up."

"Two sixteen-year-olds did this?" Phoenix asked, totally astounded. Then she looked at McAlister and said, "You need to explain all of this now, Mr. Sage."

"I could tell you this is a matter of national security, but—"

"But you won't, will you, Mr. Sage?" Kelly said sarcastically.

"By the way, Kelly," Phoenix began, "Where's your guy now?"

"I've got 'em cuffed to the shoeshine stand. He's not going anywhere."

"Don't count on it," McAlister said. "The kid's guardian was a Navy SEAL. He's probably gone by now."

"So, he was Frank Howard's kid?"

"Yeah. Howard and the kid's father went to high school together, joined the Navy together, and became SEALs together. He became the kid's legal guardian when his father died over in Iraq during the second Gulf War a couple of years ago. His mother had remarried and started a new life. The stepfather didn't want the kid, so the mother gave up her parental rights."

"I guess we better beat the wind back to the shoeshine stand before our SEAL wannabe becomes Houdini and disappears," Kelly said, smiling.

McAlister said, "Judging by the way he killed Suzette Nance with a SEAL knife from clear across the room, I'd say Frank had trained the kid. That took skill and nerves of steel."

"You've been tracking us for a while, haven't you?" Phoenix asked.

"Not you, the killers."

"But your friend here wanted to kill me because he was in love with Coco Nimburu? Was he serious?"

"I'm afraid so. I had to threaten him several times to keep him from killing you. He wanted to take both of you out from the beginning. We had orders."

"Orders?" Kelly repeated. "To kill me and Phoenix? Why?"

McAlister hesitated for a brief moment and then said, "Because no one can know that Operation Scarecrow ever existed." He paused briefly. "In fifty years . . . maybe, but definitely not now."

Chapter 81

"Operation Scarecrow," Phoenix said, looking at Kelly, remembering Bruce's online persona. "Tell us about it. Help us understand why all these people had to die, specifically my cousin Michelle and her husband, Bruce Michaels."

McAlister took a deep breath and solemnly said, "Scarecrow is the reason you won't be making any arrests on this case, Agent Perry. You're going to lay everything at the feet of the woman Fletcher killed when the locals show."

"We are, huh? Um, and why aren't we going to make any arrests again? I'm a little fuzzy on that," Kelly said sarcastically. "You've got one of our suspects already. Your friend the lieutenant just said so."

"I'm sure our people have both of your suspects now, Agent McPherson."

"No need for introductions, huh?" Kelly said. "I bet you don't even try to warm a girl up before you forge ahead, do you? No foreplay or nothin'. You just go for it, huh? Anybody ever tell you it's better for everybody when she's a little slick?"

McAlister looked at Kelly like he couldn't believe she'd actually said what he'd heard.

Phoenix laughed. "Don't mind her, McAlister. She needs a professional."

McAlister didn't laugh. He didn't even crack a smile. He was about to say something when two men dressed in paramedic uniforms rushed over to collect Carson Fletcher's remains. They put him in a dark body bag and zipped it.

One of the men said, "Our people have the area sealed off. Neil says you need to wrap this up as soon as possible." The two men picked up Fletcher's body and put it on a stretcher. The same man spoke again. "By the way, we've got the other one in custody too." And then they quickly left the scene.

"As I was saying, Agent Perry," McAlister began again, "you won't be making any arrests on this one."

Phoenix and Kelly looked at each other briefly and then at McAlister, like they were waiting for him to explain himself.

"You won't make an arrest for three reasons. One, I'm going to tell you everything you need to know about Operation Scarecrow. Two, I've got all the evidence I need to end your career and quite possibly put you behind bars for a very long time. And three, when you agree to leave this alone, the Agency is going to owe you a huge favor."

Soberly, Phoenix said, "You've got my attention."

"I thought so," McAlister said and handed Phoenix the iPod Lieutenant Mason had given him. "We found this in Fletcher's apartment."

Phoenix took the iPod and looked at it. She gasped when she saw what was on the screen. The angle of the film she was watching indicated that it was taken from a satellite with a night-vision lens. It had been four years since the event had taken place. Two months prior to September 11, she had been on top of the One World Trade Center building, fighting Coco Nimburu to save the lives of her husband and daughter.

"What's on the screen, Phoenix?" Kelly asked when she saw how utterly shocked and surprised Phoenix was by what she was seeing.

Phoenix handed it to her. Now she knew why McAlister was so confident.

"Oh, shit," Kelly said after viewing the gruesome decapitation. Seconds later, she watched Phoenix kill Director St. Clair. Conspicuously missing was the fact that St. Clair had tried to shoot Phoenix.

"Do you two understand now?" McAlister asked.

"It was self-defense," Phoenix said. "I didn't do anything wrong."

"Really?" McAlister said with a short laugh. "You'd have a lot of explaining to do if that video was ever shown on CNN. I'm willing to bet that your paperwork says Nimburu killed St. Clair. If it does, that means you falsified official government documents, didn't you?"

"How did you get this?" Phoenix asked, avoiding the question.

"Nimburu was an independent contractor," McAlister said.

"How did you get this?" Phoenix repeated, pointing the iPod at him.

"Fletcher was the contact man for the Nimburu hits. He set the whole thing up. You were not expected to survive. On the off chance you did survive, the client wanted it on film to shut you up if you wouldn't listen to reason."

"So, Coco was CIA?" Kelly asked.

"Yes. Fletcher hired her to do some contracts for a good friend of the Agency, a patriot that died the same night in her office."

"What did Bruce and Michelle have to do with all of this?" Phoenix asked.

"We don't know everything, but we believe Carson violated protocol when I investigated you during your stint at Homeland Security. He probably tapped the phones of your friends and family and discovered that Bruce was a frustrated writer. He then sent him an invitation to join Pissed Writers United. As you probably know from searching his hard drive, Bruce, like lots of authors, join online writing groups when invited. From there, we believe he fed Bruce enough information on Operation Scarecrow for him to write a book about it."

"What was Operation Scarecrow?" Phoenix asked.

"Despite the Agency's repeated warnings about Al Qaeda's growing numbers in this country, nothing was done to impede the number of Muslims migrating here. Over half of the Muslims with student visas have disappeared. The Immigration and Naturalization Service had no idea where they were, and neither did we. We had virtually no assets on the ground in the Middle East. We were restricted to using satellites only, which made it nearly impossible to have accurate information coming in. When we got wind of the 9/11 plot from the Israelis and the Germans, people in very high places suggested we let it happen in order to secure the kind of resources we needed to protect Americans."

Incredulous, Kelly said, "Excuse me? Did I hear you right? Did you say you knew in advance and you let it happen? You let three thousand people die to get a bigger budget? Tell me that's not what you're saying."

McAlister shook his head slowly, knowing how difficult it was for FBI agents to understand the big picture when it came to geopolitical matters. "Agent McPherson, it wasn't about three thousand lives that day in downtown Manhattan. It was about eight million lives in New York. Ultimately, it was about three hundred million American lives. Given the choice, which one would you choose? It wasn't about if we got hit, it was about when we got hit and what the damage would be." He paused and watched them weigh his carefully constructed words. "What do you think would happen to the economy if instead of planes flying into The World Trade Center towers, there was a nuclear detonation in Manhattan? Do you understand that we still haven't fully recovered from 9/11 economically? And that was only two planes. If a nuclear device goes off, we will respond, Agent McPherson. And the response will be massive. What do you think the Chinese will do? What about Pakistan, India, and anyone else who has nuclear weapons? As callous as it sounds, this thing is so much bigger than three thousand lives. Once the detonations begin, it may not end until we're all dust again."

"That justifies three thousand deaths?" Phoenix asked.

"On a personal level . . . no, certainly not. But on a geopolitical level, yes. It most certainly does. Believe it or not, the Agency is in the business of saving lives. American lives. Your family and my family. Does that mean we can save everybody? No. But often times, a few deaths can save millions of deaths."

Stunned by what appeared to be gross apathy, she said, "How dare you say three thousand American lives are but a few? How dare you?"

"As ugly as the truth is, somebody has to make those hard decisions, Agent Perry. We could have stopped it, sure, but if we had, given our limited resources and the limitations in our own laws, people in very high places thought it a necessary evil that would ultimately save the lives of millions, perhaps billions. We needed it to happen so that the American people would scream for justice in the form of war. We needed it to happen to ensure the passage of the Patriot Act. We needed it to happen to stave off thermonuclear war. If 9/11 didn't happen, a major event would have been unavoidable."

Shaking her head, Kelly said, "And you don't want the

American people to know you people made a unilateral decision to sacrifice those innocent people, all so you could get a bigger spy budget."

"Think for a moment, Agent McPherson. Their sacrifice may have helped secure our shores for two decades or more. Those buildings had to come down no matter what."

"Why?" Kelly said. "Planes hitting the buildings wouldn't have been enough to get the Agency the budget it coveted?"

"No, it wouldn't. Oklahoma City wasn't enough. The first attack on the World Trade Center wasn't enough either. That's how long the Agency has been screaming for someone to listen to us. But all our screaming fell on deaf ears. Those buildings had to come down, period. That was the only way to wake everybody up and hold their attention long enough to get the budget we needed to protect them from the insurgents already in this country. It was a national, if not a global alarm clock, and it got everybody's attention. You two are investigators. Investigate. Accept nothing at face value. For example, look into what really happened with building seven. How did it fall when it wasn't hit by a plane? Yet it collapsed? How?"

Even with McAlister's explanation, Phoenix was still floored by what he had said. And then something occurred to her during a moment of reflection.

"Kelly, it just hit me," Phoenix said. "If *all* our suspects were in Arlington, they couldn't have committed a murder in Fort Lauderdale. So, who killed Mrs. Devlin?"

Chapter 82

Kelly and I later learned that Mr. Devlin had fabricated his story in order to collect his wife's insurance policy. He had fallen in love with one of his students, a vivacious twenty-one-year-old English major who believed every word he told her. It was the typical story one hears almost daily about a spouse deciding they want out of a loveless marriage. Like so many irresponsible spouses, Mr. Devlin wanted his cake and he wanted to eat it too. He didn't like the idea of having to pay alimony, and I guess he figured why not get rid of his wife altogether and bilk his insurance company out of more than five hundred thousand dollars to boot? To show you how ruthless this guy was, he actually told the Fort Lauderdale Police Department, after being arrested, that his insurance paid off his mortgage if his wife died, and that he had worked too hard for that house to see her in it or to see it sold out from under him. I guess what's frightening is that this school of thought has become all too common in America. I've read dozens and dozens of articles about spouses killing each other. If you're sick of your wife or husband, don't bother going through the difficulties of a divorce. Just kill the spouse and be done with it. Absolute insanity.

If that wasn't sick enough, McAlister told us that Natasha Weir and her boyfriend, Jonathan Lambert, were going to get a government sponsored education at Yale (two more candidates for Skull and Bones) and afterwards, CIA wet work training. Wet work is code for assassinations. Both "kids" were incredibly intelligent and had virtually no moral imperatives. In other words, they were born killers, the kind of people that could do the dirty work that most Americans want done, but don't want to know about. McAlister gave us permission to question them to tie up some loose ends concerning my cousin and her husband. What those two monsters told me sent an icy chill down my spine.

It turned out that not only had Liz Clayton been married to Frank Howard, the former Mrs. Howard was also the two "kids" literature teacher. She was also a frustrated author who, after having received repeated rejection letters, decided to not only get even with the people who had cheated her and Bruce out of their money, she was going to get even with any and everybody of that ilk. In addition to that, she was having an ongoing sexual relationship with Jonathan while she was still married to Frank.

She had let Jonathan read her stories, and he thought they were the best thing he'd ever read; never mind that he was only thirteen at the time. She was flattered by the attention the adolescent was paying her. He looked at her with adoring eyes, and thought she could do no wrong. Before long, the relationship ceased to be guardian/teacher and morphed into a scandalous, nearly incestuous affair. Unlike most teacher/student affairs, this "relationship" was far more insidious in that the crime was being committed in the home, right under Frank Howard's nose. As far as we know, when teacher/student "relationships" bloom, the abused boy or girl doesn't live with the abuser. All I can say is that Liz Clayton had to be incredibly sick in the head to get caught up like she did.

As Jonathan grew older and became a high school All-American football player, the school's faculty started wondering about Liz's relationship with him. The faculty thought it didn't look good for him to spend so much time with Clayton, especially since he was a tall, well-built quarterback who didn't have a girlfriend. To silence the circulating rumors, Liz thought he should start dating someone his own age, even if it was a sham for appearance's sake. Liz thought Natasha Weir was the perfect choice. She was pretty, shy, and kept to herself—no real competition for Jonathan's affections. Making Natasha an even more ideal pick was the fact that she came from a troubled home with an overworked single mother. Her drug-addicted father had abandoned the family long ago. There would be no concerned parents to ask too many questions about Natasha's new boyfriend and inadvertently uncover Liz Clayton's secrets.

Later, when Jonathan started dating Natasha, she wondered about his and Clayton's relationship too. She asked him about it, but he denied it all. One day, she caught them kissing in Clayton's kitchen. They were there doing some work for her to get extra credit. Natasha often felt like a third wheel around them, and her curiosity grew each day. She had seen them look at each other amorously a number of times and wondered what they did when she wasn't in the room. She decided to find out by pretending to go to the bathroom. She tiptoed back down the hall leading to the kitchen and peered around the door opening. She walked in while they were in a deep, passionate kiss. She stood there and watched until they realized they had been caught.

But seeing them together didn't upset Natasha at all because she had a secret of her own. She told them about the affair she'd had with Mrs. Dixon, her gym teacher. They had gotten caught in the girls' shower after school by the school maintenance man. They were taking a shower together, kissing, and touching each other's genitals. Mrs. Dixon was summarily dismissed, albeit quietly, as not to ruin the reputation of the school. After Natasha confessed her own sins, the trio began an incredibly heated, unrestrained ménage à trois that very day.

After the divorce, Frank Howard noticed that Jonathan's behavior had changed. He didn't want to spend much, if any, time with him. At first Frank thought Liz was poisoning Jonathan's mind because of the divorce. When he confronted her about it, she flatly denied any coercion on her part. Frank began to believe it was typical teenage rebellion; the boy needed some time for himself and his friends. Next, he thought drugs were playing a role. But he was absolutely floored when he found a pair of Ms. Clayton's black silk panties in Jonathan's sock drawer while searching for drugs to explain his behavior. He called Liz and threatened to expose her for statutory rape of a minor.

But Liz begged him not to call the police. She agreed to give the marriage another chance if he let her explain how it all happened. Frank had begged her to come back to him dozens of times, so Liz knew that he wouldn't call the police before hearing her side of the affair. She told Jonathan and Natasha about the threat, and they knew what they had to do. All three of them planned and then killed Frank Howard in his kitchen. When I asked them why they were so brutal, they gleefully said because they wanted it to look like a crime of passion when the cops found him. Once they had killed Frank, they knew they could kill anybody. They knew it was time to make Bruce's novel, *Pay Day*, a reality.

When I asked them how they got hooked up with Bruce, they confirmed that they had met him in the Pissed Writers

United chat room. Jonathan explained that Liz thought it would be a good idea to seek out online writing groups. She thought that if they were lucky, they might actually meet some published authors. She never dreamed that she'd meet other writers who had been duped too. Some authors had lost thousands trusting people like Rick and Suzette Nance with their prized manuscripts. That's when someone named Agent Doom suggested starting Pissed Writers United. They had joined several groups and learned that a lot of authors had been swindled by so-called editors and agents. Many of the authors were afraid to complain because everybody knew everybody in the publishing industry. They were all afraid of being shut out of the vocation they loved before they had even broken into it.

At first the group was supposed to be a place where they shared information about the many swindlers in the publishing industry, but it quickly became a den of malicious lions who thought of intricate scenarios to track down and kill the people who deceived them. In the beginning, authors seemed to be blowing off some steam, but after a while, people started getting serious. When that happened, lots of authors left the group and only five people remained—Darth Maul, Cat Woman, The Clown, Scarecrow, and Agent Doom. They explained that they never met Agent Doom, but he had told them how to track people down using the potential victim's Internet Protocol address. Shortly after learning how to track emails and websites, Frank Howard had called Liz to confront her about the panties he'd found.

Agent Doom had a sophisticated software program that could trace the Internet Protocol address and the computer's serial number. With those two pieces of information, he could then find the manufacturer, hack into the mainframe and find the real names and addresses of the people who were ripping off authors. He suggested that temporary identity theft would work well if people actually had the guts to carry out their murderous plans.

We thought it was reasonable to assume that Agent Doom was actually Carson Fletcher, manipulating sick people to carry out his elaborate plan to kill me as payback for killing Coco Nimburu—a twisted tale indeed.

Chapter 83

By the time I got home that night, I was energized, even though I'd been up for nearly twenty-four hours. Finishing a case always made me feel alive and vibrant. I looked in on my children, who were fast asleep. Keyth was asleep, too, so I went into my office and turned on my computer. On the way home, I seriously considered what McAlister Sage had said about the September 11 terrorist attacks. I also wondered if I could trust a CIA agent to tell me the truth about anything. Wasn't lying a part of their credo? Did the CIA know about 9/11 and let it happen to get a bigger budget and to get the Patriot Act enacted? Was the CIA that diabolical? I didn't know, but I did know they had me cold on falsifying government documents and had known about it for quite some time, yet had treated the information like it was a matter of national security.

Now that my desktop was up, I clicked on to America Online and signed on. I wanted to do a little research on building demolition and implosion. I went to www.google.com and typed in WHAT REALLY HAPPENED ON 9/11 just to see what I'd get. A few seconds later, I got a litany of results. I clicked on the first link and started reading. Before I knew it, I had been reading for nearly three hours. While I'm not a conspiracy theorist, I did have to question how building seven was able to fall without being hit by a plane. I did a search on building demolition and downloaded actually footage of imploded buildings. The thing that struck me most was the dust that rose from every imploded building. It was exactly what I'd seen time and again in news footage of when the Twin Towers fell.

As I sat there watching the remarkable footage of the collapse of building seven of the World Trade Center, I heard my husband say, "Is the case finally over?"

I swiveled my chair around so I could see him. "Yes, and you won't believe who was behind all the killing."

Without hesitation, he said, "Yes, I would. I'd believe almost anything these days. Are you coming to bed?"

I lowered my eyes and looked at his erection, which seemed to be staring back at me. "Why, you wanna get a little to help you sleep?"

He didn't say anything. He just walked into my office, took me by the hand, and I followed him.

"Let me take a quick shower first. I feel all grimy from chasing Liz Clayton through the underground mall."

"Why don't we take one together and you can tell me all about it?"

"Sounds good to me."

"Okay, I'll be there in a second," he said.

As the hot water splashed down on me, I heard the bathroom door open and then close. I turned around and saw my husband approaching our walk-in shower. He was hard. When he opened the shower door, I said, "Did you lock the door?"

"Naw. The kids are sleeping."

"Lock the door first, honey. And then you can get some, okay?"

Keyth smiled and fast-walked back to the door and locked it. When he got into the shower again, I said, "You wanna hear what really happened on September 11?"

"I thought you were going to tell me about your case first."

"Believe or not, 9/11 is a part of the case."

He frowned. "What? How?"

I turned around and let the water run down my back. "Scrub my back for me, okay?"

Seconds later, I felt Keyth's powerful hands and a lathered face towel on my shoulder blades. "You're not going to believe this, but two of the killers turned out to be sixteen years old."

Keyth laughed and said, "Let me guess. They're from Littleton, Colorado, where that Trench Coat Mafia, or whatever they called themselves, killed all those students, right?"

I hit him playfully, laughing along with him. "No, honey. That's not funny." Then soberly I said, "Here's the insanity of it, Keyth. We had three suspects, but only one of the three was an adult. She was killed today. Not only was she the two minors' literary teacher, but she was sexing both of them."

"What?"

"You heard me right."

After I told him about the "love" triangle, I noticed a strange thing. Keyth was wearing the biggest smile. Intrigued, I said, "What?"

"Nothing."

"Tell me, honey," I said, smiling too.

"Well, I was just remembering one of my high school teachers. Mrs. Bell. Every kid I knew wanted to get up in that. We used to talk about it every day." He was laughing now, but I wasn't. He continued. "Remember that song by Anita Ward? It was called 'Ring My Bell.' She was a schoolteacher, too, if memory serves. And we all wanted to ring Mrs. Bell's bell. All of us." He laughed again.

Serious now, I said, "Um, so you think what she did was okay?"

"How can I condemn her for what I would have done in the kid's place?"

"Easily, Keyth. You're an adult now. At sixteen, your hormones were out of control. The adult should've had more control and used better judgment. I can't believe you're condoning what she did to those kids, especially the boy."

"Well, okay, it was wrong to sex the girl. But come on, Phoenix, the boy? Why couldn't he get his?"

"Would it be okay if that happened to Sydney? Would it be okay if some grown-ass woman took his virginity from him like it was worthless?"

"I think you're taking this thing a little too far, babe. Sydney's a boy. He's not expected to be like a girl. You have to protect girls. You don't have to protect boys. Come on, now. Be for real."

Now I was seriously pissed. "You be for real, Keyth!"

"Are you upset about this?"

"You damned right."

"Why? Because I don't agree with you? Why is that such a big deal for you? So the kid got a piece from his teacher. So what?"

"I'm upset because for the first time since I met and fell in love with you, you have truly, truly disappointed me."

Keyth took a deep breath. "I've disappointed you?"

"Forget it, Keyth. You'll never understand. You're a man."

"Here we go with this man shit. Typical female retort when a man doesn't agree with female manipulation. Honestly, I don't see what the big deal is. They both wanted to get their little swerve on. So what!"

"Typical."

"Typical? Typical how?"

I looked at him, deep into his eyes. "Tell me the truth, Keyth. Did being a virgin when we met appeal to you? Isn't that one of the reasons you wanted me? Isn't that the *real* reason you fought with the assistant director of the FBI? Isn't that the main reason you found the strength to abstain when I would have given it up to you prior to getting married? Be honest."

"Honestly, yeah. But listen, girl, no man wants a woman who's been around, okay? Please!"

"Like my father used to say, 'That be the problem right there, but you're too blind to see it.'"

A little irritated now, he said, "I'm too blind to see what, Phoenix?"

I could tell that this thing was about to explode, and I wanted to get a little before falling asleep, so I said, "Forget it, Keyth."

I turned the water off and walked out of the shower. Keyth followed me. I grabbed two towels and handed him one.

He toweled himself. "Naw. Say what's on your mind, Phoenix. You started this. Now finish it."

"Let's just forget it and get in bed. I'll tell you the rest tomorrow."

He stared at me without blinking. "Well."

I looked at him and said, "You really wanna know?"

"Yeah, I really wanna know."

"Okay. You just remember that you wanted to know. You, like most, if not all men, are blind to your own bullshit. You wanna run around bangin' as many women as you can and then when you're ready to settle down, you want a woman as pure as the driven snow. But what you simpletons don't understand is this; when you run from woman to woman, when you've busted as many nuts as you could, at some point, there won't be any pure women left. And then you cretins blame women for being loose. After you finish *fucking* 'em, what are they supposed to do, become celibate?

"No, that's not going to happen. Most women are going to fall in love with another user and let him get up in her, be-

lieving he's going to be different. Then when he's had
enough, he's gone too. So then what does she do? She finds
another who is full of flattering words and later, when he's
finished *fucking her* he moves on too. After about the third or
fourth one, she's pissed, and she's not going to take it anymore. She decides to become a taker and then men, like
Sterling's best friend, Nelson Kennard, have the nerve to get
pissed when he gets what he in all likelihood doled out."

I continued toweling myself as I walked through the
French doors into our bedroom. Keyth followed me.

"So, this is about the Nelson Kennard case. Or is it about
Sterling and Kelly?"

"All the above, Keyth. All the above. It's about my son and
your son, Sydney. It's about Savannah and one of her teachers that might wanna run up in her because she thinks he
can walk on water. It's about your attitude concerning your
son, Keyth! Damn! Why do I have to explain the obvious to
you?"

"So, you expect the boy to be a virgin when he gets married? Is that it, Phoenix?"

"Let me ask you something, husband of mine. How old
were you when you first got laid?"

"Fourteen . . . why?"

"You have good parents, Keyth. Why were you indulging
in grown-up sexual activity at that age? Did your dad approve?"

"As a matter of fact, he did."

"And your mom, did she approve?"

"I never discussed it with her."

"Was your mom a virgin when she married your dad?"

Keyth hesitated. He diverted his eyes away from me and
appeared to be thinking deeply. He sat on the bed and said,
"I guess you've got me there, but I still don't see what the
problem is."

"Blind as I said. That's the problem with judges who let

these women off when they abuse the boys. The boys learn to think like you and your daddy, and probably your daddy's daddy, and they probably go around bangin' the girls, turning them into whores before they're old enough to decide what their moral standards are going to be. When these abused boys grow up, I wonder if they end up abusing little girls. If they do, we'll call them pedophiles and put them in prison. They say the abused becomes an abuser. What if this epidemic of women teachers can be traced back to one of their male teachers, who was in turn abused by some female, perhaps his best friend's mother?"

"Okay, okay, okay, point taken. Can I get some sleep now?"

"Don't patronize me, Keyth," I said. He reached out to touch me. I snatched away from him and left the bedroom.

I went into the kitchen to get a glass of orange juice. With my emotions running high, I knew I wouldn't be able to sleep until I calmed down. I poured myself a glass and downed it like it was a shot of whiskey. I poured myself another and I sat at the table and started going through the bills. As I sifted through them, I came across a piece of mail that I had been ignoring for years now; the black and white rectangular piece of mail that had a picture of a missing child.

When the pictures of missing children first appeared on milk cartoons about fifteen years ago, I used to pay attention to them. Now, I just tossed them in the trash and forgot I even saw America's disappearing posterity. But after my conversation with my clueless husband, I was paying strict attention to this little black girl lost. I wondered what would become of her, and how her parents were dealing with her absence. That's when I decided to make the effort to pay attention again. This little girl was somebody's child. If it were Savannah or Sydney or one of Kelly's kids, or a close friend or a relative, I'd want everybody to at least look at my missing child before tossing her in the trash.

Thirty minutes later, Keyth came into the kitchen and

stood in the doorway, staring at me. "We're not going to leave it like this, are we? You know I can't sleep when things are not right between us. Maybe you're right. I never thought about it before you forced me to. You're definitely right about one thing. After I had sex that first time, I did go on a rampage. Thinking about it now, I'm probably responsible for a lot of messed up relationships because of it."

My husband had a way of talking to me that made me soften my attitude. "Are you being serious, Keyth? Don't patronize me."

"I'm serious. I thought about it, and I wouldn't want my son to hurt someone's daughter, just as I wouldn't want someone to do to Savannah what I've done. Knowing what I now know, if I could go back and change what I've done, I would."

I went over to my husband and kissed him. I caressed his crotch until he was stiff again, and then I took him by the hand and said, "Come on, let's go take care of this."

Chapter 84

My body tingled as we lay in our bed, holding each other. Keyth's head was on my chest. He was starting to breathe deeply, an indication that he'd soon be sleep again. But I wanted to talk to him about what I'd learned from McAlister Sage. I wanted to hear his opinion. I've always valued it. I think what keeps our relationship fresh is the time we spend talking to each other. After fourteen years of marriage, I still enjoy our conversations. "I want to talk to you before you go to sleep again," I said loudly. I wanted to awaken his mind to my voice so he could pay attention.

Groggily, he mumbled, "Okay, babe. Tell me what *really* happened on 9/11."

I turned on my lamp. Then I reached over and turned on his. "Wake up so I can tell you about this."

The brightness of the light stung his eyes, forcing him to squint when he looked at me. "Can't you tell me about it tomorrow? I'm tired, babe." His eyes seemed to close with each word as sleep overwhelmed him.

I stared at him until he looked at me. Then I said, "That's

why we women like to talk *before* we give it up. Once you men get yours, you're ready for dreamland."

He curled his lips, cleared his throat, and sat up. "Okay, tell me all about it."

I smiled and put my head on his chest. "Thank you, honey. Now, what would you say if I told you that the Twin Towers of the World Trade Center were brought down by highly skilled demolition men, hired by our own Central Intelligence Agency?"

"You sound surprised, Phoenix."

I raised my head off his chest and looked into his eyes. "And you're not?"

"Hell naw. I wouldn't put anything past the CIA or the government. Nothing! You wanna know why I wouldn't put anything past our government?"

"I know why."

Skeptical, Keyth looked at me and said, "Why?"

I said, "Because they fired yo' ass for putting your foot knee deep in the posterior of Assistant Director Michelson. And you did it all in the name of honor—mine, to be exact."

Keyth smiled at me and said, "Well, he shouldn't have lied and said he was doing to you what I just did to you. But no, that's not why."

"Run it down to me, honey. Tell a sista why."

"I stopped trusting the government the day we learned about the Tuskegee experiments, when they treated 399 black men like they were laboratory animals, much like the Nazis did when experimenting on the Jews. Those guys were illiterate sharecroppers, and they told them they were treating them for bad blood, when in reality they gave those guys syphilis. This so-called experiment went on from 1932 to 1972. Forty fuckin' years, babe. Forty years and they didn't know they had it, so you know they were spreading that shit to black women. When I learned about that in the eighth grade, I began to wonder what the difference was between our government and the government of the Third Reich. So, if the CIA was involved in the events of September 11 . . . what's new?"

"I think it's true, Keyth, because I went online to the How Stuff Works website and saw multiple buildings implode. The thing that struck me was that when each building collapsed, a cloud of dust followed . . . like when the towers fell. People were covered with dust, remember?"

"Yeah, I remember, but it takes structural engineers weeks to plan something like that, perhaps months for buildings that were one hundred and ten stories."

"I know. I read all about it, but how do you explain the fact that they were able to implode building seven of The World Trade Center with all that chaos going on? If it takes weeks to set up an implosion, they must have known they were going to fly those planes into downtown Manhattan. And if they knew in advance to pull one building down in the late afternoon on 9/11—building seven that wasn't hit by a plane, mind you—it had to be wired way in advance. Perhaps months, Keyth. And if that building was wired, it's conceivable that the other two that fell were wired too."

Now Keyth was fully awake and thinking. "Hmmm," he muttered and then said, "Assuming all of what you say is true, what are you going to do about it?"

"Nothing."

He frowned and said, "Nothing?"

"Absolutely."

Still frowning, he said, "Okay, I'll bite. Why not?"

"Nobody wants to believe anything other than what they think they saw. We're at war because of those buildings, Keyth."

"You don't think we the people have a right to know what happened, if it happened the way you're suggesting?"

"I thought about it, and honestly, Keyth, no. Not now."

"Why not?"

"Several reasons. First, the public really doesn't want to

know. If they knew, they'd have to deal with the issue of our government lying to us again. Second, they would probably discredit anything I say with sophisticated theories about structural physics or something; kinda like the magic bullet that killed a president. Third, if I open my mouth, the whole family will be in danger if I ask one official question or even repeat what I've discovered. Besides all that, they've got a satellite video recording of my showdown with Coco Nimburu."

"So, they know you falsified government documents too, huh?"

"Like I said, absolutely nothing. I'm ridin' the bench on this one."

"Well, at least you caught the people who killed Michelle, right? It wasn't a total loss, right?"

"I think divine justice will have to prevail on this one, honey."

"Because . . ."

"Because the woman that killed Michelle is now a CIA recruit."

"How come I'm not surprised?"

As I kissed my husband goodnight, the phone rang and jolted me. I looked at my watch. It was approaching 6 o'clock.

I looked at the caller ID before picking up the phone. Flippantly, I said, "It's a little late to be calling here."

"Phoenix, this is Director Malone. Find Kelly and get in here immediately."

"Why, what happened?"

"Famed defense attorney Myles Barrington's daughter, Portia, has been kidnapped."

"I'm on my way," I said. But before I left, I took care of my husband again and made sure he was asleep.